John James Procter

The Philosopher in the Clearing

John James Procter

The Philosopher in the Clearing

ISBN/EAN: 9783337073350

Printed in Europe, USA, Canada, Australia, Japan

Cover: Foto ©Andreas Hilbeck / pixelio.de

More available books at **www.hansebooks.com**

THE PHILOSOPHER

In The Clearing.

BY

J. J. PROCTER,

AUTHOR OF "THE RAGGED PHILOSOPHER," "THE STANDARD BEARER
AND OTHER POEMS," "VOICES OF THE NIGHT," ETC.

QUEBEC :
DAILY TELEGRAPH PRINT.

1897

At the Gate of the Clearing.

SOME years ago, when I was asked by the editor of the St. Johns *News*—who must be forgiven in that he did it in ignorance, and never dreamed of the amount of boredom he was preparing to inflict on himself and his readers—to contribute to his paper regularly, I was for a moment inclined to refuse, being appalled at the prospect of having something to write about every week. I had not learned at the time that it is the easiest thing in the world to say it when you have nothing to say, and, very frequently, the hardest thing when you have. That is the reason why the fair sex are so eminently gifted in the oratorical line, and why men are either silent altogether, or make an awful mess of it when they do speak. However, I concluded, as too many unfortunate readers are aware, to try the experiment, and then came the question what line I should take, and in what guise I should present myself. As I pondered over these things my eyes lit upon an old stump by the roadside, and suddenly there came before me a vision of the half-forgotten past when I first came into this country, and when all was an unknown land to me, even as the literary journey on which I was preparing to embark was.

It was late in the fall of one of the fifties when, after a stay of some four weeks in Montreal, I set out to make my abode in a certain village of the Eastern Townships, which was better known to its neighbors at that time by the name of Slab City, than by the one it insisted on being called, though it eventually succeeded in carrying its point. How well do I remember the long day's ride in the stage under a hot sun from St. Johns to Stanbridge East, at which point I rested from my joltings for the night! How exciting was the constantly recurring speculation as to which wheel was coming off first as we rumbled into and out of holes in which a calf might have been buried, and in which occasional cats, young puppies, and other agricultural products were! What an inventive, and at the same time thrifty genius of the inhabitants it showed when attempts at mending the worst parts of the road by filling them up with old boots, and worn-out stovepipes were observable! And, in the parishes nearest St. Johns, what a lot of children there were! All young; they never seemed to get beyond a certain age; but they made up in numbers what they lacked in maturity. Sturdy little urchins looking cherubic enough to have just come out of the garden of Eden, and about as scantily clad as if they had; some of them, indeed, being, like Horace, clothed in their own virtue—and nothing else. These, and the dogs, which formed almost as large a portion of the population as the children, and the bright-eyed smiling women that came to the doors as the stage rolled by, were the salient points of my reminiscences of that old-time ride. But the most salient points were the cahots— " cow holes " as I then understood them to be called, and I thought that perhaps they were the " buffalo wallows " of which I had read in England, and kept a bright look out for the buffaloes. But I never saw any.

"The shades of night were falling fast " long before we drew up for a few minutes at the post-office in Bedford, and the scenery between that village and Stanbridge was as indefinite as a Liberal's conceptions of a commercial policy, so that when I rose up in the morning, and looked out of the bed-room window, my eyes fell for the first time on a genuine Canadian clearing; a vast field that stretched from the very yard of the little inn to the bush in the distance, and full of stumps. Stumps of all shapes and sizes; smooth ones, splintered ones, stumps blackened with fire, stumps whitened with sun and rain. I think there was some grass, but I am not sure; I know there were lots of little pools of water, and a great many stones; and there were some ten or a dozen melancholy sheep scattered about, looking very like what the hundredth ovine must have done when it had strayed off from the ninety and nine. But the one predominant idea was stumps. Involuntarily I looked about for the wolves. I had read a great deal about the Canadian wolves, and this seemed just the place where one might expect to see them, but I didn't, any more than I saw the buffaloes. Yet this expectation was not so very absurd after all, for I did hear once or twice after of a wolf being seen in the vicinity; but he was an untruthful and delusive animal, partaking of the opposite characters of angels' visits, in that he was "few and far between," and of a politician's ante-election promises, in that he failed to materialize, or, if he did, turned out to be some stray dog out on a sheep-stealing expedition : just like a politician.

However, the scene, which is common enough, impressed me very strangely at the time with a sense of weird loneliness which I had never experienced before. And yet, when a school-boy, I had spent hours, and sometimes whole days, in roaming over the great furze and heath-covered wastes of the Westmoreland and Yorkshire mountains along which a man might travel from Kendal to the Scottish border without seeing a human habitation, or the trace of human civilization beyond the different flocks of sheep that dotted every steep hill side. But there the conflict between man and nature was ended, and peace had been signed. The time when that vast upheaval had been covered by the stately trees of the forest had long passed away, and left no trace behind it; here, the struggle was just begun, and I was looking down on one of the battle-fields still cumbered with the evidences of the strife, and the slowly decaying bodies of the fallen. There I was face to face with nature quietly contemplative in a settled order of things ; here was a state of transition ; man breaking in on the old peace. I carried that picture away with me then, and shall still carry it till all earthly pictures are effaced. It rose up before me as I was pondering over the request of the editor of the *News*, and I said to myself, "There you have it. Just fancy yourself back on one of those old stumps, and philosophize on things in general and nothing in particular."

I was, in a measure, adapted for philosophizing, too, so far as externals went. My wife complained, (as she complains with tears in her eyes to this day), that she never could get me to look decent. I hate "fixing up"; and I have a peculiar affection for old clothes, partly because they are more comfortable, and partly because one is never distressed with fears of spoiling them. It was in vain that she represented to me that I owed something to society, and that I ought to at least appear respectable. I replied that when society footed my tailor's bills, it might dictate what I should wear, but that so long as I had to perform that unpleasant operation myself, I should consult my own convenience, and society, if it did not like it, might go to Bath, and further, if it chose. It was just at the end of one of the daily discussions on the subject that I confided to her my intention of writing philosophical articles from the stump by the roadside, on which she exclaimed, " You a Philosopher ! a pretty ragged Philosopher you'd make." And this is how I came to be a Ragged Philosopher, and write nonsense. I may have sinned deeply : I am only too conscious that I have ; but I trust it will be taken into merciful consideration that I was brought into literary existence by the combined forces of an editor and a woman ; and what goodness can you expect from the influence of the one, or sense from the influence of the other ?

Pausing at the Gate. The Preface.

―――――

" There are more things in heaven and earth, Horatio,
Than are dreamt of in our philosophy ":

I am not quite certain whether that is the correct quotation, but it does not matter if it isn't ; it will serve my purpose just as well, and that is all that I care about. The reader will be kind enough to bear it in mind before he starts any objection to finding the preface to a book come in a different order to that which is generally assigned to it. There are reasons : and reasons probably that would never have occurred to him had this book not been written. In the first place, I am desirous of having something original ; not very much ; I am quite content with a limited possession in that line, being satisfied, in the main, with commonplaces dressed up and served in a kind of literary boarding-house hash for present use; but still I should like, for my own sake, a little bit of originality, and since Solomon assures us that there is nothing new in the way of human thought under the sun, I see no other means of attaining the fulfilment of my modest aspirations save by putting the preface where it "didn't ought to was." Secondly, authors may not be aware of the fact, but readers are, that a preface is never read. "Surely in vain is the net spread in the sight of any bird," and the general reader is a great deal too wary to bother himself with a preface, a thing which is usually as dry and uninteresting to anybody but the writer, as the old Sunday school books which contained biographies of " Little Mary Jane," and happy death beds of infantile saints ; or if it was at all witty and interesting was simply an exasperating button-holing of the reader anxious to plunge at once *in medius res*. Any way, interesting or not, prefaces are never read, as I intend, this to be, and therefore I am going to get it in surreptitiously, and as a sort of surprise party, for it would be manifestly derogatory to my wisdom as a philosopher to write something that I knew beforehand would not be looked at. There are other reasons also; but " enough is as good as a feast," though that is a proverb that will not stand close examination.

Having thus established, I hope satisfactorily, that the placing of a preface in the contents of a book, instead of before them, is not a totally indefensible proceeding, however startling it may appear at first sight, I am conscious that I shall meet with the objection that if I wished this of mine to be read I should not have announced it with a flourish of trumpets, and proclaimed it from the house tops. Here again, I must refer to the statement of Mr. Shakespeare with which I commenced. The fact is that I don't intend to take any chances, as I informed my publisher when he suggested that it would be a great deal more grand and heroic for me to risk my capital than to risk his. I did not dispute the assertion, but I put it to him that, as a philosopher, I could not be expected to set any value on glory and fame, which are perishable articles at best; that, indeed, it was perfectly impossible for me to consent to acquire them, and that since they doubtless would be gained by the publication of my book, he was the only one to whom they could fall. He looked dubious, but " the woman that hesitates is lost," and so is the publisher. Now either a preface is, by artful contrivance, read, or it is not read. That seems to be incontrovertible. If this of mine falls under the former category, I shall have gained a point; if under the latter, I shall have gained a point still. Not the same, I grant, but another. Did it ever strike you, (but of course it never did) what unlimited possibilities for the author there are in an ordinary preface. Secure in the knowledge that it will be passed over unheeded, he can say what he likes. He can preface a treatise in favor of Free Trade with an elaborate disquisition on the advantages of Protection ; a geography, with the statement that the world is flat, and that if you only go far enough, you will tumble off; a treatise on medicine, with a defence of the principles of christian science ; a volume of orthodox sermons, with the theories of the Theosophists ; and nobody will be any the wiser. By the aid of a preface he can even go so far as to construct, unaided, a full party programme, a thing which inasmuch as it embraces every theory known to the political world, has hitherto had to be got up in sections in this country; a little bit in each Province; and which, despite the numerous talented minds that have been working at it, has never yet been blended into one harmonious whole. But the author can do it—with a preface—and can answer any objections made to his book by the enquiry "Have you read what I advanced in my preface?" Of course the answer is "no," with probably the muttered addition, "and don't intend to." Then the objector stands convicted before the world of not having fully mastered his subject, and is silenced accordingly. This is how I stand to win on either event. Read this, and you will probably be too wearied and listless to be capable of making any complaint afterwards; don't read it, and then if you should say the book is dull and stupid the answer is that you have not perused it with sufficient care, and it is your fault, not mine.

I have chosen as a frontispiece an owl sitting on a stump. The stump is obvious enough; perhaps a little too obvious; but the owl is more debatable. I never could satisfactorily make out why that bird should be assigned to the Goddess of Wisdom: he's not particularly wise that I know of; in fact, if you catch him out by daylight, which is not a very usual thing to do, he looks particularly foolish. He bolts his food whole; and that any child studying hygiene under the auspices of the committee of Public Instruction can tell you is very injurious to the digestion. It is also a further proof of his deplorable lack of education that he does not seem to suffer from dyspepsia by the practice. He is a dissipated bird, too, and keeps late hours; doesn't do any work in the day time, and comes down to breakfast when the shades of night are gathering fast, a lamentable proof of his utter disregard for the feelings and convenience of Mrs. Owl. What he does when he condescends to leave his bed at a time when respectable birds are either in theirs or preparing to go to them, is accurately known to few, except the field-mice ; and they have nothing good to report about him ; but I have a suspicion that he drinks ; and something stronger than water too ; for if you happen to be awake in the wee sma' hours, you will hear him attempting to say " Truly rural " to Mrs. Owl when he goes home, or practising what he calls singing on some old dead branch.   A little later on you will hear him snoring ; and if you pass his house in the morning he will be hiccuping in his sleep.   Now you can't call such a bird as that a fitting companion for a prim old school marm like Miss Minerva, and I don't believe she had anything to do with him. It's all a vile slander, and was probably started by some disgruntled ratepayer when Minerva commenced her educational life as teacher of an elementary country school.   Not that I consider the owl an ass (intellectually asinine, of course) ; far from it.   He knows enough to enjoy life according to his lights, or rather, in his case, twilights, which, I take it, is more than a great many of us, male and female, old and young, wise and foolish, know how to do.   We are all of us fed with a species of providential bacon, in which the fat of prosperity is intermingled with the lean of adversity, and sorrow, and disappointment ; and we cannot take our lean uncomplainingly : it spoils our enjoyment of the fat.   We are like the old lady whose rheumatism more than counter-balanced a comfortable home, assured means of living, and good friends ; we think more of the crumpled rose leaves than the smooth ones in our beds.   You never find an owl doing that.   If he misses his swoop at a too nimble mouse, he merely remarks " Hoot, mon ! but ye're gey and lucky," and goes off in search of another without troubling himself further about the absconder. I don't know whether he ever goes home without his supper, or whatever he calls his meal, but he always goes home jolly, and saying Tooral-looral.   Bright moonlight, or murky dark, wet or dry, it is all the same to him, at any rate so far as he can be heard from, and there is no question about his enjoyment of life.   Even when he gets belated in the daytime, and is surrounded by a host of little birds reviling him, and pretending to peck at him, he sits

blinking in a humorous manner as if the whole show was got up
for his entertainment, and does not appear the least troubled with
his novel position.   He's a wise bird in his way, though decidedly
not intellectual, and has a solemn and pretentious air which is
very imposing.   I think he and I have some points of resemblance.
And now that I have made these things clear we will come down
to the business of this chapter.   Let me see! what was it? oh!
the preface—Yes! the preface!

Well, now! You must be aware that I have already reached
the limits of an ordinary well behaved chapter in getting ready to
say what I was going to say; and I shouldn't wonder if you were
tired.   What is of a great deal more importance, (to me), is that
I am tired whether you are or not, and so I am going to put the
shutters up and close the wisdom store till next morning.   What
is that you're saying? "You haven't come to the preface yet."
Now I think of it, you are right; you haven't; and what is more,
I don't believe there is any prospect of your doing so.   What does
it matter? You would not have read it if you had; and now you
are in the proud, and I flatter myself, original position, of having
perused a preface that never was written, and never will be.   That
alone is more than worth the price of the whole book.

In the Clearing. On Preconceived Ideas.

OPEN confession, they say, is good for the soul, and what "they say," must be true, though I have always been a little suspicious of the maxim, having observed that those who are most active in preaching it, are also, generally, those who are most backward in coming forward to the practice of it, and I am not sensible of any particular moral benefit that has accrued to me for confiding my preconceived notions of Canadian zoology to a heartless public that will probably laugh at me instead of sympathizing with me. And yet if I looked upon Canada in my earlier days as a paradise for young women, where any amount of bears was ready to hug them to their heart's content, and a terrible place for innocent masculine lambs like myself, whom wolves were always ready to devour, yet I was not so very far astray after all, for there *are* bears in the province of Quebec, because I've seen them ; and I know there used to be wolves, but they have since evolved into contractors, and politicians, and wander over the country amid metaphorical instead of literal stumps. In those days, however, I kept my ideas to myself as much as I could, and so avoided having them enlarged and improved, as happened to a young Englishman who had come into the country about a year before I did, and had grown confidential with the genial Collector of Customs who dwelt in Slab City and kept one eye on one side of the line, and the other on the other side. This young man had preconceived an idea, that the boundary separated two races of men as distinct in thought, speech, and appearance as the heathen Chinee, and the new woman, and he was encouraged in the belief by his confidant. " Yes ! " said the Collector, " the difference is very perceptible, and strikes the thoughtful observer immediately he crosses the line. Of course, I don't say that there is any change in the scenery close by the border, but in everything else there is a marked alteration, even in the atmosphere. However, there is

nothing like seeing for yourself, and as I am going to drive over
to West Berkshire on the other side, I shall be happy to have your
company." The offer was accepted, and the two jogged along merrily
for a mile and a half, when the Collector pointed out the boundary
stone. Now, as luck would have it, just at this precise moment
one of those pretty little bushy-tailed animals, which are as
renowned for their perfume as any city girl, had run across the
road, and the air was blue with the remarks he made, *en passant.*
The Collector rose to the occasion. " Here we are just crossing
the line," said he, " and I told you there was a difference in the
atmosphere. Perhaps you are able to distinguish it ? " By this
time they were in the full enjoyment of the odours of Araby the
Blest, and the Englishman was looking pale, and holding on to his
nose with both hands. " Yes " he gasped, " there is a decided
difference. Unpleasant, too, I should say, but I suppose the
natives are accustomed to it. I think, if you'll excuse me, I'll get out
and walk back." And he did. What is more, during his brief
stay there, nothing would induce him to go in that direction again.
His preconceived notions had been more than corroborated by
experience. It was useless to argue with him ; he pinned his faith on
the Collector and the—Sk—k.

Mutato nomine de te fabula. In these days of Vassar and
Girton there is no need of apology to the fair reader, if I have
any, for quoting Latin, but for the benefit of the weaker masculine
intellect I may translate it briefly into the vernacular, " You're
another." We all of us have our preconceived notions, and they
are all more or less erroneous and absurd. When Mr. Pecksniff
expressed an overwhelming desire to be favoured with his land-
lady's ideas of a wooden leg, I rather fancy he would have been
considerably astonished if his wish had been gratified. We cannot,
unfortunately, get at her ideas now, but I should not be at all
surprised to learn that the worthy lady's ideal of a wooden leg
took the form of a highly polished mahogany one, such as used to
sus ain th old fashioned four-poster bedsteads ; or take the case of
our M st Gracious Sovereign Lady, the Queen. Don't you, when-

ever you think about her at all, picture her to yourself as a stately woman wearing a gorgeous crown, with long trailing robes to match, instead of a stout old lady in widow's weeds, specimens of which one meets everywhere ? I know I do. When we who are outside of the pale of the noble four hundred, let our imaginations conjure up visions of the aristocracy, are they not pictured to us as be-starred, and be-gartered, clad in ermine and fine linen, instead of the common place ladies and gentlemen whom we may jostle in the streets without knowing what we have done ? Does " Maud in the light of her youth and her grace, singing of Death, and of Honour that cannot die " have any picture before her of the real smoke-grimed hero, with patched up uniform, that lies on the battle field, breathing out his life in sobbing gasps ?

As a general rule, I fancy, the notions we form of things with which we have not had a previous acquaintance magnify the reality, either in importance and desirability, or their contraries, just as the haze distorts the outlines of the objects that loom through it. We seldom undervalue a thing *in prospectu*, unless it be some obstacle to the accomplishment of our own wills. I know of but one instance to the contrary, and that was the case of the Irishman who had heard dreadful tales of the mosquitoes in foreign parts, and of their long trunks which they plunged into the bodies of their victims and through which they drained the blood. He was bound for India, and on arriving at Calcutta, the first thing he saw on the wharf was an elephant. " Howly Mother av Moses !" he exclaimed in horror, " Is that baste a muskeeter ? " What's that you're saying ? That the elephant was not a mosquito, and therefore Paddy's preconceived notions might have been right after all ? Now, that brings up a very intricate question, namely, whether things have any actual existence outside of ourselves, and independent of the attributes which we assign to them. Take a dream, for instance. Its incidents are very real to the dreamer, though when he awakes he will be ready to acknowledge that they did not, and could not exist. And yet is he so certain of that ? I remember once reading of a man who used frequently to wake out of his sleep, crying out that some enemy had him by the throat, and was trying to choke him.   One morning he was found dead in bed, with blackened face, eyes and tongue protruding, and every symptom of death by strangulation.   What do you make out of that ?   Well, now ! if the actuality of a thing depends on our own perceptions of it, then, since the elephant was, according to Paddy's inner consciousness, a mosquito, an actual mosquito he was, pro tem. and not an elephant.—Q. E. D.

"THE word 'politics' surprises by himself" wrote Count Smorltork, and, whether he meant it or not, the remark was a most valuable and true one, for politics are nothing less than a constant series of surprise parties. The derivation of the word is popularly supposed to be polis, a state, and politics to mean matters pertaining to the state, but this is an entire error: the real derivation is "polloi" "many," and "ticks," a parasite which affects sheep and other animals, many ticks, and the idea was suggested by the way in which those devoted to politics as a pursuit get into the wool of the taxpayer, and fleece him. Politics is the one blessed thing on this changing scene in which there is always money: it has various aspects, and appears under various forms; patriotism, public spirit, enterprise, etc., etc., but you can always tell it by that characteristic. If there is no money in it, it's not politics. As a late lamented friend of mine, who was first a Conservative, then a Liberal, then premier of the province and a Nationalist, and finally became a patriot once remarked, *je n'aime que la politique qui paie*. That is the only kind of politics which is real; any other is hollow sham. If you don't believe me, ask the first contractor you come across.

It is necessary that this great principle should be first laid down in order to understand why opposing parties call each other such uncomplimentary names as rogue, thief, liar, etc., while insisting at the same time on their own purity and honesty, without eliciting the faintest sign of feeling from the persons so attacked. When once you admit that true and good politics consists in the extraction of money for your own, and, incidentally, your friends' benefit from the public purse, it is easy to perceive how nothing will make those in power believe that they are doing anything but what is right, and that their opponents are false to the very nature of the thing they profess to be; and how those opponents feeling themselves as capable of the employing of the public purse for their own benefit, should conceive that they are deterred from doing so by illegal means. But they are "all honourable men;" and to bribe, or get fat contracts, or any other corrupt mode of proceeding does not detract from their honour, for the more money a man makes out of politics the more thoroughly is he doing his duty to himself: that is, to his country, or that section of it which is represented by him.

There are two classes of politicians: those who sit still, and make all the money; and those who go about the country, and make all the speeches. The former are called the supporters, and the latter are termed the leaders of the party. The supporters are so named because they maintain the other fellows, pay for the bouquets that are presented them, and the dinners that are tendered them; also for election expenses, such as surreptitious whiskey, valuable old horses, and rubber rings for interesting babies, etc., etc. The leaders get their name from heading the pack, and running the game, i. e., the public purse, down, when the rest of the hounds, (I don't mean anything personal), come up, and devour it. There is also a small subsection of the supporters, called the organizers. These act as the huntsmen: they mark out the country over which the run is to be made, whip the pack into line, and keep the leaders from devouring the quarry when it is run down. They get the antlers and haunches; the pack gets the body, and the leaders the leavings. "Only poor pickings," you will say. Perfectly correct; and that is why a cabinet minister, generally speaking, has very little to leave behind him when he dies. There remains one more element in "the party"; the little terriers and mongrels that run about fussily, and do all the yelping. These are called "the rank and file." They are not much good, except for show, and get mighty few crumbs; a couple of dollars for a vote, when it is doubtful, is a fair market price.

All these together constitute "the party"; but it is only the men that make the money, the contractors, the promoters of rail-

2

roads and canals and shipping lines, the combines, that are really the politicians. It is true that the others get a little; a very little; but that does not entitle them to be classed as politicians, any more than the employes can be looked upon as the members of a firm because they get paid their wages out of the profits. Now, it is from want of a proper appreciation of this fact that the outside public falls into a grievous error, and when it finds its pockets rapidly being depleted, or stumbles suddenly on some good fat job, blames the unfortunate government for it. It is not the fault of the government at all, but of the men who cry. "Simon says, 'Wiggle-Waggle'" to it, and who proceed to turn it out, or attempt to do so, if it does not Wiggle-Waggle as per order. Ezekiel Snooks votes for the ministerial candidate; he is supporting the government only incidentally; in reality he is voting for a railway company, a graving-dock contractor, a cotton or sugar combine; and when he casts his ballot for an opposition candidate, he is supporting men who either belong to one of these classes, or want to belong to them. It all comes to the same thing in the end, my son. "Here" said the showman describing his panorama of the Battle of Waterloo; "here you sees Bonyparty on his white horse cheering on the last charge; and there you sees the Dook of Vellinton, on his white horse, a shouting "Up, Guards, and at 'em'." "Vich is Bonyparty, and Vich is the Dook of Vellinton"? squeaked a small voice in the audience. "Vichever you likes, my little dear; you pays your money, and you takes your choice." That's what the elector does. The one material thing is the paying of the money; the choice is quite immaterial. It does not much matter, so far as the expenditure of the public money is concerned, whether the Government is Conservative or Liberal; the same class of men is behind it, and manipulates the purse strings. Does that seem a sweeping assertion? I recollect, and I dare say others are yet alive to recollect also, how a great railway corporation turned round on a government and ejected it from power, because it was on the point of establishing another great railroad company, whose rivalry was feared. There was a great deal of fuss about the "scandal," as it was then called, at the time, and it was made to do duty for years after; but the simple matter was that one set of "supporters" offered more pecuniary support to have a charter granted, than the other set either would, or could give to have it refused, and the latter turned over its support to the enemy. The public interest had nothing to do with the affair: in fact the public got the worst of it, as it generally does in these disputes, for it wasted five precious years in the contemplation of a line to consist of alternate stretches of land and waterways; as if anybody in his senses could expect a line to pay that involved half-a-dozen trans-shipments, more or less; and a lot of steel rails dumped down to rust by the honest and capable Government that succeeded the corrupt one which was turned out. If you look upon those wasted years as you would a sum of money, according to the old adage "Time is money," and calculate the interest on them up to the present date, how much do you think the advancement of the country was delayed? And whose fault was it?

HERE is not much to say about a stump from a social point of view; it is essentially a solitary thing, although surrounded by scores of its fellows, all as unsociable as itself, and has an air, half morose, half melancholy. It may be patronized occasionally by a predatory old crow, or a marauding hawk, but that gorgeous thief of the world, the blue jay, won't come near it, and the rollicking bob-o-link holds it in high disdain. It is only when a stump is regarded philosophically that it becomes a matter of interest, and then its uses are apparent; for observation, if you sit on the top of it; for meditation, if you recline at the foot of it. The person who uses it for a seat must have all his senses on the *qui vive*: he is obliged to sit up like a little man, because there is no back to it; and he is forced to keep his eyes from shutting, and his wits from wool-gathering, because if he does not, he runs the risk of tumbling off, and hurting himself. There is nothing that comes up to a seat on a stump for the purpose of exercising the powers of intelligent observation, that I am aware of, unless it be a high step-ladder. But you can't very well carry a high step-ladder under your arm to sit down on when you are tired, every time you go out for a stroll; whereas you can find a stump most any where in Canada outside of the cities. On the other hand, the foot of the stump is admirably adapted for meditation, and the closing of the dreamy eyes. The ground is generally covered with a soft mattress of moss and wild flowers; there is a nice support for your back; and the roots stretch out on both sides of you like the arms of an easy chair. The only precaution to be taken is to make sure that the spot has not been preempted by a bumble bee, or a black wasp; in which case it is as unfavourable for philosophy and meditation as can well be imagined. When I wish to pursue political researches, I sit on the top of a stump; when it is my desire to indulge in philosophical disquisitions, I lie at the foot of it. I am doing so now.

It is drawing to the close of a hot summer's day, and the air is dancing up and down in glassy undulations. There are other dancers besides the air, in the shape of myriads of small flies, that seem to me never to deviate from their respective tracks to right or to left, but to keep a perpetual alternation of ascent and descent. I call them flies; some people call them gnats; and others again, midgets : the naturalists give the merry little beggars a long Latin name, Ephemerides, and pretend that their term of life extends throughout the space of twenty-four hours. It may be so; I shouldn't be surprised if it were. I know that I should be dead myself long before the twenty-four hours had expired, if I attempted to take the violent exercise they do, and I wonder if they have any idea that there is such a thing as perspiration.

They are not social economists; that's evident. I should like to catch one of them, if I could, and explain to them of what enormous waste of motive power they are guilty, and of how much more use it would be to the world if they were to form a combine, and run a cotton mill, for instance. They could do it if they chose. Of course some one would have to build the mill for them, but they could run it afterwards and pay him off out of the profits. "Just consider, my little friend," I would say to one; "here you are raising your body two or three feet into the air about twenty times every second. It's not much of a body, it is true; but then there are thousands of you; millions; myriads I should say, if there are corresponding swarms of you round every stump in the field. And you are at this work from the minute you are born to the minute you die—twenty-four hours; that is, 86,400 seconds; and twenty times a second makes 1,728,000 times; and 3 feet at a time makes 5,184,000 feet. Now, supposing it takes ten million of you to weigh a pound, (and you really look a great deal stouter than that), and supposing also that there is at the least calculation a pound of you jigging up and down by this stump, you have exerted a force equal to raising over five million pounds a foot high during your lifetime. What's that you

say ? That you are dancing for your own amusement, and not for
men's profit ? That is a very wrong view to take. It is not moral,
and you cannot seriously entertain it. It would grieve me deeply
to think there was such a thing as an immoral Ephemerid. No !
my little friend ! We are all placed in this world to assist and
support one another, and————." May dogs defile the grave of
that mosquito's grandmother ! The rascal has bitten me on the
nose.

I wonder which of us was right; I in looking on dancing in
a practical light as a species of labour, or the Ephemerid in regarding it as an amusement. Savage and heathen nations have asso-
ciated it with religious ceremonies, and thus, combining the idea
of service performed with an expression of rejoicing and thanksgiving, have invested the act with the characteristics of both work
and play. There is no doubt that as a religious ceremony dancing
played an important part in the Jewish ritual, but Christianity
refuses to recognize it as a part of religion, and indeed some creeds
profess to look upon it as immoral, or, at the very least, unbe-
coming. And, no doubt, it would be a considerable shock to see
the Archbishops of Canterbury and York, and the bishops of the
English church, dancing a schottische in St. Paul's Cathedral in
lawn sleeves and knee breeches; or the Pope and his Cardinals
going through the mazes of a country dance in St. Peter's. We
have operatic singers to sing solos in our churches, and the musical
talent of our choirs is a great factor in gathering a good congregation ; but dancing is "a horse of another colour." We draw the
line at the music.

In proportion as the religious phase of dancing was discarded,
the heathen nations of Greece and Rome, and the semi-civilized
peoples that succeeded them, came to look upon dancing as a
labour, and one, moreover, that was beneath their dignity. It is
related of a Turkish ambassador to a European court, that when
he first witnessed a ball, he expressed his astonishment that people
should take so much trouble. " In my country" said he, " we
have girls to do the dancing, and look on ourselves."" Them's my
sentiments, exactly." I can admire the grace and elegance of girls

trained to dance, but society dances have always seemed to me
absurd and ridiculous, more especially in the male sex, the greater
portion of whom invariably look as if they would put their hands
in their pockets, were they not embarrassed by an insane desire to
put their feet there too.   Which gives them an aspect of indecision.
I don't mind confessing that I hate dancing myself; my first
serious trouble came from it, when, as a little five-year-old, I was
sent to a dancing school to learn the art.   There I met with my
fate; a wicked little flirt of sweet six, with blue eyes, long curls,
and short petticoats.   I fell madly, distractedly, in love with her,
and, oh bliss! my passion was returned.   We had got so far as to
discuss an elopement, when the usual villain intervened, in the
shape of a boy a year older than myself, who had steel buckles on
his shoes, and silk stockings, whereas I had only cotton ones, and
no buckles at all.   Then she cut me dead.   It was an awful blow,
and I have never completely recovered it.   I recollect bursting
into tears and expressing a wish to go home.   Strange how the
events of our youth repeat themselves in after life! The dew is
falling, and I am getting damp, and once more I want to go home.
I'm going.

In a Tangle.

IT is a mark of the philosopher that his trained and well regulated mind is able to perceive clearly things which are either imperceptible, or but dimly seen by other people; and it is a further mark that he can receive calmly and without surprise these quasi-discoveries which would be startling to common minds, if they came without any previous preparation for them. One of these discoveries which the true philosopher makes is that he is an ass. He is continually making it, and—forgetting it; so that when he comes upon it for, say, the hundred and first time, it has all the merit of a novel sensation. This is my hundred and second, and still it is as astonishing as when it first dawned upon me. But I don't congratulate myself; far from it. Evil was the day when I persuaded myself that a man ought to keep up with the spirit of the times; that he should leave the beaten paths of Conservatism, and wander down the sinuous byways traced out by youthful Liberalism. Still more evil was the day when, forgetting the example of my great ancestor Adam, I listened to the words of feminine lips, and hastened to guide my steps by the light of feminine wisdom. Utterly crushed and broken down for the moment, I am repenting of my folly, when too late, in metaphorical dust and ashes, and in literal brown paper, vinegar, and court-plaster. "Oh, my!" as Mr. Fledgeby remarked when he, too, had come to grief through a woman's instrumentality, "Oh, my!"

"The King's daughter is all glorious within," wrote the psalmist. She might be in those days, and she may be now, for anything I know to the contrary. I cannot contradict the assertion from actual experience, for I never dissected one; though just at present I'd dissect half a hundred of them with the greatest pleasure in life if I could get hold of them. But this I can safely say: they are anything but glorious without. Apples of Sodom are they; fair to view, but bitter to the taste; shifting sands, that under the appearance of solid ground engulf the unwary wayfarer; mossy quagmires, with nothing green about them except the fellow that trusts himself to them. Never, never, never will I listen to a King's daughter again. If I lived to be a thousand years old, and had to be married a hundred times in that period, I would keep a safe distance from courts, and the princesses that dwell in them, and choose my wives from Republican heiresses. .

It came about in this way. On a never-sufficiently-to-be anathematized day I was reading the New York *Tribune*, and I came on the following paragraph:

"At a gathering of King's daughters at London, Ont., the other day, Mrs. Graham, of Toronto, on being asked if dancing should be tolerated, replied: 'Yes! but only in the morning, an hour before breakfast, and then the woman should dance with her husband or brother."

I pondered deeply on this saying, and became convinced that I had been sinfully neglectful of my duties as a husband and master. You will observe that Mrs. Graham did not say the woman, (that is every woman in the household) "may" dance, but "should" dance, clearly meaning that it is the duty of every woman to dance, and that she should be assisted by her husband, or brother, as the case might be, in doing so. My household is singularly well arranged for such a pursuit, and we can always pair off like members of the Legislature when they don't want to have their names appearing in the division lists. There was my wife and myself; the cat, Naomi, and the dog, Jim; the hired man, Nathan, and the hired girl, Bloomah; husband and wife, as required by Mrs. Graham: the cat and dog were not exactly married, but they quarrel so continuously that they have every claim to be considered in the light of a loving couple; and as for Nathan and Bloomah, I knew that he had proposed to her a few days before, and she had told him that she loved another, but she would always be a sister to him; so there again the conditions under which dancing became a moral duty were fulfilled. You see, the household was already splendidly mated for saltatory exercise; husband

and wife ; cat and dog; brother and sister. It really seemed to me, as a sense of neglected duty dawned on me from a perusal of Mrs. Graham's words, that the finger of Providence had been pointing that way for a long time, and that everything was prepared to facilitate the performance of duty. "The woman should dance." Of course. How was it that this had never occurred to me before, though I had noticed that Bloomah was developing a tendency to fatten up like my prize pig, and was just about as much disinclined to bestir herself about her ordinary avocations ?

The hour fixed upon was also singularly convenient. We keep up the good old fashion of family prayers before breakfast, and all the household is then assembled in the dining-room. The cat and the dog don't join in, of course, but they listen very attentively, or else imitate the example of a fashionable congregation during the sermon, and go to sleep, which is as much as can be expected from animals that are not credited with possessing souls, (I am referring to the cat and dog, not the congregation), so, as I said, we are all assembled just at the proper time ; and that, again, was a manifest sign in what direction my duty lay So I concluded to begin the very next morning, and have a good dance before breakfast, instead of prayers, three times a week. Mrs. Graham did not say that a woman should dance every day, and I thought every other one, leaving Sunday as an off day, would be sufficient for a beginning. I did not take my wife into my confidence, thinking I would surprise her. So I did; and afterwards she surprised me—she and Bloomah combined. I detest combines now as much as any Liberal does. I went to bed full of virtuous intentions, and as Southey says of Bishop Hatto, who was eaten up by rats, I "slept that night like an innocent man." He adds, "But Bishop Hatto never slept again," and upon my word I feel as if I were going to be in the same predicament. "Oh, my ! I do ache so."

The fateful morning came ; but I thought it advisable previously to give Nathan instructions to ensure everything going off smoothly. " Nat," I said, " We are going to vary the religious exercises a little this morning, so keep your eye on me, and you

and Bloomah must just follow me and my wife." He looked a
little astonished, but said it was all right, and he would. So when
we stood up to sing the opening hymn, I just clipped my wife
round the waist and began to waltz round the room, singing
lustily,

> "Up and down the cobbler's bench
> The monkey chased the weasel ;
> The parson kissed the cobbler's wife,
> And Pop ! goes the weasel."

Nathan followed suit, hugging Bloomah like a bear, and dancing
like one, too. He trod on the cat's tail at the first start, and she
flew at the dog ; and the two adjourned under the table, which was
the only safe place for them, for a free fight. They had to keep it
up, too, for neither of them dared run from under the table while
we were whirling round in the giddy maze, and when the waltz
came to an end there was as much hair and fur on the ground as
would have stuffed a decent sized mattress.

Feeling a little tired at the end of five minutes, I dropped my
wife on the sofa, and Nathan dumped Bloomah into the rocking-
chair for a brief intermission. Before they could either of them
get enough breath to speak, we had them off again ; this time to
the strains of "Ta-ra-ra Boomdeay," which we afterward toned
down to "Two Little Girls in Blue," for the pace was killing.
What was left of the cat had taken advantage of the pause to seek
refuge on the top of the high cupboard in which we keep the
crockery ; at least, I saw a tail as thick as a stovepipe waving up
there ; I don't know if there was any body to it. As for the dog,
he couldn't be seen anywhere ; and I afterwards heard that when
he was found, he was under the sofa trying to cover the unwonted
nakedness of his hinder parts in one of my big fishing boots, and
the corresponding baldness of his pate in the other. He has completely lost one eye, and, to make things even at the other end, has
only two inches of his tail left.

We had another intermission, but I delayed too long, humming over "After the Ball," which I thought would be a fitting
tune for the conclusion of the ceremony. This gave time to my

wife and Bloomah to recover from their surprise; they did not recover breath for two or three minutes more; and the first intimation I got of it was a whack on the back of the head from the flying coffee pot, the spout of which got jammed between my collar and my neck, and poured the whole of the boiling liquid down the small of my back. Nathan basely turned tail, and bolted, but, I am happy to say, the women finished him off in the kitchen after they had done with 'me. What they did, I cannot precisely say. I have a confused idea of a storm of flying cups, saucers, plates, knives and forks, spoons, toast, eggs, and other articles too numerous to mention; and when these were exhausted, of being assailed with all the opprobrious terms that were ever known to man, and a whole dictionary full of more that were specially invented for the occasion. Let me draw a veil over the scene. A woman when she gets mad is the very—hem! and there were two of them. You may imagine the rest. King's daughters, indeed! Bother the King's daughters, and very particularly bother Mrs. Graham, if they can't do better than lay down rules that a fellow cannot follow without making a martyr and an ass of himself; and getting anathematized into the bargain.

"ENFIN, *me voilà!* On my end, here I am!" I am not
quite certain which end it is, but I think it must be the
latter one, having been brought so near it in consequence of my
imprudence in listening to a King's daughter, and not having had
much time to make progress on my recovery. And I am the
more supported in this conclusion because, if I may trust to
appearances, I am sitting on my old favorite stump, the companion
of my meditations, and my tried friend when the conjugal sky is
overcast. I say, "if I may trust to appearances," because I am
not much disposed to put my trust in anything, and I think
David might have spoken out like a man instead of half way
when he said, " Put not your trust in princes "—he ought to have
added, " or in princes' daughters either " : then, I should have been
all right. However, I am the gainer after all by my late experience,
for I have deduced from it a very important rule of life, and that
is, don't regulate your conduct to a woman by the advice given
by other women, especially if she happens to be your wife or your
hired girl. I don't mean to say that the feminine mind is not
profound—it is too profound for ordinary intellects—or that it is
lacking in common sense. It is certain, however, that its precepts
are not intended for the guidance of the sex. As the poet very
correctly remarks, "The proper study of womankind is man," and
woman recognizes the justice of the sentiment. The sole object
of her thoughts is man : how he should behave, how he should
dress, what he should say, and what he should and should not do.
She studies man in all his pursuits and vocations, from the
minister in the pulpit to the politician in the caucus; she sizes
him up, and tones him down; she contemplates him as a possible
husband, and a certain lover; she torments his life out by day,

and dreams about him by night ; and all her schemes are devoted to the moral, intellectual and social regeneration of man. She never condescends to bother herself about her sisters, or, when she does, she picks them to pieces, and dismisses them with contempt. If I had seen this clearly before I attempted to start a family dancing school, I should not have needed the chastening of experience ; and, after all, I am not so much disposed to blame the King's daughters. It was not their fault if I did not understand that in any scheme they may have for masculine regeneration, the way in which other women will view it when put into practical operation never enters their heads. Their view of creation comprises but two things, man and his regenerator.

At any rate, I am in a fair way for recovery ; and I have been greatly helped to this by reading the reports of the proceedings at the recent quarterly meeting of the Protestant committee of the Council of Public Instruction. I am delighted to find that that body has at length awoke to the perception of what I long ago pointed out, namely, that it is absurd and unjust to devote so great a part of the public aid to education to the support of schools in large and flourishing centres, which are fully able to support themselves, both in scholars and in money, while poor and struggling communities are left to die of inanition, and are put off with aids which are useless, except for the purpose of mockery ; one school, which I instanced, actually receiving twenty-five cents as the Government grant ; a sum which barely covered the postage on the correspondence with the department. It is true that this tardy recognition of what I pointed out some years ago is only as yet partial and half hearted ; the committee still clings to the leaven of the Pharisees, and still adheres in a modified form to the principle of apportioning grants by the results of examinations. It apparently contemplates the withdrawal, or, at any rate, the reduction of the grants made to schools which are, or ought to be be, self-supporting ; but it still professes to be convinced of the propriety of being guided in its distribution of the public moneys by the results of the public examination, and the reports of the inspectors combined.

Let me try and clear the situation once more in as few words as possible, and explain the principles which are at issue. The system of payment by results is a system of prizes; and prizes are awarded, not for the aid, but for the encouragement of education. It is important to note and insist on this distinction, because it may be urged, and with justice, that whatever encourages education helps it. This is true enough, so far as it goes, but the help extended is incidental only. The prizes given to the classes in a school are no doubt of material assistance in stirring up emulation and encouraging study in the scholars, and, in so far, they are of advantage both to these, and to the school itself; but they are no more aid, properly so called, to education, than are the desks of the latest modern fashion, the system of ventilation, the blackboards, and other school appliances. In fact, without an efficient staff of teachers, all these things are worse than useless. Now what the books, and medals, and diplomas are to the scholars, that, and no more, are the government grants on the results system to the schools. They are prizes for the encouragement of efficient education in a community: the only difference is that instead of being given to the scholars, they are given to the ratepayers, as represented by the School Commissioners, or the Board of Trustees. I think that this position is so plain and obvious that no one will attempt to controvert it; at any rate I have not yet met with any one who has done so.

Now I admit, at once, that this principle is a good one, and attended with satisfactory results under certain well defined conditions; my objection to it is that these conditions do not exist in this province. They exist only in old, and well settled countries, where every community, however small, is able at least to pay for a sound elementary education, by which I mean "the three R's, Reading, Riting, and Rithmetic," without extraneous assistance. Then, the prize system of government grants works satisfactorily and without doing any injustice, because it has a good basis to work on. It encourages competition, because, however small may be the grant received by a school, the sum can be applied to the improvement of its education, and is not needed for its maintenance.

In this country, and more especially in this province, the case is different. It is sparsely populated, and all over it are little struggling communities that have about as much as they can manage to provide for their own maintenance, and to whom the scanty pittance which they pay to the raw young girls whom alone they can get as school teachers is a heavy burden. No prize system can awaken any spirit of competition in them, from the simple fact that any advance is just as much beyond their reach as the sun is, and from the other simple fact that when a man is struggling for a bare crust of bread, visions of glory and of fame are not wont to flit before his eyes. What such schools need is help, not encouragement. There are communities again in which the Protestant element is so small that they are either obliged now to send their children and pay their taxes to the Roman Catholic schools, or soon will be. I know of one, and in a tolerably large city too, where the only thing that keeps it from being struck off entirely from the list of Protestant schools is the presence of French Roman Catholic children who make up half its number. An exceptional case? Well, so far as its being in a tolerably populous centre goes, yes; in other details, no. I have been a teacher, amongst other things, in my day, and I have taught in elementary schools as well as academies, and I call to mind two of the former where the government aid was $12 a year, and where the grant received from the Society for the Propagation of the Gospel in England was much more. I don't know whether they have it now; I rather think they haven't, but I do know that one of them afterwards received that munificent aid of twenty-five cents to which I have referred, and by this time, at the same rate, it is probably paying the government five cents a year instead of receiving anything.

There is no need to go any further. Now, perhaps you will understand why I say that the system of apportioning the public money "by results," is a false and pernicious one in this province, and that the true principle in the present condition of Protestant education here is to apply that portion of the money which is devoted to common and elementary education according to the needs of the smaller and poorer communities. To many of these latter it is a matter of life or death, to all it is one of simple efficient instruction. It is all very well to exclaim against the incompetency of the teachers, and to endeavor to educate them thoroughly, as is still done. In the name of common sense, if such a thing is known in educational circles, what well educated and accomplished young man or young woman will bury himself or herself in a little obscure rural hamlet, with all its discomforts of living, for a salary not greater than most servant girls get, and infinitely less than that of a good cook, housemaid, or waiter? Educate! Yes! and the educated will go off as clerks in stores and mercantile firms, as type-writers, as book-keepers; some few may be trapped into a so-called model school, or even an elementary school in a big village. But into an out-of-the-way rustic hamlet, —"not if I know it, Sammy: no! you don't."

A Winter Fantasy.

FOREMOST among the pioneers of civilization, and the benefactors of mankind are the North American Indians. It is true that they were uncultured, and their attentions to strangers were more energetic than conventional, and more warm than agreeable, but then every nation has its customs, and there are fly-specks on the best of us. If they made their captives run the gauntlet, out of that they evolved lacrosse, and would have evolved football too, if rubber had not been scarce; if they made incursions in the winter, and burned down villages without any regard to the feelings of the inmates, or the fact that the thermometer was 20 below zero, they invented snow shoes for the purpose; if they organized summer surprise parties which ended by their sticking the surprised with lighted pine splinters as full as a hedge hog is of quills, and finally dismissing them in a grand pyrotechnic display, they called into existence the toboggan in their more sedate moments. Lacrosse, snowshoe clubs, toboggan slides, these grand things civilization owes to the Indians. Eh! "Rather different now to what they were in the time of the aborigines?" Of course. If a man cannot improve on what his ancestors did he had better have been born before them, and besides, it's a great deal easier to improve on a thing after it is invented, than to invent it oneself. The criticism is irrational. How is a man going to perfect any idea before it has occurred to any one, I should like to know. Therefore the Indians were the pioneers of civilization, and the benefactors of mankind, Q.E.D.

Look at snow-shoeing; only look at snow-shoeing. Could there be anything more invigorating, more exhilarating, more delightful? That is when you get accustomed to it, and don't trip yourself up at the first deep snow drift, and make a frantic attempt to stand on your head on the ground five feet below, while your heels wave wildly in the air, a human semaphore. But when

these preliminaries are over, oh the glory of that steady swinging
tramp over the crisp snow that sparkles in a million diamond facets
under your feet, while the pure bracing air rushes to meet you
laden with the breath of spruce and pine, and fills your lungs with
the elixir of life. It also converts your beard and moustache into
a fairy grotto of icicles, so that you could not get within two inches
of the lips of the pretty girl at your side, however much you might
feel tempted to do so, and a convenient turn in the line of march
might afford an opportunity. Never mind; "there is a tide in the
affairs of men," and besides your nose is looking a little too blue
for sentiment. Hark! How the mounting spirits break out into
song; no birds ever sang more heartily. "Ho! Ho! Ho! over
the snow, with the blue above and the white below! Hearts stout
and light of the blue and white, over the sparkling crust to-night!"
What's that break in the song and a roar of laughter instead?
Tompkins gone to grass? There's no grass now. Pull him out and
set him on his legs again. Nose frozen? Rub it with snow, or
stop! Ask Miss Maude there to "kiss the spot and make it well."
All right, old man! off we go again. The glory? Ay! and the
health and the pleasure and the good fellowship of it. The air is full
of laughter and joke and song, and the snow under the feet sings like
an accompaniment of fairy bells. Talk about summer birds! Why
here is the very essence of music and poetry. Who is that
swearing up in the big old pine there? A squirrel, and he's not
swearing either, he is laughing till he can scarcely hold on to the
branch. See how his head bobs down and his tail jerks up in
a very ecstasy of fun. "Bright eyes," Miss Helen? It's your own
you see reflected in them.

> Diamonds glance from the branching pines,
> Diamonds cover the sleeping vines,
> Diamonds star the skies above
> But brighter thy clear pure eyes, my love.
>   Sweet eyes! sparkle when blue skies darkle
>   When night comes down with her starry crown
>   Ere the bridegroom sun hath his race begun
>   And sleep still fosters country and town.

What's that? "Close up in the rear there and don't fall
behind." Close up, it is; only stopping to admire the squirrel.
Take my arm, Miss Helen, we'll get along faster to catch them up.

Yes! snow-shoeing is a grand invention, better than tobboggan-
ing. I don't care much for tobogganing : one has no time to——
admire squirrels. You can't talk soft nonsense when your whole
attention is devoted to holding on to your toboggan and your
breath, and your whole soul is wrapt in an earnest prayer that
when you reach the bottom it may be only your leg that is broken,
and not your neck. It is very nice just as you are getting ready
to start, but when that toboggan begins to make play you get a
vivid idea of a sudden leap into eternity. Earth vanishes, and
becomes a chaos of whirling phantasms ; the heavens—there is no
such thing as the Heavens ; nothing but a swirling blue mist amid
which all the stars, fused into one single comet with a tail five
million of billions of miles long, dart like the arrow of doom. What
was that? An earthquake or a volcanic eruption? or did that fiend
of a toboggan slide out from underneath and hit me on the
back ? Only a jump ? Next time I want to jump I'll go up five
miles in a balloon. It would be more comfortable. Where's my
breath ? I shall have to advertise for it when I get to the bottom,
if I ever do get there, which is doubtful. I don't believe there *is*
a bottom. Somebody has stolen the other end. We have been
travelling at the rate of a hundred thousand miles a second through
countless years, and we ought to have been there, wherever there
is, or if there is a there at all, long before this. I wish I had made
my will before I started ; I wish I could remember a prayer; I
wish I had been a better man when I was alive ; I wish I was off
this toboggan now that I am dead. I wish——Hah ! It's stopping,
and I've not been dead at all. Thank Heaven! If ever again I
go !—Jack ! Lend a hand to pull the toboggan up, and let us try it
again. Man ! it was grand.

Musings at Night Fall.

NIGHT seems to me to come to a clearing with a more gentle tread, and to hush it to sleep with a more tender whisper than she does elsewhere. The homestead is full of life, and eager anticipations of the morrow ; the graveyard has nothing but the dust of the dead and the memories of their yesterday ; the clearing combines them both ; tells of the waving forest of the past, and foreshadows the golden grain fields of the future. Whilst the farm house, the hamlet, and the town represent life in its vigorous activity, and the cemetery represents a vanished life, the clearing is at once the close of one existence and the beginning of another. What does the night-breeze whisper among the stumps ? A regret for the forest glories, and a sigh for the present desolation ; or a vision of the beauty to come ? Who knows ? Does the man, or woman, far advanced in years, know whether in the depths of the heart, the regret for past joys, the consciousness of failing powers, or the prospect of the newer and better life is really the most predominant ? Does he cling to the memories of youth and maturity, or does he say with the poet,

> " The saints are dead, the martyrs dead,
>   And Mary, and Our Lord ; and I
>   Would follow with humility ?"

I wonder whether I could put his thoughts into verse, and whether they would run much in this way.

> Is there a sigh for the days of yore
>   When the soul looks back on the beaten track ?
> Is it " ah, for the days that shall be no more,"
>   And alas ! for the present, all gloomy and black ?"
>   God knows—not I ;

For the soul of man is strange in its ways,
An unsolved riddle, a tangled maze.
    It mingles its gladness with sorrow,
    Its present and past with to morrow ;
    Dashes its triumphs with whispered fears,
    Mixes its laughter with hidden tears ;
    It chants in a psalm of thanksgiving
    The beauty and glory of living,
    Whilst all through the notes of its pœau fly
    The undertones of its agony.
    As the ways of a nesting plover,
    As the heart of a maid to her lover,
    As a dream that we lose in awaking,
    As a flower that is crushed in the taking,
    As the joy that has fled in the grasping,
    As the love that has died in the clasping,
    As the vapour-born lights of the fen
    Are the souls of men unto men.
Have we a yearning sigh for the past,
Or a smile that the end is coming at last ?
       I know not—I.

Smooth is the pathway that children tread,
    Traced out by love, and all hedged in by laughter,
With never a care, and never a dread,
    And never a thought of the coming hereafter ;
With the soft hand stroking the golden head,
    And the dear voice cooing its dove to rest,
And the sweet face bending above the bed,
    And watching the birdling in its nest !
    Ripple of laughter all day long,
    Patter of little feet, trilling of song !
Oh ! the sweetness, the sweetness, the sweetness
   Of the innocent days that have long gone by !
And ah ! the fleetness, the fleetness, the fleetness
    Of Time that has left but their memory !

Fair was the road when youth was strong,
    When the pulse beat high, and the heart was gay ;
When the breezes whispered naught but a song,
    And flowers studded the pleasant way ;

When the vines were laden with purple and gold,
    And the apples of Eden hung from each tree ;
When the cup of pleasure was easy to hold,
    And the beauty of woman fair to see.
Oh ! the gladness, the gladness, the gladness,
    The rapture of youth in the days of yore !
But ah ! the sadness, the sadness, the sadness
    Of elusive joys that return no more !
For the apples were apples of Sodom, dust ;
    And the poison of asps was the juice of the grape ;
And the heart's desire but an empty lust ;
    And the beauty of woman a soul-less shape.

Hard and rough was the road for the man ;
    Rugged and hard, to be trod alone,
With toil and trouble, and plan upon plan,
    And frequent stumbles o'er rock and stone ;
When the heart was dead to all joys save one,
    The making, and keeping, and massing of pelf ;
And if ever there entered a ray of life's sun,
    'T was lost in the growing gloom of self.
Children and wife, he toiled for them,
    He said to himself in a dreamy way,
He laboured that they might take their ease,
    And who was there that could say him, nay ?
Oh ! the gladness, the gladness, the gladness
    Of seeing the toil-won wealth increase !
But ah ! the madness, the madness, the madness
    Of ever dreaming that gold brings peace.

For if the apples of Sodom are dust,
The gold of Ophir is iron rust.
It might well be in the first beginning
That wealth for loved ones was worth the winning,
But habit grows, and hardens, and grows
Till it kills the stem upon which it rose,
And the heart lies torpid, unable to bleed,
Sucked dry in the grasp of the devil-fish, greed.

And is it " oh ! for the days of yore,"
    As the soul looks back again o'er the past ?
Or is it " Thank God that they come no more,
    And the long sought rest approaches at last "?
        God knows, not I,

Which it shall be in the solemn day
When the visions of earth are passing away,
       A smile, or a cry.
We are mocked through our years by shadows that flee
     Still as we strive to grasp them.
And our joys are dreams of t e memory,
       E'en as we clasp them.

Oh Thou, who seest not as we see,
Look on us when we come to Thee:
          Miserere, Domine !
....And lo ! when at last he has run his race,
    There rests a smile on the dead man's face.

By The Water Courses.

THERE is a little stream runs through the clearing, and down into the cultivated lands below. Up above, in the bush, it is quite a respectable brook, with miniature water falls, and small rapids, and chatters along from stone to mossy stone in a sociable manner that is very charming. It is not what you might call sparkling, for the great trees crowd its banks, and shut out the sun light, but it is very merry for all that. The wild birds use it for a bathing place, and after having carefully selected a spot where it is about a quarter of an inch deep, and there is no fear of being drowned, proceed to read the Riot Act over it, as over a tumultuous assemblage of water drops, and disperse it with much fluttering of wing, and jerking of tail; while the squirrel running over a fallen trunk at some deeper spot, suddenly catches the semblance of another squirrel running along another trunk down below, and halts to give his opinion of such conduct, with bushy tail quivering with indignation, and a perfect storm of bad language which culminates in a shriek, and a flash of red lightning. Down below, in the cultivated lands, it holds a direct and even course, and, if it looks more like a drain than anything else, is yet undoubtedly a stream. But in the clearing it is simply an ooze, where it is not a puddle. It has been so blocked up in one place by decaying trunks, and in another by tangled brush that it has lost all heart, and dribbles off here and there in devious ways and unexpected directions. There are trout up above in it, I know, for I have seen them, and trout below in the drain which it becomes, not very big ones of course, but still undeniable brook trout, but I won't believe that there are any in the clearing. There is not water enough in any one spot to cover the knee joints of a middle aged grass-hopper; and yet Nathan brought me a fish weighing about five ounces which he vowed he had caught not far from my stump.

He wouldn't say how far; only winked, and said he wasn't going to tell me of the hole, and I believe he had the best of reasons for declining.

The demoralizing influence which a fish has on the average human conscience is as strange as it is notorious. I am not referring merely to "fish stories," or to all the petty deceptions to which an angler resorts to magnify himself and his catch in the eyes of the world, but to other things besides. Above all other pursuits, angling promotes selfishness; there is the disposition to give misleading advice to a brother angler as to the best fishing resorts, and the best places in them; and the innocent air with which one fisherman will recommend another to use flies which he knows to be altogether unsuitable, is only equalled by that with which a girl lures a young fellow into proposing and being rejected. And a fish puts to rout all previously acquired religious habits. I have known grave and reverend church wardens, and elders, men who raise their hands with holy horror at flowers on the Communion table, and emulate the example of the deaf adder when they hear of choral services, who would nevertheless start off on a Saturday afternoon after a hard week's work, and go to some distant lake or river to enjoy a Sunday's fishing; and they would come back on the Monday, too, with a goodly string of trout, or ouananiche, or pickerel, and never think of trying to make amends for their evil doings by sending me any. It's very curious, by the way, how fish seem to encourage Sabbath breaking. You may flog a stream, or a pond, from Monday morning to dewy Saturday eve, without getting as much as a rise, and lo! on the Sunday there is a perpetual hail storm of leaping fish all through the day. I know the same sort of thing has been observed about a crow; gun or no gun, you've got to keep out of range of him on week days, but on Sundays you can get almost near enough to put salt on his tail; and it has been urged from the consideration of the behaviour of birds and fish in this respect, that long experience has taught the lower animals that on one day out of seven they have nothing to fear from the average civilized man. I doubt the soundness of this conclusion. You will observe that there is nothing tempting about the crow. He is not good to eat, and he is not used as an ornament for a lady's hat. I have no doubt that he wonders why people shoot at him, and when the day of rest comes, he accepts the fact like the philosopher that he is, and makes no more ado about it. He doesn't stroll in your barn yard, or crow on your roof, and say " Here I am ; get your gun, Johnnie, if you dare." But a fish knows that he is good to eat, and a thing to be desired, because he himself has eaten lots of other little fish in his day, and enjoyed them amazingly. When he leaps up on Sunday, he is tempting man and boy, and he knows it, the wicked beggar. I am not sure that I grieve deeply when he meets with retribution, even if it be unrighteous ; though, of course, I wouldn't do it myself on any account ; that is, if I thought the village was likely to know it ; and I know plenty of other men who hold the same views on the subject.

Besides being the tempter to Sabbath-breaking, the fish is an inspirer of what I may delicately term deceptive imaginations. When he is brought to the scales he is invariably found wanting, but it is when he takes his own scales away with him that he is prodigious, and only inferior in size to the lies that are told about him. Yet sometimes a fish appears to be possessed of a conscience of its own, and a sense of what is due to veracity. I recollect a case in point when a friend of mine got a well merited rebuke for trying to palm off a " fish story " on me. We had been out on a sporting expedition together to Lake Kiskising, and one day he took the canoe and went out on the pond, while I, having found a nice little spot where I could fish from the bank, and smoke comfortably, remained behind. A couple of hours elapsed, during which I won't say how many I caught, for fear you would think I was lying, which I never do, but it was a good many, when my friend made his appearance round the point and hailed me. To his enquiries as to the luck I had had, I answered by pointing to the string at my feet, and then asked after his welfare. " Only a couple of dozen," said he ; " they were taking the fly splendidly, but just as I was getting warmed to the work I hooked a splendid fellow. By Jove sir, I never saw such a fish in my life before, or

you either. I don't wonder now at the tales of sea serpents. I
played him for an hour and a half, nip and tuck ; up the lake ;
down the lake ; across the lake." "How on earth did you manage
that ? " I interrupted ; " You couldn't play such a fish as the one
you're talking about and row at the same time." "Right you are
Philosopher," he said " but, you see, when my line was all run
out, I just held on to the butt of the rod, braced my feet against
the sides of the boat, and let him tow me. And he did it, sir !
For an hour and a half did that fish pull the heavy boat at an
express rate, till, about five minutes ago, he found he was getting
into shoal water, (a little over five feet, for I sounded it afterwards),
and then a sudden idea seemed to strike him. Instead of making
out for the deep again he stopped, stood straight up on his tail with
his head and shoulders out of the water, gave a sort of a twirl
round that broke my line, and then swore at me like a trooper for
having what he called ' such a confounded heavy old tub.' ' It's
lucky for you,' said he ' that I've been gaining flesh, for last time
I was scaled I only weighed 149 lbs, 5 ounces ; but I've toned up
since, or you wouldn't have had such a fine run.' What do you
think of that ? " I was going to tell him, when a little trout
about six inches long leaped out of the water, with a yard of line
hanging from his mouth. "I don't know what he thinks," it
squeaked, " but I think you're a confounded liar." And he splashed
into the water again. You never saw a man so taken aback.

I was very glad of it, myself, for I detest anything like
exaggeration, or the slightest deviation from truth, and I knew, by
sad experience, that my own actual catch that day would have
been dwarfed into insignificance besides the relation of what he
might have caught, and ought to have caught, but did not, so that
when we got home I should have been obliged to sit on the empty
cracker box in the back corner of the post office and general store,
while he sat on the counter, and held forth to the admiring
assemblage. That's the sort of way he always used to serve me
when we went out in those days. But this time I had him ; and
when I got back and said I had caught a land-locked salmon that
gave us three square meals a day for four days, and then we had

to throw the greater part of it away, because it would not keep any longer, he could only groan and turn up his eyes.   He did open his mouth at the conclusion of my story, but I went on to add : "You may think, boys, I'm romancing, but, after all that's only a small fish for that Lake.   Here's Bob will tell you he has known fish there that were six feet long, and weighed over 149 lbs. Haven't you, Bob ?"   And Bob jumped up and said, "Come along, boys, it's my treat."

Products of the Clearing. Weeds.

A clearing in its infancy is a very unpromising thing to look at. At the first glance you would say that to call it a wilderness would be to pay it a wholly undeserved compliment. It is not even a waste, though it looks desolate and wretched enough for one. It is an extent of unsightly stumps and decaying logs, with stones and rock interspersed, puddles of water here and there in the wet season, and small basins of dead vegetation in the dry, and with a few scanty blades of coarse grass, which barely suffice to whet the appetites of the two or three cows, or sheep, that are turned in to get their living as best they may, and that generally do so by breaking down the fences, and wandering off into the bush beyond. The berrying season is the only time at which the clearing appears to any advantage, for there the wild strawberry blushes furiously over the mounds and hillocks, and the raspberry clings to the outskirts of the bush, or, later on, mounts over the heaps of piled stones. How they got there is a mystery. You don't find them in the middle of the bush, but directly the overshadowing roof of the forest foliage is taken away, up they pop, like as many vegetable Jack-in-the-boxes. And with them, the little violets, purple and white and yellow, and the great dog violet, the wild oats, the wood anemone and the Mayflower. If you are very lucky, you may come across a trillium ; the purple one, be it well understood, not the white; but this is of very rare occurrence. These are the spring treasures of the clearing, as the berries are its summer ones, and it hides them very carefully from view; so carefully, indeed, that to a casual observer it presents much the same aspect in the first half of the year that it does in the fall, only it looks a little less dusty and brown. But it has not the slightest hesitation in obtruding its weeds on notice. Thistles and burdock and mullein thrive on its bosom, as if they would say "Yes! here we are, and here we mean to stay. You don't like us? That is a matter of taste. We are the natural products of neglect, and this is our rightful place. By and by, we will overrun those beautiful fields of yours, and give you a deal of trouble, but in the meantime as we stand here we have a beauty of our own, and possibilities that only lie latent because you do not think us worth your attention." I am not so sure that they are not right. I know that the wheat and grains that feed millions to-day have been developed by care and cultivation from coarse and worthless grasses; that when left alone they degenerate into the condition from which they were raised. I know that some of our choicest flowers were originally weeds; that the crab tree is the distant ancestor of the Fameuse, and the sloe of the plum. There is a great deal to be got out of weeds if you only go the right way to work about it, and have the necessary patience. I think, amongst other things, there is a lesson of charity.

Just a few moments ago a tramp passed down the lane, and looked into the clearing. He was unsavory enough in appearance, and I doubt not would have been equally unsatisfactory to the olfactory nerves if I had been near enough, which I fortunately wasn't. There is no need to describe him in detail: tramps are not black swans, and a rarity on this continent; or indeed any other; and as they are, with rare exceptions, very much alike in their salient points, you may imagine what my tramp was like from those you have seen for yourselves. He did not see me, and after leaning on the fence and spitting meditatively over it for a minute or two, passed wearily on. What was it I was talking about just now? Weeds? well! here was a two-legged one. I wonder whether, if he had seen me, he would have said to me as that burdock was saying when he came up, " we are the natural products of neglect, but we have possibilities that are only latent because you despise us, and do not think us worth your attention." And, again, if he were to say so, I am not quite sure that he would not be right.

The tramp family is a large one, and embraces widely differing varieties. It is also an ancient and aristocratic one. The wise

king of Ithaca, Ulysses " who saw many manners of men and their
cities " was one of its members.   When the Grecian army was
disbanded after the capture of Troy, he did just what a lot of
soldiers do in similar circumstances at the present day, and went
on the tramp.   He was just the fellow for it too ; unscrupulous and
truculent at heart, and plausible in speech.   I have no doubt he was
an adept at wiling the pie of indigestion from the housekeepers of
those days, as well as at extracting a meal of cold meat and
potatoes by menaces whenever he thought he could do it safely.
And he never did a stroke of work, that I can find out.   Coming
further down the roll of time, we find musical tramps, yclept
Troubadours, and wandering minstrels ; religious tramps, such as
the mendicant friars ; literary tramps, such as the poor scholars of
the universities in the middle ages.   Guttenberg was a fine example
of the printing tramp ; Columbus of the nautical tramp ; and
political tramps abound now.   King and soldier, priest and
scholar, musician and politician, discoverer and explorer, they have
one and all had the same characteristics ; they have religiously
abstained from doing any hard work themselves that they could
possibly avoid, and they have got their living out of the fears or
the foibles of the rest of the world ; and yet they have been held
in honour.   They have never been called bad names, or had
the dog set at them.   It is only the tramp *par excellence*, the
avowed and unmitigated tramp, as represented by my friend of a
few minutes ago, for whom such treatment is reserved.

Well ! I suppose he merits it.   He is dirty, lazy, (in the sense
of having no settled occupation), brutal ; and it requires a great
deal of Christianity, of which we have none of us any too much,
to tolerate him ; loving him as a man and a brother is far beyond
our reach.   But have you ever considered through what a sad and
terrible experience he must have passed to become the wretch and
outcast that he is ?   There are tramps that have been such from
the time almost that they were able to walk ; whose babyhood
never knew a mother's love ; whose childhood was passed amidst
blows and curses, picking its scanty sustenance out of the garbage
of the gutter ; taught, and forced, to lie and to steal ; forced not

merely by those to whom they belonged, but by the great well-to-do world that would afford them the means of existence on no other conditions ; knowing nothing of God and the Saviour except as convenient names to round off an oath ; nothing of virtue, and everything of vice—starved, cold, naked, without sympathy, without love, without means of enjoyment save in the gratification of the coarsest sensual appetites. What else can they grow up to but what I have just seen ? "Do men gather grapes off thorns or figs off thistles ?" And if some kind hand is stretched out to help them ; to feed and educate them, and send them to some other country where there is more work for them to gain their living, what is the cry that is raised ? You know it yourselves. "Keep your scum at home ; we want men, it is true, but they must be men with money." You needn't look indignant. That is what you say, only I have put the thing in plainer words than you care to do. I have spoken of the born tramp : there are others that are not born, but forced into the ranks. Tramps that have been honest, hard-working men, and have lost their work through sickness, accident, or the competition of others, and, having lost it, have not been able to recover it again. Others, again, have wandered from their homes in the hopes of "bettering themselves," and have not done it. Some of these men give up the struggle at once, and commit suicide, as the man who falls overboard on a dark stormy night in mid-ocean will, after the first few instinctive struggles, perceive their futility, and cease from them. But the most of them join the great army of tramps, from which, having once enlisted, there is no possibility of desertion. Perhaps you think that these cannot fall so far as the others. I am not sure that they don't fall further, with the memories of the past honest life gnawing at their hearts, and the prospects of the future that lies before them. Like Sir Bedivere in King Arthur, they "Hear the deep before them, and a cry behind." How, do you suppose, Lucifer felt, when he was driven out of heaven ? Suffering may ennoble a man, but suffering without prospect or hope of release makes him a devil.

I am not pleading the cause of the tramp as he is : but such as he is, such has he been made by the world. Is there nothing

significant in the fact, that as the army of tramps increases so do
the numbers and the wealth of millionaires? There never was a
more infernal doctrine than the Free Trade maxim, sound economy
though it may be "Buy in the cheapest market, and sell in the
dearest," for it has led to the grinding down of the labourer, and
the reduction of his wages to the lowest living point; to shoddy
and skimped work, and to the introduction of machinery by which
one man can do the work of fifty men before. Oh, yes! we are
living fast; and we are dying fast too. The trouble is that we
don't die sufficiently fast, and there is a superabundance of the
human materials. We make astonishing progress in the arts and
sciences, in civilization and luxury and wealth, but we are sadly
backward in the art of dying, and the most unreasonable people in
this respect are the poor and the tramps who have been thought-
fully provided with every inducement to shuffle off this mortal coil,
and persist in refusing to do it. It is plainly, their duty to do it.
Somebody has got to die, and it is preposterous to suppose that
we who are comfortably off, who can throw away a few thousands
on a supper or ball, and a few hundreds on a bouquet or a pair of
garters, who dress in broadcloth and fine linen, and fare, some of
us, sumptuously, the rest of us comfortably every day, should be
called upon to quit, what, after all, is a very pleasant life.
Certainly we are our brother's keepers. We don't make the mistake
that Cain did, when he knocked Abel on the head. We keep our
brother in a different way now : insist on his mortifying the flesh by
abstinence ; remembering that it is hard for the rich to enter into
the Kingdom of Heaven, take the hardship all on ourselves, and make
the entrance easy for him ; and if he still needs further affectionate
keeping, tax ourselves for gaols and reformatories, and penitentiaries
wherein to keep him more carefully. It is quite astonishing after all
this, that he should be so ungrateful as to rob, and steal, and commit
an occasional murder, is not it? What was it the burdock said?
" We are the natural products of neglect, but we have possibilities
that only lie latent because you do not think us worth your attention." It may be so; but it is a great deal easier to swear at the burdock
as a useless and mischievous encumbrance, and to cut him down.

My Cousins, the Ants.

THERE goes an ant. He has got a dead fly about four times as big as himself in his mouth, and is progressing backwards, pulling, not pushing. I suppose Sir John Lubbock would consider that a proof of intelligence, a knowledge that strength is better expended in pulling a thing toward you than in pushing it from you. "That ant," or pismire, as our great grandmothers used to call him, Sir John would say, "has evidently been indoctrinated in the rudimentary principles of statics and dynamics." And this would be a strong argument in the favor of the evolution of the monkey through a long series of stages from protoplasm, and of man from the monkey. But just wait a bit. Presently you'll see that accomplished insect climb painfully up a blade of grass, and, when he has reached the top, stand on his hind legs and endeavor to thrust that dead fly into the jaws of space. I thought so! There he is poking the corpus delicti, (for I am convinced that he assassinated that fly) to all quarters of the compass, as if expecting some heavenly visitant to relieve him of his burden. He'll be uncommonly lucky if the said heavenly visitant does not come down on him in the shape of a bird. And I am willing to make a small bet that this is not the first time he has played this trick, and, if he gets home safely, it won't be the last. Now will anybody tell me that my little friend is possessed of the reasoning faculty ? He knows as well as you or I do what a blade of grass is ; and he is perfectly aware that there is an end to it ; and yet, simply because it happens to stand in what he fancies his way home, he must needs run up it, and stand waving himself about like a lunatic on its summit until his jaws ache with his burden, and he descends a sadder, but not a wiser ant, for he will do the very same thing when the next occasion presents itself. "Go to the ant, thou sluggard," says Solomon, as if one could learn anything from such an insensate proceeding as that I have just witnessed. Well! I don't know after all but what he may have had some reason for his advice. I rather fancy that most of us who are in a hurry to attain some wished for end, are apt to take the first way to it that presents itself, without much consideration as to where it may lead us. Perhaps we mayn't regard it as a way; perhaps it may be an obstacle instead; the result is much the same in either case; we go at it without reflection, and we find ourselves "up a tree." There's a great deal of human nature in the brute creation, or of brute nature in the human creation; which is it?

Now, when that ant came down to solid earth again, you will notice that he had lost his way. I never knew an ant yet that got out of sight of his home, and the highways that lead to it that didn't lose his way. He finds it again, of course, by some mysterious process or other, or else by making successive casts in every direction till he comes across some landmark he knows, or meets with some other ant who is able to tell him; but he loses it all the same for the time being, though he takes very good care not to lose the fly. He is like an Englishman in that respect. It is very hard to make John Bull let go of any property that he has once managed to get hold of; as witness Egypt. Our cousins, the Yankees, are the only people that I know of that have ever induced him to part with any of his worldly goods; and they generally do it by what is vulgarly called "bamboozling," combined with a judiciously safe amount of bluster. They got a big slice of Maine in that way; and another of Oregon; and I shouldn't be at all surprised if they get another of Alaska. But John Bull never loses his way; the ant does. I have noticed the same peculiarity about many insects—humble-bees especially. Even when they are quite close to the entrance to their home they seem puzzled, and unable to find it for a few minutes. The carpenter-wasp is another instance. He will poke his head into half-a-dozen holes and crannies before he finds the right one, and this nearly every time he returns to his residence. It is a very curious peculiarity, and has often puzzled me. You may take a cat away in a bag, and get rid of it twenty, fifty, or a hundred miles from its accustomed domicile, and it will return. Or a dog. The homing pigeon flies back to its nest with marvelous accuracy and celerity.

But these little creatures seem liable to a sudden loss of memory, or whatever is equivalent to it. Once get them out of their ordinary routine, and they are hopelessly at sea; for a time at least.

The meanest thing that has life evinces the possession of reasoning faculties which are totally distinct from what we call instinct. It is instinct which teaches the duckling to swim, and the chicken to peck directly it comes out of the shell; which leads the young of mammals, (including babies) to suckle; instinct probably, though not certainly, which dictates the form and fashion of their nests to the birds; but besides and beyond this there are evidences of the power of thought and reasoning in the lowest living thing which seems inseparable from the principle of life. I make no exceptions. The lower we go in the scale of animated creation, the fewer and fainter are the traces of this, till, when we come to the realm of botany, they almost entirely disappear. Yet even in plants they are not altogether wanting. It is something more than mere accident that leads a vine to send out rootlets in search of the nutriment to be derived from bones buried some distance from it, as it has been known to do; that induced a tree, annoyed by the fretting against its trunk of a branch of another tree, to throw out an excrescence that grasped the offender tight, and strangled it. It seems hard to attribute such things as these, and others that I could name, to thought; the thought of a tree! But what then was it? Certainly not accident, but purpose; means adapted to a definite end; and what is that but thought, or, if you take refuge in instinct, what is that again but unconscious thought?.

I take it, then, that the confusion of my little friend when he came down from his perilous elevation on the top of a blade of grass, was a suspension of the reasoning faculty, and hence an evidence that it previously existed. Instinct would have taken him straight home; even though, by so taking him, it had for a time got him "up a tree." When he got down again he would have trudged off with his burden in the most unhesitating manner. But he didn't. First he ran a little bit one way; then he ran a little bit another; then he came back and went up the blade of

grass again, as if he wanted to get a good look at the country.
Plainly, he was vexed, and nervous, and would not reason out
matters coolly. I have seen my hired girl, Bloomah, do much the
same sort of thing when a bad-tempered cow originated an
impromptu chaos of milk, milk-pail, milking maid, and barn-yard
manure, with a single elevation of one of its hind legs. Bloomah
was dazed: she did not know which to pick up first; the milk, or
the pail, or the manure, or herself; and she tried to do all four
things at once; just like my little friend the ant thrusting his fly
into the faces of the four winds of heaven from the top of the blade
of grass. When she finally got up, she did not know where to
look, or where to go, or even what to say. It's not often that you
find a woman totally incapable of an energetic expression of her
sentiments, but she was. She couldn't even say "gosh!" Now a
man would not have hesitated for a moment, either in action or
word. He would have seized a stick, or in default of that, the
milk stool, and have left that cow under no mistaken impression
as to his sentiments in the matter. And he would have been at
no loss for a proper, or rather improper vocabulary either. Now
this similarity of conduct of Bloomah and the ant under totally
unexpected and annoying circumstances, shows a similarity in the
reasoning powers of the two, contrasted as it is with the dissimilarity of conduct of the higher masculine intelligence. Nobody
would deny Bloomah the possession of reason because she looked
and acted like a fool when she was swimming in milk, and when
she recovered her erect position; and nobody should deny the
same faculty to the ant, because he looked also like a very foolish
ant on the blade of grass, and when he came down again.
Bloomah recovered sooner than the ant did, and while the latter
"returned to his muttons" and climbed up the grass again, she took
very good care not to come near the cow that night, but, seeing me
laughing at her, impressed me into the service, and made a fool of
me. Now this was evidently a grade of intelligence much higher
than that of the ant, to whom it never occurred to make me carry
the fly home for him, and is a further proof of thought pervading
the whole of the inferior living creation from woman down to

a cabbage-head, and in a gradually diminishing ratio. In unforeseen crises man alone has the perfect intelligence ; man alone is lord of himself ; man alone knows what to do, and what to say.

I wonder where the ant—he's gone now, and I can't ask him. I wonder where he got that fly. It couldn't have died of its own accord, for it is the middle of summer, and no fly would think of shuffling off this mortal coil till the first chills of autumn came, unless he was forced to do so. Just at this season the fly is particularly lively and wide awake. When he was young, and not well acquainted with this wicked world, you could occasionally take advantage of his infantile artlessness and want of caution, and hit him a whack. If you attempt to do it at this period of his life, you only hit yourself. Now how did that ant get that fly ? It looks very much as if I had been the witness of an insect crime ; of an assassination, or rather the results of one ; an accessory to a foul murder. It does not much matter now, for the ant is off, and I couldn't find him again if I were to try, but I should very much like to learn how he did it. It would be something useful to know next time musca domestica uses my nose as a parade ground when I want to go to sleep. It takes a great deal of serious thought and planning to circumvent a lively fly, and I'm beginning to think that perhaps I was wrong in assigning but a limited reasoning power to the pismire. I hope he will get home safe with his booty, and that he and Mrs. ant, and the little cousins will all have a good supper to-night. I know it is wishing well to a man, I mean a pismire, whom I believe in my heart to have been a murderer, but then, remember, his victim was a fly. There are cases in which murder is only righteous retribution. I know some among my friends and acquaintance whose taking off I should feel tempted to consider in that light, and I dare say you have the same experience. Very likely, this class will be enlarged, when this book comes to be criticized, if I hear my critics. Moreover I have no doubt that there are some who regard you and me in the same way ; to wit, that they would not be very indignant if we were assassinated. And that class also will be increased when this book comes to be read.

"Dulce et Decorum est."

WHEN contemplating the pismire the other day, my sense of justice, combined with the love of truth, compelled me to finish by claiming for him a limited possession of the faculty of thought, or reason, which I hold to be the distinctive characteristic of all created life, and the line that divides it from matter. If I had been left to my own predilections I should not have done so; I would much rather have shown him up as a perfect idiot, for though an ant may be, and doubtless is, an object for the imitation of the rising generation, yet viewing him with a philosophical eye he is a nuisance; an abstract nuisance, I mean; that he is a concrete one anybody can easily prove to himself by sitting down for a quarter of an hour or so in some place where the little nation most doth congregate. But taken abstractedly, and considered totally apart from his vicious little nippers, and his small body and legs, he is to me, at any rate, a nuisance, for he is a perpetual reproach. He is the personification of energy and directness; the incarnation of the "You mind your business, and I'll mind mine" principle, the solution of the problem of perpetual motion. I don't believe he ever sleeps; I am certain he never philosophizes. Now I don't mean to say that energy and indomitable perseverance are not great virtues; in fact, a man in this nineteenth century cannot get on without them; but then even these may be carried too far, and when they are, they become vices. The ant is a great deal too restless to be really good.

You want to know what all this has to do with patriotism? Who said anything about patriotism? I didn't. It is true that the chapter is headed dulce et decorum est, but I didn't finish the quotation with pro patria mori; and there are a great many things that are sweet and fair-seeming besides dying for one's country. Nobody does that now-a-days; there is nobody now that will deliberately leap into a gulf purely for his country's sake, as the old Roman did in ages long since past. Men risk their lives for titles, or fame, or money. Tommy Atkins will stand up to be shot at for tenpence or a shilling a week, and very well he stands up too, when he is called on to do it. But the absolute certainty of losing one's life never appears to be so dulce et decorum when it is presented to a man. A whole congregation will stand up and sing

> " Ah me ! ah me ! that I
> In Kedar's tents here stay ! "

Or, –

> " O Paradise ? O Paradise !
> The world is growing old ;
> Who would not be at rest, and free,
> Where love is never cold,"

but if the chance of getting out of Kedar's tents right straight off, and of being "at rest and free where love is never cold" were offered at the conclusion of the hymn, there is not a man, woman, or child in the whole congregation that would jump at it. They would all say " Oh ! this is so sudden," like a young girl to a proposal of marriage, and want a little time to reply to the offer. And the longer the time, the better they would be pleased. No ! we are none of us enamored with the prospect of death, either for our country or any other object, that is to say, of our own death. Anybody else's is a different matter. Man is a great humbug. I don't say he is a hypocrite, because he really believes in himself ; but he is a humbug, and humbugs. There is nothing that catches him so soon as a high-sounding phrase ; what politicians call " a good cry." He never stops to consider whether he believes in it, or not. And that, I take it, is the reason why there are so many scoffers at the Christianity of the present age, because its beliefs are only half, or sentimental beliefs, and the practical half is so often absent. The popular religion is an emotional one of noble thoughts, fine aspirations, eloquent discourses, rapturous hymns and music, pomp and flowers ; and because it is an emotional one and cannot be kept up unintermittingly, it is reserved for Sundays, and laid aside on week days.   It is not hypocrisy, heaven forbid! It is real enough so far as it goes, but it does not go far enough; and in that it is unreal.   The man who feels his bosom filled with love and charity to his neighbor on the Sunday, will pay his workwomen starvation wages on the Saturday following, and will spend the intervening period in trying to get out of his fellow-men the very utmost he can without infringing on the strict letter of the law.   "I see the better things and approve of them," said the old Roman poet.   "I follow the worse."   The approval of the better is as sincere and real as the practice of the worse.   Why? Because, unconsciously, we have only a half belief at the bottom of our hearts in what we say.

No!   I am not going to sing the praises of patriotism, or any other of the virtues that are more on our lips than in our heart, and in our professions more than in our practice.   Stretched at my ease on a nice little rug of moss, and having before my eyes the irritating example of the busy ant, I am meditating a laudation of laziness, about which there can be no humbug, as it is not generally conceded to be an estimable quality.   But before I begin to do so, let me remind you of what I said about energy and indomitable perseverance, viz : that when carried to excess they become vices. Similarly, (and don't you forget it) laziness, which is a very good and estimable thing in itself, becomes totally reprehensible if you indulge in it too much.   In that, it is like everything else in the world, wickedness excepted, concerning which the same law holds good for all, that it is the excess which constitutes the sin and not the use.   I don't claim any originality for the remark.   Solomon said the same long ago, when he observed "There is a time for all things," and St. Paul reiterated it afterwards in the declaration "All things are lawful ; but all things are not convenient."   Now if these authorities are to be relied on, it is manifest that there is a time when laziness is lawful, and also a time when it is not convenient ; and that is tantamount to saying that it is good when not pushed to excess.

Some people don't think so.   The ant does not believe in it ;

neither does my wife ; neither do women generally as a rule.
They are always in motion themselves ; (I really don't see how the
world would get along if they weren't), and they want everybody
and everything else to be in motion too. In their eyes, idleness of
any kind is the eighth, and worst, of the seven deadly sins, and an
unfortunate male that comes within the swoop of a feminine whirl-
pool has just simply got to do something. He must not take an
after dinner nap ; he must not sit and smoke ; he must not sit and
read ; sitting is an abomination, and lying down is worse than
heresy. He must stir about and do something, no matter what ;
and if he doesn't know what to do, he must still stir about till he
does. If Providence had not endowed man with a blessed mulish
and obstinate disposition, woman would have worn out creation
long before the appointed time. Bloomah is just as bad as my
wife. If she sees me unoccupied, she always finds out something
to be done. She wants a pail of water, and the hired man is out
in the garden ; or else she wants wood, and there is nobody about
to saw it; or the pig has got in the potato patch ; or, if she can't
invent anything else, "The Missus is a looking for you, Sir."
Anyhow, I've got to stir ; and stirring on a hot day is provocative
of perspiration and profanity.

Now that is all wrong ; it is uncomfortable ; it is unnatural,
and it is unscientific; uncomfortable, as everybody knows that has
ever had a woman in the house when he wants to be quiet ;
unnatural as the action of our own hearts may teach us. We have
a fancy that our very lives depend on that sanguineous little organ
keeping up its work without intermission ; that, in fact, if the heart
stops beating we die. If we consider that that is tantamount to
expecting it to keep on working without intermission for perhaps
seventy or eighty years at a stretch, it will be readily seen what an
extravagant demand we make on it. But the truth is that our
hearts do no such thing ; they have fits of laziness—physiologists
call it "relaxation of the muscles,"—about seventy times a minute
in a healthy adult, and the consequence is that they get a rest of
eight hours in the twenty-four. No married man ever gets that.
Moreover, to object to laziness is unscientific. A high authority

has recently discovered that the longer a man sleeps in the twenty-four hours, the longer he will live ; so that if he were to sleep the whole time he wouldn't die at all. Herein lies the secret of immortality, and in order to prevent man from making use of it when discovered, animals like my wife Polly, and my servant girl Bloomah, were created. If there were no women, we should all go peacefully to sleep ; there would be no wars, no strikes, no famines, no doctors, lawyers or politicians ; no programmes of committees of public instruction ; no schools, no prisons, no taverns, no nothing. A blessed and peaceful repose would reign in the world, and a quiet only broken by snoring. Just think what a Utopia would exist under the reign of pure and perfect laziness !

Wouldn't that be "dulce" ? Wouldn't it be "decorum" ? A whole world reposing under its blankets and counterpanes, snugly tucked in and snoring the snore of the just ? What is that you object ? That there would be no civilization, no progress, no heroic deeds, no noble aspirations ? and pray who would want them ? It is your unquiet body, who is always poking up himself and other people, that makes progress and all the rest of it necessary ; creates competition, and in so doing, is the originator of combines, mono-polies, and election campaigns. Man was born to be lazy ; it was only when he was turned out of Eden that he had to begin to work ; and if Eve had been asleep, as she ought to have been, instead of rambling about, falling in with serpents, he would never have had to leave it. The most famous (and the most sensible) beauty in history, is The Sleeping Beauty, who was all right, and everybody and thing about her was all right too, till the "fairy-footed Prince" came along and woke her with a kiss. Misguided young man ! I fancy that in after years there were times when he bitterly repented of that kiss.

> "And o'er the hills and far away
>   Beyond their utmost purple rim,
> Beyond the night, across the day,
>   Through all the world she followed him ;"

There was no getting away from her after she had once woke up.

After Sunset.

HERE is one great drawback to a clearing, so far as I am concerned, in the absence of shade ; for I don't call that shade
which is afforded by a four foot stump, to avail yourself of which
you have to sit on the ground and submit to be walked over by
ants and spiders, and other creeping things. At the same time it
must be remembered that I am but a unit of the unnumbered
habitues of the place, and that the birds and chipmunks, the mice,
centipedes and other insect populations, find shade enough and to
spare. Since then·the ideal of government is the greatest good for
the greatest number, it cannot properly be said that the fact of my
being obliged to sit and brown in the sun whenever I want to muse
in the clearing is a drawback to it. There is a great deal of
philosophy in this reflection, and, viewed in a right light, it is one
that is eminently conducive to contentment under adverse circumstances. You recollect the fable of the Boys and the Frogs : how
the latter, on being pelted with stones every time they popped
their noses above the surface of the pond, appealed to the sense of
justice in their persecutors, and adjured them to reflect that what
was fun to the terrestrials was death to the amphibious partners in
the joke. The statement was not strictly true, or, indeed, true at
all, for that matter. I have thrown lots of stones at frogs in the
water in my time, and have known plenty of other people that
have done so too, but I never hit one myself, and I never knew
anybody that did. Do you ? Now, it is an impossibility to kill
a frog by missing him with a stone, so that the croaking orator
misrepresented matters as thoroughly as any party newspaper, or
stump politician, ever does, and his appeal might very properly
have been ruled out as not founded in fact ; but I want you to
observe that, supposing for the moment it had been, the true
question at issue was not whether it was a matter of life or death

for the frogs, but whether they were in the majority or not. If
they were, then they were justified in protesting ; but if they were
not, then the principle of the greatest good for the greatest number
should have been held to prevail, and the deaths of the frog
minority more than counterbalanced by the fun accruing from
them to the puerile majority. Obviously, therefore, the frogs
should have been contented with their situation, and if they
deplored anything, should have felt bad about it every time one of
their number escaped having his brains knocked out ; obviously,
also, I have no right to call the absence of shade in the clearing a
drawback, and the proper and philosophical course is to accept the
situation as it is, and make myself as comfortable as I can under
the circumstances,   I generally do ; with the aid of an umbrella.
It looks un-dignified and unphilosophical, I admit, to sit on a stump
for an hour together holding a big cotton umbrella over one's head,
and it's just a little trying on the arms, *mais, que voulez-vous !*
As the Kukuana chief said to Macumazahn, no man can put out
the sun.   "The sun is stronger than man who looks at him."
Now, that you can't put out the sun is no reason for being put out
yourself.   That is a very good thing to remember when you are
arguing with your wife.

But the day comes to an end sometime, as everything else,
you and I included, will do, and then the little breezes that have
been asleep in the nursery on the top of the trees wake up, and
their sisters that have been dozing in the soft mosses and the arms
of the violets and speedwells do the same, and there are gentle
whispers calling to each other far overhead in the forest, and a
rippling murmur breathing responsive in the grasses beneath.
The robin at the edge of the clearing is singing his mate and little
ones to sleep, preparatory to going to bed himself on a near branch
of the elm or maple, and the frogs begin their love songs in a not
altogether unpleasant whistling treble, with the bull frog playing
the bass accompaniment.   Did you ever catch froggie when he
goes a-wooing, and whistles as he goes ?   I have ; but only very
rarely ; directly he becomes conscious of an illegitimate audience,
he pockets his instrument in an instant, and looks as innocent of

music as if he belonged to a Ladies' Matinee Musicale." What is his instrument ?" Well ! You would never guess it, but when Rana is in love, he becomes a bagpiper. Where he gets it from, or how he does it, I don't profess to know, but he has a thin semi-translucent membrane which he puffs out in the form of a bag under his chin, and from the air contained in it he draws out the long whistling trill that you hear in the spring evenings and summer nights. It was a long time before I found this out ; I thought till then that frogs could do nothing but croak, and that the whistling sound proceeded from lizards, (though a college student once assured me that it was from wild ducks, and started off to get his gun to shoot them). Fancy the astonishment of a serenading froggie at getting a charge of duckshot about his ears ; it would be worse than the stones with which the boys pelted his ancestors. However, I once caught a damp troubadour in flagrante delicto. He must have been head over ears in love to let me get near him, but I did ; and I watched him swell out his little bag and trill till all the air in it was exhausted, and he had to pause for a fresh supply of breath. Then he saw me ; and, presto ! the bag disappeared ; he put on an air of "Please, Sir ! it wasn't me," and tried to make me believe he was out after mosquitoes. I pretended I was con-vinced and walked gently away, but the moment my back was turned he was at it as loud and as shrill as ever ; rather more so indeed, as if he wanted to make up for lost time. Ah ! it's a wicked and deceitful world, and there is no trust to be placed in any creature when it is courting.

In middle air the evening becomes vocal with the hum of mosquitoes ; not that that is anything new, for he has "been making things hum" all day ; but as night draws on he seems louder and more hummy than before. It is the contrast, I suppose. Night always seems to me to have a still silence peculiarly her own, and so subtle that it is felt rather than perceived. I have read that in the tropical forests night is the noisiest portion of the twenty-four hours, for then the birds and the beasts, and the insects that have been, so to speak, lying flattened out under the oppressive heat of the day, spring up into vigorously resonant life, but for all that, I cannot believe that the peculiar silence of the night is affected by it. I know that I myself am conscious of it, even in the lecture, or the concert room, or at home conversing with my friends; and those who will watch for it carefully, may, if I may use the bull, hear it themselves amidst all the sounds that surround them. Night is like a mother watching the gambols and hearing the laughter of her children, herself grave and silent, with the tender light of love in her eyes. "Verily, the darkness is no darkness with Thee."

"Fanciful." Well perhaps I am. Strange fancies crowd into a man's head, as he sits alone with the Creator in the gathering shadows of the twilight, and I cannot think that they are altogether wild and unprofitable, even if they should be wholly destitute of reality. Call them but waking dreams, as visionary and eccentric as those which visit us in our sleep; they, at any rate, are under the control of the will and the intellect, and it depends on the will of the dreamer himself whether they shall bring a blessing, or leave a curse; whether they shall make the life purer, nobler, more tender, or haunt it with a hideous nightmare. This fancy of mine respecting the indestructible stillness of night came to me originally when I was lying on a sick bed, given up by my medical attendant, and all around me, and all but given up by myself. The same thing may come to all who read this book; must come to most of them; and I tell this fancy of mine for their benefit. It is no light thing to lie alone save for the half hidden watcher by the bedside, weak and in pain, listening to the loud ticking of the clock telling out the sands of time as they drop into eternity. Have you ever noticed the ticking of a clock, when that was the only sound audible? How ostentatiously loud it is for a space, and how it gradually sinks into a whisper, and then dies away altogether, till, just as you are beginning to think that the clock has run down, it bursts out again as uproarious as at the first? That clock used to harass me more than I care to say; I suppose I was nervous; but at any rate I used to lie awake listening to it, and almost frightened at it, till one night the fancy came, and I caught the outside stillness of the night pervading and embracing the sound and making it part and parcel of itself. It was the realization of perfect rest and peace to which the activity of the clock was necessary, and yet wholly subordinate; not the rest of that "land where all things are forgotten," but the rest so grossly misinterpreted of the Epicurean deities who sit on the heights of Olympus, intelligently viewing the storms of the world ; not indeed unsympathizing or scornful, as the poet represents them, but untouched in their conscious security by them.

"Thou art about my bed and about my path, and spiest out all my ways." It may be that others cannot grasp this fancy of mine as I have grasped it ; "Non cuivis homini contingit adire Corinthum ;" but it is well worth making the attempt to do so. There is a wonderful sense of watchful protection and care in this feeling of the predominant silence of night that amalgamates all sound with itself.

The sun has gone down and overhead the clouds that gathered round his parting rays, and the clouds that did not venture to show themselves before, are a billowy mass of colour ; smitten into flame, bathed in blood, till they tone down into golden and rosy lights, and so, through tender shades of green and gray, into the sombre hues of the dark. The day is dead, but how lovely in dying ; how lovely in its death after the glare and heat and turmoil that preceded it. And now there is a fresh and totally different world, yet still the same. New voices break upon the air, which is cleft by new wings ; new footsteps steal across the lands ; new lights break out in the skies. Consider well the meaning of the story thus written on the daily page of the book of the world. Is death then such a terrible and abhorrent thing as we represent it to ourselves to be ? Is it a suspension of life, even for a second ? Ask the day when it dies ; ask the night when she covers life with her veil, if that life has been arrested, or—changed.

5

The Learned Pig.

IF my eyes don't deceive me, that is my pig that has just made his way under the bars into the clearing. I had fondly thought that his education was progressing satisfactorily, and that he had got too much of a corporation on him now to be able to squeeze under the bars. It seems that I was mistaken, and that so far from attaining to the dignity of being erected into a municipality, he is nothing more than a struggling little hamlet; two hamlets rather, with the as yet unfulfilled possibilities of hams. Perhaps this seems rather confused, and unintelligible, but that is accounted for by a slight feeling of disappointment which his sudden appearance has evoked, and may be set right in a few words. You see, I do not regard a pig scientifically, as an animal of the genus sus; or vulgarly, as a pig in the concrete; but philosophically, politically, and theologically, as a very estimable food-product. Philosophically the pig may be regarded as concentrated intelligence: potted head; politically, he may be looked on as a growing corporation: flitches of bacon; and theologically, he may be considered with reference to his latter end: hams. When you come to analyze him carefully in this way you will perceive that he is a very complex arrangement, and a very nice one, too; and that anything that tends to disturb this arrangement, must necessarily produce confusion, not only in the pig himself, but in the philosopher who is contemplating him. Now when a moderately stout gentleman pig undertakes to squeeze himself underneath the lowest rail of a clearing fence, and gets scored along the back by a projecting knot, the probabilities are that he will be very much disturbed for the time being. Mine was, I know, because I heard him squeak. You will readily perceive that when the subject of meditation becomes "kind o' mixed-up," the ideas suggested by it must in consequence be themselves mixed up also. After all, the confusion in my case of hamlets and hams, corporations and pigs, was not altogether an unnatural one. There is not much difference between some corporations and hogs : ask the ratepayers if there is.

Now that I have cleared up matters satisfactorily, as I hope, (and if I haven't, the fault must lie with the reader, and not with me ; which, of course it doesn't), I will proceed to reiterate the statement with which I started, namely, that I was disappointed at seeing my pig enter the clearing, because it showed that he had not advanced as far in his philosophical education toward becoming perfect food-product as I had fondly hoped. I am not proud. I don't object to having a pig as a companion, provided he keeps his proper distance. Neither am I jealous. I readily admit his superior advantages in the matter of legs ; and, I don't envy or covet his possession of a snout to dig up potatoes with when he makes surreptitious visits to the potato-patch ; or his æsthetic curly tail, with a lovely little kink in it, which was evidently given him as an adornment, for he does not use it to steer by, and it is of no manner of good in brushing off flies. No ! I am neither disdainful nor envious. My distress at his sudden appearance arose from the obvious fact that he was not yet too fat to squeeze under the bars, and had therefore manifestly not made the most of his opportunities. And these were many and regular every night and every morning. Had they not been so, I should have still felt as disappointed as the parent who sends his boy on odd days when he can be spared to the district school, and finds after a couple of years of the course that he has not got out of the Second Reader. As it was, I felt as if I had given him all the advantages of the latest educational discoveries as set forth in the nearest academy, and he had failed to pass his examination. That made matters worse. I myself stood towards him in the relation of Principal, with Nathan A. M. (able man-of-all-work) as assistant ; and I could not very well lay the blame on the educational staff, which is generally the parental resource.

I have reared and educated a great many little hogs in my time, and though they were the objects of my greatest solicitude and fondest care, they all died at a comparatively early age. Yet there was a great sweetness in their thus passing away. "Whom the gods love die young," is applicable to the affection which,

whether we confess it or not, the human race generally bears to the
pig. Moreover, whenever a vacancy in the porcine population was
created, there was always the consoling thought, amounting to a
moral certainty, that I should meet him again, or part of him at
any rate, under happier circumstances, and at the festal board. I
always had the prospect of an experience similar in kind to that
which fell to the lot of the author of that touching ballad, "Old
Dog Tray." You remember how he speaks of the love, amounting
to that of a brother, with which he regarded his canine friend : how
that love was rudely broken in upon by the heartless government
myrmidons who insisted on the payment of a two-dollar dog tax
annually ; how this brutal conduct on their part necessitated the
administration of a dose of prussic acid, hidden, as a last tribute of
heart-broken affection, in a savory dish of bones and potatoes : and
how the bereaved survivor grew thin and wasted from sorrow, and
found no pleasure in life, even going to the length of leaving his
beer at dinner untouched. Yet in an unexpected moment the two
friends were reunited, and the heart of the mourner was comforted.
Let me tell it in his own affecting words :

> "Old Dog Tray I met again, though.
>   To eat they persuaded me one day,
> With some tempting mutton pies,
>   In the which I recognize
> The flavour of my Old Dog Tray."

In my boarding school days we were served at dinner on
Saturday with a pie, popularly believed to be composed of all the
scraps that had been left on the dinner plates during the week,
which we christened "resurrection pie." It must have been a kind
of resurrection pie that once more restored dog Tray to his master.
Ham sandwiches have just the same effect when a pig is in the case.

Education is a very difficult matter, and the education of a pig
is no exception to the general rule. An uncle of mine adopted the
theological, or sectarian school principle, and brought up his pigs
in what he denominated pews, namely pens in which they had no
room to turn, and when they had eaten their breakfast had to

walk backwards into their sty to digest it. By thus securing their continuance in a straight way, he maintained that all independent exercise was prevented, and that an improved tendency to corpulence was effected. Moreover, he fed them on a fixed and unvaried diet; of oatmeal and potatoes as far as I can recollect; and encouraged them in the practice of temperance by giving them only water to drink. I forget how the experiment turned out: I think the pigs all died of fatty degeneration of the brain, or some such thing. For my part, I tried the national school system. I fed them with anything and everything; I crammed them till they could not even grunt. The plan worked well up to a certain point: that is with those who lived through it; for some died of brain fever, and others got weakened lungs, and had consumption; and some went idiotic, and were unfit for food; but the others grew and thrived up to a certain point, and then instead of increasing in fatness they began to grow lean again. I could not understand it, till I consulted the principal of our academy. A principal of an academy nowadays knows everything that can be known, and a great deal more besides, so he was able to give me the key to the enigma. Taking me to where the pump stood in the yard he filled the bucket up to the brim. "Now," said he, "watch." Then he pumped again for five minutes before he stopped, and when he had finished there was absolutely less water in the bucket than when he began. "There!" he went on, "the receptivity of anything is only limited. If you try to put in more than it can hold, you drive out that which was already in. If you din a heterogeneous mass of lessons into a child's brain before it has had time to stow away what it had previously learned, it will forget them in a short time; and however long you may keep pumping in, the new knowledge displaces a part at least of the old. If you keep a pig's stomach continually filled without giving it time to digest, it won't digest, and it won't fatten. It will eventually die, either of dyspepsia or inanition. You can starve a pig by giving him too much, just as you can stupify a child by giving him too many subjects to learn. You can't more than fill a full bucket." Since that time I have given up cramming.

---

*J*F you listen to astronomers, and other scientific people, they will tell you that the stars are in the skies during the daytime, and that the reason why they are not seen is that their light is overpowered by the superior brightness of the sun's rays. It may be so: in fact, I have no doubt that it is so; the stars must be somewhere during the day, and if they are not in the sky, where are they? It was rather a pretty fancy that accounted for their invisibility during the day by regarding them as so many myriad electric lights, lit up by the angels every evening, but even then, they must be in the heavens all the time, lit or unlit, and we can rest assured of that without going into any abstruse astronomical calculations. The reason assigned for our not seeing them is however less indisputable, (I am speaking unscientifically) and it does not seem reasonable that the light of worlds, some of which are as much bigger than the sun as that luminary is than the earth, should be swallowed up by him, although he does happen to be a great deal nearer. Still, we have got to believe what we are told at school, and I suppose it is of no use to advance any other theory; I may be allowed, however, to point out that there is a reason for all things, and that there must be a reason why the sun should be allowed to temporarily extinguish the stars. I believe it to be because the latter are not wanted in the day time.

Now don't jump at hasty conclusions. I am not retailing the old joke about the moon's not giving her light during the day because she wasn't needed: my remark lies deeper than that, and is based on a philosophical consideration of the uses of starlight. For the purpose of illuminating objects and rendering them visible this light is almost worthless; you can neither read nor write by it; you cannot sew by it; you can pursue none of the ordinary avocations of life by it, as you can manage to do by moonlight; but you can meditate by it. Of course you can do that in the day time, or when the moon is up, or in the dark hours of the night if you can keep awake; but starlight meditations have a vastness and solemnity peculiarly their own, which the busy turmoil of life during the day is unfitted for, and which the darkness of the night is not qualified to give. "The Heavens declare the glory of God, and the firmament showeth His handiwork." It is when the overpowering light of the sun, and the shadowing light of the moon are taken away; when the veil of the cloud-burdened atmosphere is rent; that then system after system of created worlds come into view, and man stands in the presence, and gazes into the eyes of infinity without being overwhelmed by it.

Look up, and you see spread out before you creation in all its stages, from the dead world of the moon, to the masses of incandescent vapour condensing into nebulæ, and from nebulæ into suns with their attendant planets, if we may believe the now generally accepted nebular hypothesis. The field of view is seen with them in every stage, of every size, and far as the eye or the telescope can reach, and even further, as the sensitive plate records for us. The light from these numberless incandescent bodies fills the interstitial spaces, and coming to our atmosphere blends them into a whole which we call the firmament, and the vastness of its extent may well paralyze the imagination. But there is something behind vaster still, and which is given only to those who visit the underworld to see. Probably you never thought on the subject at all; probably also, if you ever did, you came to the conclusion that what was presented before your eyes, and you could see, or acquire the knowledge of by the sensitive plate was continued beyond your powers of ascertaining, indefinitely: in point of fact, that the succession of worlds is endless, and the presence of matter every-where. Hard as it may be to conceive an infinite series of solar systems throughout space, it is harder still to conceive of any portion of infinite space where such systems do not exist; that is to say, an absolute void, as far as matter is concerned. I do not say a perfectly absolute void, for that is as inconceivable as a termination of space; but absolute as regards matter. Yet if we

can find grounds for such a supposition we are driven to the
conclusion that matter is finite in regard to one thing, space, and
to the presumption that it is equally finite in regard to the other
thing, time.   In other words that it is neither infinite nor eternal,
and as such is not self-existent, and has been created.

I am not advancing here any theological theory based on
Holy Writ, which, for my present purpose, may be put out of the
question.   It is perfectly impossible for the human mind to
conceive of any beginning of time, or any ending of space : we
assent to the propositions of Eternity and Infinity, not because we
can understand them, but because they commend themselves to our
reason.   It is also possible for us to conceive of Eternal and
Infinite matter, knowing that its destruction is a mere matter of
appearance, and is really a change of form.   Even then, we should
be driven to admit of the existence of an eternal, infinite and
intelligent personality, for the essential characteristic of matter
is inertia, that is, it is unable to set itself in motion and needs an
extraneous impulse which must be given to it by some thing
immaterial in the first place.   Now we know of no force in nature,
even the most subtle, that is not operated by matter in motion, and
there must evidently be something to produce that motion.   So
that even granting the properties of eternity and infinity to the
material atoms, we have still to supply something else before we
can get at what we call, and truly, the visible creation, and the
argument (wholly rational) for the existence of a Supreme Being is
not affected by what I have further to say.

There is a very curious phenomenon noticeable in the sidereal
map of the Southern Hemisphere which is, I believe, popularly
known as the "Coal-Sacks."   These are two vast gaps in the
firmament, of the most intense blackness, in the which, so far as I
know, the most powerful telescope that could be brought on them
has failed to discover star, or nebula, or luminous vapor.   They are
absolutely destitute of light.   Recalling this to my mind as I look
up to the brilliant display overhead, and recollecting that in no
other part of the heavens does this phenomenon occur, I am
inclined to believe that in gazing at the Coal-Sacks a man is looking

beyond the vast concourse of worlds into that realm where no matter exists or ever has existed. Of course we cannot say positively that the space has never been filled up, but if it has been it has been swept clean. Elsewhere, the eye is arrested by worlds upon worlds, and worlds beyond these again ; here there is absolutely nothing so far as we can conceive ; nothing but the deepest and most intense darkness. Do you remember that significant expression of the Saviour speaking of the ultimate doom of the wicked where He says that they shall be cast into the "Outer darkness"; the darkness of that space which is outside the realm of created matter ! It almost seems to me that in the Coal-Sacks we have an evidence of the existence of that region.

In fact, where ever there is matter, however attenuated its particles may be, there must be light of some sort, not necessarily visible to our eyes, as is evidenced by the X rays, but potentially visible to senses differently constituted to our own, for light is a vibration of molecular particles which may or may not be perceptible according as it is obstructed or arrested by other molecules. At least, that is my theory of it, how far correct I am not able just now to say without looking it up in a scientific treatise. Not being scientific, but only philosophical, it does not much matter to me whether it is correct or not. I am satisfied with it. After all, the agnostics have some show of reason in asserting that we know nothing. We don't even know, I mean that we cannot be certain, that we don't know. Looking up into the starry space above my head, I am confounded with the unsolved questions that it presents, and the inscrutable enigma that lies behind it, and yet pervades it. "The heavens declare the glory of God," and "what man by searching hath found out God ?"

Instead of puzzling myself with vague speculations, let me turn my meditations to a more practical use, and enjoy the calm loveliness of the scene spread out before me. How many eyes since the foundation of the world have looked, as I am looking, and guessed as I have been guessing? And where are the gazers now ? Their material part has restored to earth what it took from earth, to the air what it took from air, to the water what it took from water; but was there nothing in the individuals besides all this; were they nothing but automatons set in motion by a spring which we call Life, and ceasing to move when that spring grew worn out? In that case, but in that case only, Death is the end of the man. There may be a reincarnation; the materials may in the lapse of countless years come together again fortuitously, a fresh spring be supplied, and the mechanism work again for some brief time; but is man a mechanism merely? If not, where has the other part of him gone. What he drew from earth he returned to earth at death: to what did he return the remainder? Matter to matter; but the will, the intelligence, where is that to go to? Here is the question which materialists cannot answer. There is the immaterial part of man which has to be disposed of, and to which they can assign no place.

Daybreak.

IT is a very difficult thing to take a philosophical view of day-break; extremely difficult. You may take a poetic or a prosaic, a sentimental or a practical one, but a philosophical one is more difficult to attain to. You must see this yourself. You must be conscious that it is hard to keep your temper with daybreak; that he is an impertinent intruder; a fellow that thrusts his nose in just where he isn't wanted. If he would come a little later on in the day it would be all right enough; but to come before you have scarcely settled down into a sound sleep, and before the sun has warmed the atmosphere sufficiently to make it healthy out of doors, is very annoying. What renders it still more exasperating is that the period immediately preceding the dawn is the darkest of the whole twenty-four hours; and, being so, is the most conducive to sound slumber. I don't mean that a man is only just getting to sleep at daybreak; if he is, he doesn't deserve to have any sleep at all. The odds are about a hundred to one that he has been into some mischief, hurtful to himself, or other people, or both. No thoroughly honest and respectable man, or woman, will stay up till daybreak, unless under very exceptional circumstances, such as a club meeting, or a ball; and every wise man or woman will have gone to bed and to sleep long before that period; but it is only then that he or she begins to enter with enthusiasm into the business, and carry it on with promptitude and despatch; only then that the snore of the sleeper attains its full volume and mellowness of sound. Before, the slumber is light, easily broken; and the snore is irregular, faint at first, and only heard in melodious nasal ejaculations. Abrupt and brief at first, sleep is like a spirited horse when you first take him out of the stable after a long rest, skittish, and given to shying, and to breaking off from his pace, whatever that may happen to be; later on it is like the same horse after a breathing stretch of four or five miles, warmed up to his work, and laying himself down to a steady trot along the level road. Now, just fancy yourself in such a position, with a good horse under you, a well-kept road before you, and a bright breezy day, not too hot, and not too cold. You have got over all the little differences of opinion that showed themselves at the starting, and have established that essential to the perfect enjoyment of a ride, a thorough sympathy between yourself and your horse, when just as you have entered on what you intend to be a long sharp trot, a turnpike gate rises before you, and you have to pull up. The case is analogous to that of the sleeper when the day begins to break, unless he has taken the precaution to let the blinds down before he went to bed, or long continued lazy habits have rendered him impervious to the stealthy approaches of light. If he has not been fortified with one of these two things he has to wake up when day comes, especially in the country. He may go to sleep again, and probably will; but he is almost sure to wake up then, even if it be but for a moment, and it is too bad; it is really too bad, after all the trouble and hard work one has had to attain sound slumber, to have to do it all over again. It is a waste of energy.

And besides this, the hour of the dawn is the coldest in the twenty-four. I have always understood that to be the case from others, and have found it so myself on the few occasions that I have not been making a tour in Dream-land at that time. That does not matter so much in summer time, I allow; nay! it is then rather an inducement, though a deceptive one, to early rising; but in the winter it is a very different thing and renders the turning out of a warm bed doubly difficult, as any married man will testify. In the summer time there is no difficulty about getting the fire started in the morning: the women folk, always an unquiet and restless race, are alarmingly ready to take that duty on themselves, and then, Macbeth-like, murder sleep with clash of pans, and clatter of dishes, until the male folk get up in despair. You don't catch them doing any such foolish thing in winter, when the snow is on the ground, and the mercury has gone into retirement, and when if you put out a foot from under the blankets, you get your toes half frozen off before you can slip them into a stocking. "Oh dear, no! Not for Joseph if he knows it." The female population of the place is then hybernating like so many dormice, and has no intention of stirring until "the house gets warm." It has come to that wise decision by instinct, I suppose; but any way that is the principle for which I am contending, namely, that no one should get up before the house, (or the air, which amounts to the same thing), gets warm : only I am consistent, and uphold the principle in summer as well as in winter. My wife, who would have me start up like a Jack-in-the-box, directly the sun shows the top of his head on the eastern sky, argues that in summer time the only enjoyable hours, and the hours in which work can best be done, are those in the early morning. I suppose a man is entitled to choose how he will have his enjoyment, and if I prefer to take mine out in sleep, having been too hot and uncomfortable to do so until it really does get cool, I hope such a choice will commend itself as eminently reasonable ; and as to doing work! Well! I am not an enthusiastic admirer of work in my own person, and since I can perform all that I have to do in the hours that I am up and stirring, I really don't see why I should be expected to undertake any more. If I arose as suggested, I should only be engaged in pulling up dewy weeds, and dirtying my fingers, or disturbing poor little caterpillars and potato-bugs at their breakfast. Besides, if the later hours of the summer day are hot and uncomfortable, as there is very little doubt that they really are to every thing but the lizards, grasshoppers, crickets and such small deer, is that any reason for getting up early, and, so to speak, partially acclimating yourself ? If you were going to be baked alive, would you prefer to be put in a cold oven, and have the fire started under you, or to be put in a red hot one at once ?

No doubt "the early bird catches the worm." What of that ? The early bird is a murderer. Would you have me imitate him ? Would you have me resort to cowardly assassination to procure my living ? I know it is said, "The more fool the worm for getting up first," but this defence of late rising can not be maintained for an instant, on enquiry. The fact is that the worm had not got up first; he was just going to bed. Night is the worm's day : he is not made for the heat which would dry up the moisture of his body, or the light which is of no use to him. He had been enjoying the cool dews, and probably expanding his mind by foreign travel, or cultivating social virtues by a visit to his cousin in the next worm-hole, and was returning home full of news and gossip for Mrs. Worm when the early bird saw him. The early bird had no business with him at all; he was a citizen of the upper, as the worm was of the under world. If he must needs have fleshy food, there were the caterpillars, the flies, the mosquitoes, the slugs, and a host of other diurnal pests ready for him, and mankind would have applauded his eating them. Instead of that, he falls foul of an unoffending worm that never did him, or anything else, harm, and that acts as a sort of subsoil plough for the farmer, bringing up to the surface in a properly digested state, and fit for the farmer's purposes, the cold and sour underlying earth which the agricultural implements do not go deep enough to reach ; and not content with assaulting this benefactor of the human race, the early bird murders him ; and not satisfied with murdering him, he eats him, the blood-thirsty cannibal! Eats him raw, too! Behold the disastrous effects on the morals and conscience of too early rising! Is that an example worthy of imitation ? Rather than expose myself to the risk of becoming such an infamous scoundrel as the much-lauded early bird, I would even consent to take my breakfast in bed, if anybody would bring it to me. And I should look on this as self-denying virtue, not laziness.

Let me be just, however. The intelligent reader will perceive that all that I have just said refers to the practice of getting up at daybreak, either to admire it, or for more practical purposes. I have nothing to object to the dawn itself; in fact, I have no doubt I should be considerably disturbed if it did not come up to time, even for one day. I am perfectly willing to concede to others, if they wish it the privilege of watching the sun rise, and I must confess that we have been favored with many beautiful descriptions of what takes place then by those who have either seen it or imagined it. It is conceivable by those who have not viewed it, for it is the very reverse process to sunset : the voices of the night die away, and those of the day swell the morning hymn of praise and thanksgiving in their stead ; the sombre clouds swoon into the gray and green shades, that in their turn blush rose pink, and then flame out in orange and burnished gold ; and the life of joyous and bustling activity, of light and sound, takes the place of the noiseless things that moved invisible under the sheltering veil of night. To each his appointed time ; to youth the dawn with its cool caress, and its promise of future glories and joys ; to man, the bustle and the fervor of the full day ; to old age, the calm and repose of sunset ; and to all, night. Who shall exalt the one at the expense of the others ; who shall extol the beauty and desirableness of one to the depreciation of the others ? As the wind is tempered to the shorn lamb, so is the burden of the day to the strength of the shoulders that bear it ; so is the beauty of the day to the eye that gazes on it ; so is the happiness of the day to the soul that receives it. To the strong, the greater burden ; to the clear eye, the greater beauty ; to the pure soul, the greater happiness. He who despises and wastes the hours of dawn is less fitted to endure the heat of the mid-day ; he who has not toiled in the mid-day cannot appreciate the rest of the sunset ; and for him for whom the sunset of life has no real repose, night, the long night that comes to all, has no sheltering veil ; is nothing but blackness and a void.

Under the Maple.

THE maple does not properly belong to the clearing. Those who attacked the virgin forest did their work well, and were no respecters of trees in a vertical position. Prone on the ground, they represented dollars and cents, lumber or cordwood, but standing upright they were mere cumberers of the earth, defrauding man of his natural and inalienable heritage. So one after another they came down to the music of the ringing axe, the largest and stateliest first, and the others in succession, till finally even the under brush was cut down and burned, and the clearing stood out in its unadorned beauty, which the poet informs us is "adorned the most." He may be right: I won't venture to contradict him; all that I care to remark on this subject is that the utmost adornment of a clearing is nothing to brag about. I doubt whether there is anything uglier to be found on the face of the earth. It lacks the beauty of the cultured land, the solemnity of the waste, and the majesty of bleak sterility; it is "neither fish, flesh, nor fowl, nor good red herring"; yet I love it; for it is to me an "Ugly Duckling" that will, in the lapse of years, materialize into a beautiful white swan. In its present state, however, it is bereft of all trees, and their places are taken by wild raspberry tangles, or clumps of alder at the best. Thus the maple does not properly come under the scope of my observation; but that does not matter, as I dare say the readers of these rambling discourses have long ago discovered. "Homo sum, et nihil humanum a me alienum puto"; which means in my individual case that all is fish that comes to my net, and I put it down just as it comes. Being a married man, I am denied the privilege of lengthy conversation, and so have to talk in writing. Also, and for the same reason, I have got into the habit of being discursive, and talking nonsense. "Evil communications corrupt good manners."

The maple does not belong to the clearing, but it does the next best thing, it looks in over the fence, a vegetable Peeping Tom of Coventry, and is quite big enough to be seen. Moreover, it is one of the national emblems, and as such deserves notice. Why it should be looked on as emblematic of Canadians it is hard to discover. It makes the very best of firewood, but I should be sorry to say, (at any rate till I got out of the country), that Canadians were preeminently fitted for the burning; when it is green, it is very green; but I never met a Canadian yet who was especially distinguished by greenness. It is sappy in the spring time, and the sap can be boiled down into sugar: you might boil a Canadian down till he evaporated into thin air, but you would get no sugar out of him; you might get "sand," and plenty of it, but no sugar; or, if you caught him down in the lower parishes on the St. Lawrence, you might distil him; but in that case you would only get contraband whiskey. The maple turns red when it is nipped by the frost; the Canadian turns blue. The more I think of it the less able am I to discover any points of resemblance between acer saccharinum and homo Canadensis, and I will give up trying. Stop a bit! The maple is a very pretty thing to look at, and so,—no! Well, yes! So are the Canadian girls.

I fancy that different birds have preferences for different trees, but, not being a very close observer, cannot speak with certainty on the subject. Of course there are cases in which the preference is easily accounted for; as for instance those birds which build their nests with moss select trees whose trunk and branches are more or less moss-stained; but I imagine I have noticed a bird distinction of the maple which cannot be explained in this way. I mean the different manner in which the tree is treated by the robin and the oriole. The robin will sit in the maple and sing there all the day long, but he will not build in it if there is a convenient elm anywhere near; the oriole does just the reverse; when you want to find that clear voiced songster, look for him in the elm; if you have occasion to call on Mrs. Oriole, the chances are ten to one that you will find her comfortably seated in the maple. I

6

don't say that this is the universal rule, or that the exceptions to it
are few, but from what little I have noted of the habits of the two
birds I have got the impression that the robin prefers the maple
for a concert room, and the elm for a family mansion; while the
tastes of the oriole lie in just the opposite direction. I should be
glad to learn if anybody else has entertained the same fancy.

The fly-catchers, too, are great friends of the maple, and if
there are any about you are pretty certain to find them in its
branches. They are quaint merry little things, but dreadfully
vulgar. They have not the slightest respect for position. They
will catch and eat a fly upside down, just as unconcernedly as if
they were right side up: they will do it with their tails pointing
to the ground; or their beaks; or their backs; it makes no difference
to them, and it makes no difference to the fly either, which is
satisfactory to think of.   Another great frequenter of the maple is
the tree grass-hopper, the cicada, who whistles through the hot
summer day like froggy when he goes a wooing, but not so melodiously, and with a sort of chirr that makes you think he has got
a spring running down inside him somewhere.   He is rather
hard to find, but not so hard as the little tree frogs, who may also
be come across sometimes on the maple, and whom I half suspect
of the whistling, only they don't seem big enough.

The maple—my particular maple I am talking of now—
bears numerous scars on his trunk for from four to five feet from
the ground, as if he had been in the wars.   I rather fancy that
others of his tribe present the same peculiarity if they grow anywhere in the reach of man or boy.   He has undergone several
surgical operations, and has been tapped; not for the dropsy, but
for sugar.   There have been various attempts at odd times to
secure an accurate definition of that animal, man.   One eminent
scientist of ancient days thought that he had solved the riddle, and
defined him as a "featherless biped," but was put to shame and
confusion by an irreverent scallawag, who caught a rooster, stripped
him of his feathers, and invited the philosopher to recognize him
as "a man and a brother."   He has also been called a reasoning
animal, but apart from its being generally conceded that there are

other creatures that can reason quite as well according to their lights as a man, everybody knows some men who are altogether unreasonable, (they are married men, generally) and to be unreasonable presupposes an inability to reason. Another definition of him is that he is a cooking animal; but that again will not hold universally good, if we include woman, as I suppose we must, under the general term man. There are plenty of women, (worse luck!) that are by no means cooking animals: they can concoct messes productive of dyspepsia and indigestion, and equivalent to slow poisons, but they can't cook. Looking at the maple and his scars, the thought suggests itself to me that man is an animal that gets something or other for his own benefit out of everything he comes across. If he doesn't, it is not for the want of trying, but because the idea has not, for the time being, occurred to him. What other animal would ever have dreamed of getting sugar out of a tree? or would have taken so much pains to do it, when, as we all know, sugar can be obtained by merely going to the nearest grocer's for five cents a pound? You don't find any other animal tapping trees, or even going to the grocer's for sugar; and yet they are all fond of it. I had a little smooth-haired English terrier once, whose character was utterly demoralized by her attachment to sugar. She would watch her opportunity, and if the breakfast or supper table was left unguarded a moment, would jump upon it, and making for the sugar bowl, monopolize its contents if she had time; converted herself in fact into a canine sugar combine. Remonstrance and threats were useless; whippings were absolutely thrown away upon her; till one winter evening it occurred to me to burn a piece of sugar in the candle, (we had candles in those days), and present it to her. The consequence was that her nose was burned as well as the sugar, and ever after that, if the pleasure of her absence at table was earnestly desired, it was only necessary to show her a lump of the once-coveted sweet. She would walk out of the room if the door was open, or under the table if it wasn't, with her caudal appendage between her legs, and a growl that sounded marvellously like a suppressed anathema. She was possessed of a highly developed reasoning faculty; but

man, if he wants sugar, will burn his fingers, and suffocate himself
with smoke, and make himself dreadfully sick with latire, rather
than not have it. It is not because he cannot do without it, but
because his natural instinct impels him to make the most he can
out of everything he comes across. Hence he will fight for ter-
ritory, and steal, and cheat, and run away with his neighbor's
wife, and drink all the liquor he can get hold of, though it's a
great deal too much for him, and do many other reprehensible
things. It is his nature. He conceives that everything he sees
was made for his own especial benefit, and is subordinate to his
own especial interests. Even the whole of creation. There are
some men who will maintain that no world but our own can be
inhabited. One is too hot; another too cold; one too far from
the sun, another too near; one is too solid, and another not solid
enough. And he treats the unfortunate brutes, birds and beasts,
that he controls, as if they had no rights or feelings; ·Noah's ark
animals, to be maimed, and bruised, and cast aside just as it suits
him. He was placed upon earth, he thinks, to get all he can for
himself out of everything and everybody, and if he makes any
return, it is with an eye to future profits.

The Choir of the Clearing.

THERE is music in the clearing, and quite a large and accomplished band of songsters, but they are not feathered ones, as might perhaps be imagined ; at least, if some of them are, it requires a microscope to ascertain the fact. We are not rich in birds in the clearing, the regular *habitués* being confined to the little ground sparrows, whose song, such as it is, does not amount to much. The birds that move in the upper musical circles do not shun us absolutely, it is true, but their recognition of us extends only so far as what among human beings is termed a bowing acquaintance, a passing notice in the street, and never gets to familiar intercourse. The robin and oriole overlook the clearing from the elms or maples at its edge, and sing at it, not for it ; the bob-o-link does the same thing from the fences at the sides. The first named bird, indeed, will not unfrequently drop in to breakfast, or dinner, for there is a good square meal to be had here when it is not so easy to find it elsewhere, but the bob-o-link, seldom, and the oriole never, visits us. The wood-pecker is a more frequent guest with his tap, tap, tap, on some decaying stump, but who ever heard of a drum-major in a choir? and the crows come along pretty frequently, after they have dug up all the seed corn, and, *faute de mieux,* the seed potatoes that come handy ; but the crow is not musical. He may not be of this opinion himself ; in fact we know from La Fontaine's fable of the crow and the fox, that he is not ; but there is no going against nature, and nature has endowed him with a chronic bronchitis. Of the two, I should say that there is more melody in a bull frog. The blue jay makes his appearance here, too, in the fall, especially if there should be a ripe corn field close by, but he is chiefly intent on plundering purposes, and not on practising songs or psalms, and when he does open his mouth—Well : all I can say is that I have heard better singing at a village concert got up in aid of the church. Our only other bird visitants are a very exceptional owl who has got drunk over night, and lost his latch key and his way at the same time, and the hawks, sparrow and hen, who are by no means exceptional, and of whose approach you become aware before they are seen, feathery twinkling stars high up in the heavens, by the sudden hush of whatever bird conversation may happen to be going on at the time. To expect a bird choir in the clearing is to expect a vain thing, and to be disappointed.

Nevertheless, we have a numerous and well appointed choir of our own, the female members of which are recruited from the insect population, and very obligingly helped by the frogs, who represent the gentlemen, and sing bass to their treble. The ants, who are very numerous, don't count, for an ant is always too intent on business to sing, and I don't believe she could if she tried ; and it is hopeless to try and make anything of the bees. They have a musical turn if they would only cultivate it, but they have no application ; they will do nothing but hum their tunes. However, the mosquitoes and gnats make up for all other insect deficiencies, and they chant from morn to dewy eve without intermission. Of course they have their drawbacks just the same as in human choirs, though I must do them the justice to say that they don't seem to quarrel among themselves, and they keep time with each other, whilst the members of a human choir generally do the first thing, and don't do the other. But in the matter of causing the superintendent or director to wish that he had never been born they are very much alike ; whatever occasional quarrels they may have among themselves, they have always an outstanding one with him. " 'Tis true 'tis pity ; pity 'tis 'tis true." I wish I could say otherwise, but wherever there is a man ready like a lamb for the slaughter, there the lady choristers, insect or human, are gathered together to immolate him by slow torture. I don't so much mind in the case of the clergyman, for clergymen were created especially for women to caress and flatter and—sting, and serves them right, too, for if there were no clergymen there would be no marriages, and no endless enquiries as to whether marriage is a failure or not, and no thinly-veiled laudations of adultery by gentlemen and lady novelists; but when the matter affects me personally, and as superintendent of the clearing and all that goes on in it, I have to sit on a stump and listen to the practising of the lady mosquitoes, I protest against their copying their human sisters. I say "lady mosquitoes," because I am informed on high scientific authority that it is only they who bite; the gentleman is, like all other males, a poor harmless nonentity. If this be true, as reason and analogy alike forbid me to doubt, the feminine mosquito population is greatly in excess of the masculine ; as is the case with other races besides the mosquito, and would be still more markedly so with the human one, if that wise and ancient nation, the Chinese, did not drown a great proportion of their female babies as soon as they are born. I leave for the consideration of political theorists whether this practice may not account for the prolonged existence of the Flowery Empire, and have obtained for it its distinguishing epithet of Celestial.

The gnats are not so pertinacious, nor so vicious as the mosquitoes, and hence, I believe, though I have never been rude enough to attempt to confirm my belief by enquiry, that they are the married members of the choir. For I have observed that marriage is a great soother, or chastener, which ever you like to call it, of the animal spirits, and tones down the natural disposition of the individual in a truly astonishing manner. I have observed, too, and I am sure every choir-master will corroborate me, that the spinster members are always the most unruly and dangerous. It stands to reason that it should be so, because the married ladies have always a husband ready and convenient, whom they can "take it out of" at home in curtain lectures. The unmarried ones have no such resource : they may have, and indeed they are certain to have, one or more young fellows dangling at their heels ; but these are uncertain, and if the worst comes to the worst, they can always get away. The husband can't. Hence the spinster variety is the most wicked, and to be carefully avoided ; that is, when she is disengaged. When she has her hands full, or in other words is engaged, then she may be approached in comparative security, for

she is all sweetness and light. Generally, but not always; it is
not safe to be too confident. As Henry the Fourth of France
remarked,

> " Souvent femme varie,
> Bien fou qui s'y fie."

Or as Verdi subsequently put it most melodiously,

> " La donna e mobile,
> E sempre variabile."

both which sayings are endorsed by Sir Walter Scott,

> " Oh ! woman, in our hours of ease
> Uncertain, coy, and hard to please."

The gnats also have another distinguishing characteristic :
they join dancing to their singing, and very pretty and graceful
are the movements of the tiny creatures. They never tire. They
seem carried away and out of themselves by the exquisite joy of
their simple existence of a day. Their span of life may, for aught
I know to the contrary, seem quite as long to them as our allotted
space of seventy years does to us ; longer perhaps, for, for them,
death has no terrors, and is not a thing to be shrunk from. They
have no skeleton at their feast. And this peculiarity in the
Ephemerides, is also a peculiarity more or less marked of all the
lower classes in the scale of creation ; a thorough and pure enjoyment of the fact of living. I think that traces of this may be
found in early childhood, shown most plainly in the baby that
laughs and crows in its sleep in the cradle, from which the pretty
fancy has arisen that its angel is talking to it in its dreams. So
he is ; the angel of Life. Pain and sickness may obscure for a
time this exquisite pleasure of living, but it cannot efface it utterly ; not in the lower animals at any rate. It may be destroyed
in man, but it is his own doing, or the doings of others like himself ; and it is destroyed by sin—sin in ourselves, and sin in
others. With the lower animals it is not so : they, like ourselves,
are subject to pain and disease, hunger, thirst, weariness, slavery ;

but when these are removed the happiness of living reasserts itself, and shows itself plainly in their actions. Hence there is a very real and absolute meaning in the words of the Psalmist when he says " All thy works praise Thee, O Lord ! " and in the opening verse of the Song of the Three Children, " O all ye works of the Lord, bless ye the Lord, praise Him, and magnify Him for ever."

Is there not here one answer at least to the question " what were we sent into the world for ? " Were we not placed here for our own happiness, and that we might prize and enjoy the gift of life which is bestowed on us ? Not to pass it in morose discontent, affecting to despise it and the things of earth, and the means of enjoyment which the Master has given us ; nor in unnecessary mortification of the body and spirit ; unnecessary, mind ; for subject as we are to passions and evil desires, discipline of the flesh and mind are necessary, but only so far as they effect the end aimed at, and do not destroy the other aim of our innocent happiness. I take it that we were originally placed on this earth that we might make it an abode of innocent pleasure, and thus praise Him who loves all His creation, and would fain see it happy. If we have fallen from this state, and the service of God now consists mainly in obedience to the laws which He has revealed to us for our guidance, let us remember that these laws are intended to restore us to the estate from which we have fallen, and that in the keeping of them we may obtain that happiness of simple existence which we have lost. There is a lesson to be learned from these little choristers praising God for the life he has given ; and yet another. If this life be so sweet to even these tiny mites, how do we sin against their Master, when by cruelty, greed, thoughtlessness, or selfishness, we unnecessarily inflict pain on them !

A Summer Day-Dream.

Here, where I lie in rest outspread,
　　With mossy carpet girt around,
The great trees green above my head,
　　And flowers bespangle all the ground.

Low drowsy murmurs go and come
　　Among the spikelets of the pines :
Close by, I hear the wild bees hum
　　'Mid strawberry and arbutus vines.

Above my head the wood-pecker
　　Drives coffin nails in giant boles :
And all the maples are astir
　　With clear-pitched notes of orioles.

And somewhere near, (I know not where),
　　Like to the voices of a dream,
Far off, yet near, the hazy air
　　Shakes with the laughter of a stream ;

A little noisy rill that brawls
　　In mimic cataracts through the woods,
And whirls its pebbles over falls
　　Of inches into inch-deep floods.

I cannot see it, but the ear,
　　Can track its thousand fantasies,
Now rippling on distinct and clear,
　　Now loud with little angry cries.

I know that, as it flows along
　　With dancing sand-specks in its train,
Some stone has jarred upon its song,
　　And turned its gold-motes back again.

And there it pants, and foams, and raves,
   (As we, too, rave o'er little woes)
Till myriad bubbles fleck its waves
   And gather, whirling, round its throes :

And then a rush, a fairy cry,
   A crash along its water ways,
And all its rage and agony
   Are drowned in songs of peace and praise.

. . .There comes a butterfly, and flits
   To yonder fern-top's dizzy height ;
Folds for a while his wings, and sits ;
   Then opes them, quivering, in the light,

And dallies with the sunbeam's kiss,
   And shuts his wings, and opes again
In such great ecstasy of bliss
   It almost seems a throb of pain.

So fair, so frail ! So weak, so strong
   For happiness in little things !
So mute ! yet e'en the voice of song,
   Sounds poor by those wing-quiverings.

. . . .Hither and thither, in and out,
   Amid the wilderness of grass
The ants, a busy motley rout,
   Prospect and scout, pass and repass.

And as I watch them running by
   With eager footsteps to and fro
I fall to wonder, lazily,
   What mighty passion moves them so.

Not love, nor anger. Each alone
   Pursues his independent way.
None gather by some way-side stone
   To waste in gossip half the day.

Nor see I in the varying throng
    That passes and repasses by,
Some portly insect wend along,
    Slow-paced, in wealth's own dignity.

Some aim directs the varied ways
    Of all the pigmy multitude ;
Some business that allows no stays,
    Some pleasure eagerly pursued.

And yet, methinks, their rush of feet
    Is with a stronger passion rife,
And through their slender pulses beat
    The dancings of the joy of life ;

In secret haunts of sweet perfume
    To work and play the hours away,
Companions of a world of bloom,
    And flower-shaded from the day ;

To feel the tangled grasses stirred
    With the cool breeze's soft caress,
And hear, high up, the brooding bird
    Croon little notes of tenderness ;

And midst such scenes as these, to take
    And do their work, however small,
For Him who made ant, flower, and brake,
    And loves the service of them all.

So, as in dreaming sympathy
    With all this little world I lie,
Its happy spell comes over me,
    And pierces me with ecstasy

So great that when I fain would seek
    For words, they loom up faint and dim ;
And well I ween them all too weak
    For simplest notes of Life's glad hymn.

Oh Lord Omnipotent, how just,
    How strong in love are all Thy ways.
Who peoplest grass-blades, and the dust,
    And from such worlds perfectest praise ;

Who deckest out with loveliness
    The meanest creatures of Thy hand,
And watchest to protect and bless
    Lives, smaller than a grain of sand.

Above me, the breath of the pines
And the songs of the birds in the maple trees ;
    Around me the scent of the flowers
    That blossom among the woodland vines
      To greet the summer hours,
And the drowsy hum of the bees,
    And the busy unrest of the ants,
    And the varying voice of the rill
That sings, and sobs, and rages, and pants
    In its course from the hill.

What heart can paint the perfect bliss
    Of Heaven in nature's second birth,
When Love reigns in such scenes as this,
    And such strong joy in things of earth.

The Ground-bird.

THE principal of the feathered residents in the clearing is the ground-bird; indeed, I might say that he is the only one who may fairly lay claim to the title of resident, for he builds here, sleeps here, works here, and does what he calls singing here, which no other bird does. He is a quiet, unassuming little fellow, not particularly handsome unless you look at him closely; just a mite incredulous as to the possibility of good intentions on my part at first, but after he has convinced himself on that point, supremely indifferent to my presence; dismisses me from his mind as something not worth notice, at any rate so long as there is anything to be found that is fit to eat. When the supplies begin to grow scarce he turns up his little round head, and throws a reproachful glance at me from his little black eye, as if he more than suspected that I was to blame, but was too polite to say so, and flies off a few yards to look for happier hunting grounds. He generally makes his first appearance alone, and pretends to be a bachelor, free and independent, but it is not very long before I hear Mrs. Ground-bird calling to him from some little distance away, and wanting to know where he is, and what he has been doing all this time. Of course, he is obliged to tell her, and I must do him the justice to say that he generally does this at once, without any attempt at evasion or concealment, which shows that he has been well brought up, and not only knows that part of the catechism which enjoins respect and obedience to the powers that be, but puts it in practice also, and then she makes haste to join him, and the two continue their search after small game in a cosy and comfortable manner, keeping up a desultory conversation all the time. And that bird-talk is the only ground of complaint that I have against him. It may have subtle inflections and delicate shades of meaning which escape my grosser and untutored ear, but to me it sounds terribly mono-

tonous. Cheep! cheep! cheep! Directly he comes into view, he
introduces himself with "cheep;" when he flies away, his parting
remark is "cheep;" when he discovers anything to eat, he says
"cheep" before meals, and "cheep" afterwards; when he thinks he
is going to find it and doesn't, he still says "cheep." I don't
remember ever coming on a word before in any language that I
am acquainted with that was put to such a variety of uses; it even
beats the Chinese words that have an indefinite number of
significations according to the accent laid on them, and the tone of
voice used, for it has no accentuation, and only one tone. It is no
use asking him what he means by it, for he appears to mean
anything and everything, and Mrs. Ground-bird understands him
thoroughly; but my failure to comprehend him annoys me perhaps
more than it ought to do; and I feel uncomfortable in my mind
when he looks at me before flying away, and says "cheep." I
wonder if he spells that word as I have done, or with an a; and if
the latter, whether his remark is not personal and derogatory, and
expressive of a very poor opinion of me on his part. If I could
only be sure that I was right in this misgiving, I declare I would
pick up the first stone or stick that came to hand, and throw it
after him to teach him better manners.

Yet he is a well-meaning little fellow, and a harmless one,
which cannot be said of all well-meaning persons. There are
people in this world who are constantly going about picking up
their means of living, and crying cheap, cheap, cheap. Cheap
goods, cheap houses, cheap money, cheap everything. Ay! and
cheap lives and cheap souls too. I recollect when Cobden began
the anti-corn law agitation in England which grew till it finally
resulted in her present Free Trade policy. It was in Huddersfield,
I think; at any rate in one of the great manufacturing centres of
the day that he was inveighing against the corn-laws, and appealing to his hearers to assist him in securing their abolition on the
ground that it would bring cheap food to the working men. Of
course the argument told with his audience, but there was one old
weaver there that pressed the argument closer, and saw the results
a little more clearly than he was intended to do. "Cheap food,"

he growled, "hang thee, 't is cheap wages thou meanest." He never spoke a truer word in his life.

The great progress made by science in all its branches within the last half century, the improvements in machinery, the natural increase of population, and the occupancy of hitherto uncultivated lands, and the discovery and development of new and rich beds of mineral ores of different kinds have tended legitimately to cheapness in all the articles in common use, by the increased production of the raw material on the one hand, and the increased facilities for manufacturing them at a less cost on the other. In so far as lowness of prices, (which is what is generally meant by cheapness) is effected by this, the result is natural and innocent. It is only a truism to say that the more abundant, and the more easily obtained anything is, the lower is its value in public estimation, and also its value as an article of trade and barter. Increased production, from whatever source it originates, brings with it decreased prices, until it reaches a certain limit, and then there comes " a glut in the market,". and there is virtually no sale at all. The opening up and settlement of vast areas of good farming land, where agricultural operations can be carried on at comparatively small cost, has at once handicapped the occupiers of the older and more artificially cultivated districts, and has increased the available amount of food products to a very large extent; the substitution of machinery for manual labour, and the continuous process of improvement which it is undergoing have at once diminished the number of those able to find employment, and increased the output of manufactured products. The inevitable consequence in both these cases is the lowering of prices, or cheapness; and it can only be remedied by a cessation, partial, or complete for the time, of production. Such a cessation, of course, diminishes the profits of the producer, and throws out of employment a number of persons engaged in the production; but it is, as I have said, inevitable, because there is a point beyond which cheapness cannot be obtained except at a loss; and the natural causes are constantly tending to this point. They tend to create cheapness for a more or less lengthy period, and then a reaction ensues, and prices rise, when they come into action again. There is a tide in all the affairs of men upon earth, and a regular ebb, and flow, and high tide : or, to use a perhaps better simile, mundane matters are like the pendulum of a clock—the sweep may be long or short, but it always eventually returns to the point from which it started.

So far then, there is nothing objectionable or morally wrong in cheapness : it is only when man interferes with natural laws that things go all astray. But is the cheapness dear to most hearts, and especially to the feminine mind that is always hunting after bargains, one which is created by natural laws, or an artificial one ? I am very much inclined to believe it is the latter. The cheapness to which I allude is not caused by the laws of supply and demand, or attributable to competition, and the blame of it rests not on one class but on all, on those who suffer by it, and on those who profit by it, for the same madness seems to affect every body, and a thing is prized the more in proportion as it can be got cheap.

This may not be at first apparent in the wealthy few, many of whom value a thing mainly for the high price paid for it, yet I rather fancy that if we could see below the surface we should find that the real satisfaction, even here, in the purchase of any article, lies in the belief of having got it "a bargain." But, whether my fancy be true or not, the rest of the world will scarcely purchase any article, not imperatively needed, unless it be cheap. There are two evils that arise out of this ; the manufacture of worthless goods, and the adulteration of food in the first place ; the grinding down of the poor in the second place. Of the first evil I don't complain much : there are alleviations. If, for instance, coffee at 25 or 30 cents per pound satisfies my taste as well as that at 40 or 45 cents, I am perfectly willing to call it coffee, 'though I know that that bean forms a very small portion of the whole compound, and that the rest, if I am lucky, is composed of Boston Baked Beans, and Chicory. I say ' if I am lucky,' because there is some-

7

times tobacco dust mixed in. I am perfectly willing to allow that cottolene, or oleomargarine is creamery butter; not the very best, of course, but butter, and cheap at the price. I have no objection to solid gold rings at 25 cents, and diamond pins at fifty; if the one is not gold, and the other is not a diamond, they are sufficiently like the real article to pass careless muster—"Don't disturb Camarina"; don't enquire too curiously into what you eat and drink, and wherewithal you are clothed. The fruit of the tree of knowledge has never agreed with any one since the earliest days of our race. An English sailor, according to the late Mr. Leech, once landed at Canton, and feeling hungry, went into a Chinese restaurant where he was served with such a delicious ragout that he cleared the dish. If he had paid his bill and gone quietly out, he would have been all right, but he didn't. He must needs know what the delicacy was, and as he could not speak the language resorted to signs. Pointing to the dish, and patting his stomach, he remarked enquiringly to the waiter "Quack-quack?" and that functionary with a solemn shake of his head answered "Bow-wow!" Before Jack reached his ship, he might just as well have eaten no dinner at all. Better! Where cheap Jack reigns it is not well to enquire too closely into the nature of things.

Polly, and Bloomah, and the whole tribe of their sisters occasionally visit the cities, and bring back with them bundles of all sorts of articles got cheap—some of which they assure me they would not make for the price—women's blouses and capes, men's shirts, towels, all sorts of things. Take a white shirt for instance, which I have seen occasionally—(on Sundays and holidays)—and therefore know something about. The women tell me that they couldn't buy the cotton, or linen, and make the article at the price they paid for it. And they plume themselves at having got it "so cheap." But what does that shirt mean to me? It means that somewhere or other, a poor famished creature has been doing the work on it, and others like it, for twenty-five or thirty cents a dozen; it means that this, and other articles of "cheap ready made clothing," are wrung from the suffering of brothers and sisters ; that they represent starvation, dishonour, suicide. They are the garments of Death, and the "latest fashions" of Hell. The trader will not be defrauded of his profits though he sells in the long run "so cheap," and has "bargain days" and "slaughter sales," and "thirty per cent discounts," and "reductions below cost prices"; it is out of the working man and woman that the cheapness comes, and the general public must have cheapness.

Rabyahs Last Ride.

I cannot get out of my head to-day an Arabian legend I once heard or read, it is so long ago that I forget which, and had forgotten the tale itself, till it suddenly rose up from the grave of memory, and has been haunting me ever since. We all of us, I fancy, have had some such experience, similar to that of Mark Twain pursued by the refrain,

> " Punch, brothers, punch ; punch with care ;
> Punch in the presence of the passengaire."

In such cases, when the phrase, or the tune, or the memory is persistently obtrusive, the best way is to let it have its full swing, and more ; just as you cure a horse given to running away by compelling him to keep on when he gets tired and wants to stop ; so I have put this tale into verse, and so killed it ; I nearly killed myself at the same time with the effort, and I shouldn't wonder if the reader wished I had done so altogether. However, that is his affair, not mine ; so here is the tale itself. It would have been a fine poem if I had not adhered as faithfully as I could to the original, which has given it, so to speak, a flavor of prose, and may lead some to recall Hood's title for a volume of tales and poems, " Prose and Werse." It is called

RABYAH'S LAST RIDE.

This is the tale of a man, Rabyah, the son of Mokaddem,
Chief of the Beni Firaz, of the eldest sons of Adam,
Lords of the waste and the desert, who dwell in the midst of the sands,
Who live by the bow and spear, and thirst for no other lands.

Wide are the sands of the desert, and on their borders the beast
Of the infidels tears up the graves, and laughs o'er his loathly feast ;
And the tribes that dwell by the wells where the lordly palm trees soar,
Start as they lie in their tents at the lion's thunderous roar.

* *
*

But we are the Beni Firaz. When Allah moulded the clay
Of which they say all things were made, we were the men of the day.
The sun never shone on the world, since ever a man was on earth
But he smiled on the Beni Firaz that took from Adam their birth,

* *
*

And went out into the desert. To whom else could Allah give
With the shifting sands, and burning suns, and the dread simoon to live ?
Who but the Beni Firaz could have drawn in the desert's breath,
And nurtured women and men in the very jaws of death ?

* *
*

Death ! It is no great thing, and we face it every day,
The spear of a foeman may bring it, or a swerve from the beaten way.
Death is the infidel's bugbear : no son of our tribe is afraid
To die as his fathers died, and be laid where his fathers are laid.

* *
*

We are the men of men, the bravest of sons of Adam,
And chief of the Beni Firaz is Rabyah, the child of Mokaddem ;
And this is the tale of his stand when the fatal shaft had sped,
And the Beni Suleiman curs yapped from afar at the dead.

* *
*

The Beni Suleiman pressed us ; pressed hard in the ancient days :
They swooped upon us like eagles ; they rode upon all our ways :
For a blood-feud had risen between us, and though the price had been paid.
The road that was safe for men was unsafe for matron and maid.

The land was sere, and the wells were dry as a jackal-gnawed bone,
When up to the Ghazai pass came our women, unkept, and alone ;
Unkept save by Rabyah, the son of Mokammed, who brought up the rear ;
The matrons and maids of Firaz the charge of a single spear !

* *
*

The mother of Rabyah turned her head, " What, son of my heart, dost
    thou see ? "
" A whirlwind of dust, and the glint of spears, and horsemen riding free ;
But speed thou on, my mother, until the Ghazai be past,
And I will stay here and hold back the foe that cometh on fast.

* *
*

And there as he turned and drew rein a wind clave the dusty cloud,
And he saw the sparkle of steel, and the rush of a mighty crowd ;
And lo ! at its head was Nubaishah, of whom it was said that Death,
Nurser of Vultures, rode by his side, and lived in Nubaishah's breath.

* *
*

But the sister of Rabyah shrieked when he drew his bridle rein,
And the cries of her women re-echoed her wail o'er the arid plain ;
But his mother knew better her son, " Fools ! what is the cause for fear,
Though the curs of the Beni Suleiman bark, if Rabyah be near ? "

* *
*

Then they left him standing alone, and swift as an onrushing flame,
Three of the best and bravest of all Beni Suleiman came ;
But his first shaft pierced the throat, and the second sought out the heart,
And the third went straight through the eye to the brain; so sure was the dart.

* *
*

And the men of the Beni Suleiman shrank, as a man might shrink
From the eyes of a lion couched by the spring at which he has stooped to drink ;
And Rabyah pressed them hard with his arrows, and drove them back
As the South winds push back the storm, and melt into tears its rack.

Then he turned to follow the women, and Beni Suleiman turned,
Yelped on the track of his good grey mare, panted, and thirsted, and burned ;
Burned, and thirsted and panted, till he paused once more in his path,
And again the arrows sped home, and again they shrank from his wrath.

* *
*

So through the long hot day the combat surged to and fro,
And still as he made a stand, they shrank from his deadly bow ;
And still as he turned, they followed, until our pass was in sight,
And the sun was behind the hills,—the light was the eyes of night.

* *
*

And so as the dark came down the pursuers and pursued
Drew to the Ghazai pass where the great hills watch and brood ;
And into the edge of their blackness he rode for the final stand ;
But his quiver had lost its last shaft, and there was but the spear to his hand.

* *
*

The great black horses were weary, their sweat fell from them like rain,
As the well-filled water skin sweats in the heat of the desert plain ;
But Rabyah's mare was as dry as the jackal's bone is dry,
And the flame that breathed from her nostrils was shade to the fire in
    her eye.

* *
*

But against him thundered Nubaishah, Nubaishah of whom 'twas said,
That he rode with the Nurser of Vultures, Death, who covered his head ;
When there came a cry from the pass, "The victory is not won ;
Give them the sword and the spear ; give them the spear, my son."

* *
*

E'en at the word he charged, but Nubaishah drew bridle rein,
Poised his spear for a space, then sent it hurling amain.
Strong was the arm of the chief, and straight was the aim, and true ;
And the steel met Rabyah oncoming, and pierced him through and through.

Loud laughed Nubaishah then, as he saw how the shaft had sped ;
'' Take thou my love-gift, Rabyah, that soon shalt be with the dead.
Here will I wait through the night till the earliest dawn of day ;
Then, if thou hast a mind, try thou to bar my way. '

* *
*

But Rabyah turned as untouched, though ever his entrails flowed
From the mouth of the wound as he went, and tracked out all his road.
And there at the mouth of the pass he saw his mother, and cried,
'' Give me to drink, my mother, or I shall fall as I ride.''

* *
*

Give me to drink ; for the fever is coursing through all my ve'ns,
And fiercer the thirst of Death than the thirst of the burning plains.
I have ridden my last ride, mother, have fought my last good fight ;
Give me to drink that I die ; but speed thou on through the night.''

* *
*

She dropped the veil from her face, and stood before him unveiled
As none but his father had seen her, and e'en in the doing, paled ;
Then flushed again as the daybreak flushes and pales, and flushes
Ere the rising sun comes up, and the sky at his coming blushes.

* *
*

She stooped and kissed his wound that gaped like the camel's lips
When he shows his teeth with a grin, white-set with their cold blue tips ;
'' To drink is to die, my son, and thou must fight to the last.
Lo ! we go, as thou sayest ; stay thou till the strait be past.''

* *
*

'' What is thy thirst to thy wound ? What is thy wound to the shame
That, failing thee, will befall the women that bear thy name ?
What is the death of a man to the honor of maiden and wife ?
Take thou my kiss for thy drink, my Rabyah, my soul, my life ! ''

Parched and bleeding he waited alone, and watched for the foe
That stole through the darkness upon him, till he saw them down below,
And charged with a shout upon them, and sent them reeling, until
The jackals whined over the plain ; but silence kept the hill.

* *
*

At the mouth of the pass in the dawning was standing the old grey horse,
And the lance of her rider was couched in rest—the lance of a corpse.
But the Beni-Suleiman shrank ; shrank back from the levelled spear,
And circled about the pass ; circled in doubt and fear,

* *
*

Till the great round sun uprose, and the maiden, morning, flushed
At the touch of his crocus fingers, trembled awhile, and blushed,
And then Nubaishah saw that the hero drooped his head
A little, as if in sleep, and knew that the life was fled.

* *
*

Called to a bowman and asked, " Hast thou an arrow, my son,
Left to thy bow ? " and was answered, " Master, I have but one,
And that is my life, my master ; my life, for Rabyah is near ;
And his rush is Azrael's rush, and Azrael guides his spear."

* *
*

" Nevertheless, must thou shoot ; but do thou shoot at the mare,
Neither to kill nor to wound, but aim thou to graze the hair,"
So he shot, and the grey mare swerved from the bolt, and her rider fell
Prone on his face to the ground midst the Beni Suleiman's yell.

* *
*

The dead man lay in the pass, and over his body the foe
Halted, and mused, and wondered that such a man should lie low ;
But the women were safe in our tents, and we waited for news till there came
The riderless steed of Rabyah, foam flecked, with her eyes aflame.

And then we rose as one man ; our horses devoured the way,
Till we came to the mouth of the pass where the son of Mokammed lay,
And there we raised him a cairn ; and there to this day it stands
Looking out from the Ghazai pass over the desert sands.

* *
*

Rabyah, son of Mokammed, thy grave is heaped up with stone,
But under the desert cairn thou dwellest not all alone,
For wherever thy tale is told, the women give thee a part
Of their life and love, and thou livest ever more in their heart.

* *
*

. . . Now this is the tale of a man.   A tale that is easy to read,
    But one that is hard to be fashioned out into manly deed,
    For men now die for their lust, but Rabyah died for the right ;
    Stood for the honor of women, and, dying, won the fight.

* *
*

What are our women to us ? Slaves to our bow and spear,
Bought and sold in the market without or a blush, or a fear.
Men ! Do we call ourselves men ? In the face of Heaven, we lie !
We trample upon the weak, but not for the pure ones die.

* *
*

We are a race of cowards ; robbers that steal away
The purity of our women, and think it the daintiest play :
Vultures that feed on corruption, ourselves corrupt and debased,
With the stamp of lust on our hearts, and our mother's image defaced.

* *
*

But wherever a woman is honored, there too shall Rabyah's name
Be written upon the heart in living letters of flame ;
And wherever the tale of a man, a loyal man, shall be told
Women shall tell how Rabyah rode in the days of old.

Along the Cow-Path.

"CO' boss! Co' *boss!* Co' boss! Bossy, bossy, bossy!" There's
Bloomah at the gate of the clearing summoning home
"the milky mothers of the herd," or, as Nathan calls them, "them
ere pesky critters." Nathan is not very enthusiastic in his
admiration of the cows, for at certain seasons of the year, when
they are turned into the clearing to pick up what they can get,
they are apt to make for the other end of it as soon as they fancy
no one is looking at them, and explore the recesses of the bush.
Then, when the voice of the charmer, Bloomah, is heard at the
gate at eventime, some of the animals, generally the young
heifers, are out of the sound of its fascination, and Nathan has to
go and hunt them up; an exercise which sometimes keeps him
employed till night fall. The old cows do not as a rule play truant
in this fashion; they are just as ready and willing to be milked as
Bloomah is to milk them, and I see them coming out one by one
from the woods, and sauntering leisurely down to the gate, nipping
off a blade or two of grass on their way, just about the time that
that fair damsel may be expected. But the younger members of
the bovine family are not so reliable; whether they have not yet
gained experience sufficient to enable them to tell what o'clock it
is, or whether they prefer the freedom of the bush to the restraint
of the farm yard, or whether they stray too far off and lose their
way, I cannot determine, but certain it is that they frequently are
conspicuous by their absence at the proper time, and equally
certain that Bloomah is not going to trouble her head about them,
and will start Nathan after them on her return as soon as she sets
eyes on that much ruled individual. And he doesn't like it.

I suppose I shall be told that I ought to keep my fences up.
The remark is not an original one, and it betrays a very superficial
acquaintance with the nature and peculiarities of clearing fences,

which differ considerably from all others. I am not writing an
agricultural treatise, neither am I engaged by Government as a
professional member of the Society for promoting agricultural
knowledge among farmers, or I would take the opportunity to
deliver a lecture on fences in general, and clearing fences in
particular. I simply remark that in these latter, there is always
one irreclaimable gap in the side bordering on the bush, sometimes two or three. Indeed, I have known many cases where
farmers, recognizing this peculiarity, have dispensed with a fence
on this side altogether, which simplifies matters, but does not mend
them. Where they have not adopted this plan there is, as I have
said, invariably one gap at least in the fence, and it has this peculiarity, that there is not the slightest use in mending it. Fill it
up in the evening, and before noon next day it will yawn as wide
as ever. Whether this is a natural defect of the clearing fence, or
the cows are responsible, or the wood nymphs, is a moot question,
but the fact remains, though unexplained, and the wise man
recognizes it, and acquiesces in it accordingly. I am myself rather
inclined to put the blame on the cows, though they look so innocent about it, as I have observed that there is a well beaten track
leading straight from the gate to the gap, and this is the cow-path
par excellence. There are other little paths converging into it
from all quarters of the enclosure, but these are faintly defined,
and obviously accidental byways; private lanes debouching on
the cow's highway.

Now it may not strike you as a very remarkable thing that
when you travel along this path, it all depends on the direction
you take whether you get home to dinner or supper, or get lost in
the woods. That looks too obvious to merit any notice whatever.
But did it ever strike you that in the ways of human life the same
thing happens? That your happiness and comfort, and safety, all
depend on the direction towards which you set your face? Perhaps
you will say that you did not give the thing any particular thought,
but that you are fully aware of it, all the same. Well, then! let
me press the matter a little further. Have you ever thought what
life really is; and what is its real duration? Do you consider it

to be rather indefinite as to term ; lasting with some eighty, with some sixty, with some forty or thirty or twenty years? **Then you are wrong.** Life is a very definite term, inasmuch as a thing can be said to be truly yours only so long as you have certain possession of it ; and there is not a created being on this earth that is secure of life beyond the present moment. Of course, we all of us know that, though there are few of us that act as if we believed it ; as, indeed, it is morally certain that we don't believe. Men are willing enough to confess that there is a possibility that they may die the next moment ; but they never admit the probability. If a human career is cut off sooner than we anticipate, we call it sudden death. All men die suddenly, however much they may have prepared for it ; " The Son of man cometh at an hour that ye think not." Safety at home, or loss in the bush, depends on the direction of the face at the moment.

Nor is this consideration of less value in matters not involving eternity. The rule is the same in every transaction of life, that its success or failure depends mainly on the way in which we set about it, the direction from which we approach it. The lesson of the school child is mastered just so far as there is the desire and the will to master it ; it is unlearned just so far as these qualities are deficient or non-existent ; when it complains that " the lesson is too hard," it is either because the courage to overcome its difficulties is wanting, or the will. Many men are but grown-up children in this respect, and hence the remark of the poet, " The many fail, the few succeed." Moreover, there are always two ways of doing anything, the right way, and the wrong one. Take the right way, and you come out at the gate ; take the wrong way and you will spend the night in the bush. " You pays your penny, and you takes your choice." And you must recollect that this choice is to be made at every instant of your life, and at every step in the matter in which you may be engaged, be it one of business, or one of pleasure. In either case if you go the right way to work you will come out right ; if you don't, you won't.

I want you to cast your eyes on this track again : it is well beaten, tolerably straight, and serves a distinct purpose, that of travelling from one end of the clearing to the other. So long as the cows keep to it, there is no harm done; it is only when they go beyond it that Bloomah cries till she is hoarse; and Nathan subsequently travels along it as sulky as a bear with a sore head. From which I draw another deduction, that all things are made for use, and that it is only when they are abused that they become pernicious. I know that I shall tread upon a great many corns in laying down this sweeping general assertion, but I believe it to be true, and I further believe that it is more dangerous to hide or deny the truth than it is to confess it at once. Neither do I say that because everything is made to be used, and enjoyed, it should be so used under every circumstance, and without further restriction than the knowledge that it is injurious to abuse it; I remedy the indestructible gap in my fence, by putting boards over the eyes of the young heifers that wander through it and get lost; there are things whose use is so easily perverted that it is right and prudent to surround them with restrictions; but I don't block up my cow-path. I may go further, and say that I certainly should so block it up if the face-boards proved totally unavailing, and Nathan's journeys became of daily occurrence. But in that case I should not say that the cow-path was a wrong thing, never meant to be used as a road. This is the mistake that a great many worthy well-meaning people fall into; they see that a thing is often abused and leads to a great deal of crime and misery, (there are other things besides liquor, so don't fancy that I am referring especially to the temperance question), and they wish, some of them, to restrict it, some to forbid its use altogether. I am prepared to support them, but it is one thing to forbid for sound reasons the use, and another thing to deny the usefulness. We never gain anything in the long run by distorting or exaggerating the truth.

"Co' boss! Co' boss!" There come the cows at last. A cow is a favorite study for landscape painters, and it is a very easy thing to draw. At least it used to be when I was a child, and was drawn on strictly mathematical principles; also, on our slates at school. You took a rectangular parallelogram for the body of the cow; affixed an equilateral triangle at one end for its head, in

which were three circles representing the eyes and mouth; two
truncated ellipses represented the ears, and two quarter-circles the
horns: the line of beauty curving gracefully to the ground depicted
the tail, and four straight lines, of unequal lengths, and at different
angles, were placed under the parallelogram, two at each end,
which were legs; and there you had a beautiful cow. It is very
interesting from a philosophical point of view, and may be of use
to the advocates of evolution, to observe that this cow was the
triumphant result of an attempt at depicting minor animals; we
began with the cat, or the dog, according to the sex of the artist;
went on next with the dog or the cat; mounted to the horse, and
finally reached the culminating point in the cow, which, having
horns, was the most complex animal. I say this may be of use as
tending to prove the theory of evolution, because the original
conception, the mental idea of the animal was the same throughout,
and (with the exception of the horns) the same drawing served for
cat, dog, horse, and cow, the only difference being the size, and the
direction of the tail. This last in the cat was curved gracefully
between her legs; in the dog, over his back; in the horse it was
fore-shortened and not allowed to touch the ground as it did with
the cow. In fact, the evidence of one simple original plan
pervading all was so marked that to prevent mistakes we had to
write under our drawings THIS IS A KATT; THIS IS A DORG; and so
on. Later on, we grew more expert; our portraits then had a very
short and straight tail; and we wrote under it THIS IS A BARE.
Finally we made our drawing stand up; removed the ears, put the
two fore legs on at right angles, shortened the hind legs, and
abolished the tail. So we arrived at "the human form divine."
If you have followed my description carefully, you will see how
the evolution was carried out by a simple modification of the tail.
Man, as we all know, is not perfect, though nearly so, and
anatomists inform us, I believe, that he has got the rudiments of a
tail yet, though overgrown with flesh. Our men were perfect, and
the evolution was complete in their case; they had not even the
rudiments of tails.

Br'er Turtle.

THE little stream that comes out of the woods and runs through the clearing empties, a couple of fields off, into a brook, and the brook into our river. It is not much of a river, being what we should have called in the North of England a "beck;" but such as it is, it is the biggest stream of water we have, and we call it, politely, a river. In the summer time it has a little thread of water, a few mud-bottomed pools, lots of stones, and some sand and gravel banks. It also has turtles ; mud ones. Now, I am aware that a mud turtle, however estimable an amphibian he may be, cannot strictly be classed among the denizens of a clearing ; but we must not be too accurate, even in philosophizing, and Br'er Turtle, as Uncle Remus calls him, if not one of the inhabitants of the clearing, is a distant connection, (through the brook and the stream) and may be looked upon as a fifth or sixth cousin. Cousins five or six degrees removed, unless they happen to be young and pretty, and of the opposite sex, are not generally held to be of much account ; neither is Br'er Turtle ; at the same time, we are compelled by common fairness to allow that since they are brought into the world they must have some right to exist, however difficult it may be to discover it sometimes ; and, by a parity of reasoning, the same right must be conceded to the mud turtle. Generally speaking it is so conceded, just as we grant it to the distant cousins, by ignoring him completely, beyond, perhaps, a passing bow, or, what is in his case equivalent to it, a stone thrown at his head when he is sunning himself on an old log, or sand bank ; but when the small boy gets hold of him, his existence is trammeled with conditions that would make life utterly insupportable to a less phlegmatic animal, and even as it is I don't think he always likes it, though he puts up with it and "says nuffen." I remember in the earlier days of the now flourishing grammar school of Bishop's College, Lennoxville,

how one of the boys, in his half-holiday wanderings, once came on
a very juvenile specimen of Br'er Turtle, and captured him before
he had time to make good his retreat into the water. He was, (the
turtle, not the boy), a very, very little fellow, about the bigness of
a Mexican silver dollar, but not so pretty to look at, and of still
less value in commercial transactions. Neither was he good to eat.
I never knew of anybody eating mud-turtles, though I have been
assured that the thing has been done, and also that they were
delicious eating, which I doubt; but in any event this particular
turtle was not fit for that purpose for the very sufficient reason
that there was not enough of him to make a bite of. Take away
his upper and lower shell, his head, his little tail, and his flippers,
and what was there left of him? I suppose he had a stomach,
but, if he had, that was about all, and you can't eat a turtle's
stomach. So his captor, (which his baptismal name it was Charlie),
was puzzled what to do with him when he had got him; a thing
which is peculiarly exasperating to a boy. Long time he stood,
"dividing the swift mind this way and that," till finally it occurred
to him that he possessed à steel watch-guard, but no watch, and
that, *faute de mieux*, young master Turtle would serve as a time
piece. He was just about the size, and very nearly the shape of an
old fashioned silver hunting watch, and besides being of use in keeping the watch chain in a proper position relative to his waistcoat
pocket, possessed the obvious recommendation of being qualified in
this manner for surreptitious exhibition during school hours, and
also for being constantly at hand whenever wanted. So Charlie
picked him up, and carried him off home. But when he got there
an unexpected difficulty arose. How was he to be attached to
the chain, or the chain to him? The easiest solution of the
question appeared to be to run the guard right through him from
end to end; but, apart from the difficulty of getting master Turtle
to open his mouth wide enough for the purpose, Charlie had very
natural doubts as to whether the operation would not seriously
disturb the digestive faculties of his prize : he could not be certain
of the turtle's internal economy, but it looked as if it might be

8

that way, and he concluded to take no risks. There only remained the method of boring a small hole in the under shell, and this would have been easy enough if he could only have been sure which was the right end. For little Br'er Turtle had gone into retirement at the moment of his capture, and stayed there. He tucked in his head and covered it with a pair of his flippers; and he drew in his tail, and guarded it with the other pair, so that however closely you inspected him you "couldn't tell tother end from which." Now the burning a hole in a gentleman's coat, even if it is a bony one, is not calculated to evoke feelings of the liveliest satisfaction, and Charlie was rather afraid that if he made a mistake, and took the wrong end, he might chance to get his fingers nipped during the operation. So as older scientists have done before him, he proceeded to make experiments to test the truth of his theory as to which end of the animal the head was at. He got a little bit of stick and prodded; but the more he prodded the closer were the flippers drawn in, and it was evident that no result could be expected from that end. So he tried the other. The effect was magical. Almost at the first touch of the stick the head flew out at the opposite end, and a very emphatic hiss proclaimed the owner's disgust at the liberty taken with his tail. The most convincing argument, and the one that never fails to tell, is the argumentum a posteriori. The question was solved triumphantly, and for many days after Master Charlie lightened his scholastic labours by pulling out Master Mud Turtle to see whether it was time for intermission yet. I forget what became of the latter. I fancy that one night when his owner was asleep, he managed to free himself from the chain, crawl out of the watch pocket, drop to the ground, and disappear. " He never came back any more," and probably by this time has grandchildren, to whom he relates how he used to study in his younger days when he was preparing for College, and who look up to him with the same deep awe and reverence with which we contemplate a Rural Dean, or the Chancellor of a University. It is now nearly forty years since, but Charlie's use of the turtle has since then been improved upon, and not very long ago, young men and women used to wear little lizards attached to chains to make themselves more attractive. We are only big boys and girls after all, however old we get to be.

There are many points of similarity between Br'er Turtle, and man, and also many points of dissimilarity; the latter of necessity, as otherwise there would be no telling the one from the other. Among the former, I notice, for instance, that he can get along in the world without brains; doesn't appear to miss them when he loses them; and is supremely indifferent as to whether he has them or not. The loss does not affect his health, or his appetite, or his enjoyment of life. There are a great many men in the world who pass through this troublous life much in the same way: they have no brains, but they prosper just as well as if they had, and they are inclined rather to despise than admire others who are better endowed than themselves. It does not sound quite orthodox to advance such a proposition as this, but then just ask yourself whether you have not often virtually admitted it in your thoughts. Run your mental eye over the list of your acquaintances and friends, and see how many of them there are whom in your heart of hearts, though of course you are too polite to say it openly, you consider to be " perfect fools," and wonder how on earth it is that they manage to get a living at all, to say nothing of being, very often, more prosperous than yourself. You will find a great number, if you will only deal truly, and the most of these will be in the inner circle of the men that you really have the warmest affection for. " Pity," says the poet, " is akin to love," and probably this is the reason why the superior intellect is seldom beloved, though it may be regarded with feelings of admiration and esteem, while the whole heart goes out to the inferior understanding, especially if the possessor of it is of a happy accommodating disposition, and contributes to your amusement without getting into your way. I am fully of Br'er Turtle's opinion; I don't regard the lack of brains as an altogether deplorable deficiency; and I speak with authority, and as one well qualified to know; for I am perfectly content with my lot; I possess plenty of friends, and, so far as I know, no enemies; and this happy state of affairs I attribute, under Providence, to the fact of which I have been so repeatedly assured, both privately by my intimates, and publicly by gentlemen of the press, that I am a person of weak intellect ; and, indeed, some people are so kind as to pronounce me an " unmitigated idiot."

But lest this should fall under the eyes of some boy or girl, as from the tendency of modern youth to devour all sorts of literary trash it is not unlikely to do, and he or she should jump at the conclusion that the bigger fool a man is, the greater prospects of success in life he has, let me hasten to guard my position with a qualification. The old term for an idiot was "a natural," and to prevent any misconception on the subject the adjective "born" was added to it ; "a born natural," and these were held to be the especial care of Providence. An artificial idiot, that is to say, one who does not use and cultivate to the best of his ability whatever intelligence he possesses, is not supposed to be the subject of any special interposition in his behalf; he is not a fool, but simply " stupid ; " in a state of intellectual coma ; whereas the fool, as everybody can testify, is wide awake, and very much alive. Now a man or woman who passes through life in a comatose state, can never make it a success ; by which I mean, cannot pass through it at peace with himself and his neighbours, content to enjoy the moderate blessings which may come to his lot, without too eager grasping after more, and envy of those who are in a better pecuniary condition than himself. The stupid man will spend the whole of his life in the blind pursuit of riches or station ; and will be torn by envy and jealousy ; the fool will not. He does not run after things to which he cannot attain, or for the attainment of which he must sacrifice all his natural innocent enjoyments to find that he gains his end too late ; but that does not prevent him from exerting his intellectual faculties, such as they are, to the utmost. Br'er Turtle, when he has a brain, uses it ; when scientific gentlemen deprive him of it, he makes the best of things as they are, and he is wise in doing so.

Br'er Turtle, as is evident, has a singular power of adapting himself to circumstances, wherein is the secret of life. Had you or I been unfortunate enough to have our brain removed, we

should probably have made a fuss about it, and declined to continue
to exist under such altered conditions. Br'er Turtle does no such
silly thing; he just waddles off, and if it is about his dinner time,
sets to work on the first article of food that comes in his way.
He altogether declines to acknowledge that he has no brains: the
fact is not altered thereby, it is true; but that makes no difference
to him. "No brains? Well! I'll get along without them as long
as I can. I'm not going to break my heart about it." When
Master Turtle was transferred to Charlie's vest pocket, with a hole
bored in his lower shell, and a chain fastened to it, he did not kick
and fume about it; he tucked himself comfortably in and appeared
to go to sleep. He was biding his time, knowing that "all things
come to the turtle who waits," and when his time came he acted
with decision. Until then he adapted himself to the circumstances
as well as he could.

Snakes.

ARRIVING one day a little later than usual at my accustomed stump, I found the ground preempted, and a little snake about eighteen inches long lying stretched out and basking in the sun between a couple of the roots that buttressed him on either side. Whether he was bona fide asleep, or was merely in a philosophic and meditative mood, I cannot pretend to say : which-ever it was, I got quite near him before he was aware of my presence, and then, presto, he coiled himself up, with the slender head and neck elevated, the bright eyes glancing, and the delicate tongue rapidly vibrating, and in this attitude he followed every change of base on my part. It was a very pretty, and very audacious attempt at bluff, for, on advancing the point of my stick a little nearer to him, down went the little head, out flew the coils, and the rogue had disappeared before I had breath enough to make use of Nathan's favorite ejaculation of surprise, " Gosh ! " As the illustrious poet remarks, " He was off before you could say, ' Jack Robinson'."

I have no doubt that all the time my little friend was putting on his brave show of resistance he was in a dreadful fright : I dare swear that his heart was beating three or four times faster than it usually does ; and not without reason. If it had been Nathan instead of myself, the little lithe body would have been lying maimed and writhing in the death agony before it had time to make good its escape : if it had been Bloomah, the poor reptile would have been saluted by a volley of screams " fit to deave the dead," and driven into a state of temporary idiotcy, as I once saw a lady do to a rat. She mounted a small table, and keeping her skirts gathered tight about the ankles, screamed at him till he finally lost his senses, and tried to hide under some impossible place, I forget what exactly, but I think it was an old envelope,

and so fell an easy victim to his male pursuer, to wit, myself.
And in this, I consider that the rat was fortunate; had he been
alone with the lady, those terrific and ear-piercing screams must
have continued, penetrating to him in his ill-judged asylum, and
inflicting on him all the tortures of horror and despair. I picture
to myself that rat, after vainly attempting to stop his ears with
the flap of the envelope, emerging in a state of desperation, and,
lying on his back in the middle of the room with his four legs
straight up in the air, exclaiming "Now let me die." To be
brained by a philosopher with a kitchen poker was, in comparison
with such a death, bliss ineffable.

I don't think my little friend would have waited for Bloomah
to reduce him to this state of mental incapacity. He would have
glided away leaving her to scream herself hoarse at her leisure,
which would have been in about ten minutes, unless she had succeeded in attracting a male deliverer before that time. In that
case her inarticulate yells would have given place to a gasp of "Kill
him! kill him!" There is a great deal of unreasoning cruelty in
the feminine heart, but it is the effect of over-mastering fear, and
not of an inherent brutality. It is an instinct very similar to that
which will sometimes lead a dog to snap at a person on being suddenly awakened, and is more frequently the cause of the attacks of
wild beasts that we are generally disposed to believe. If you come
unawares on any animal, lion, or tiger, bird, or reptile, if it
possesses any weapons of offence whatever, it will attack you in
ninety-nine cases out of a hundred; not because it really wishes
you any harm, but because it is afraid you may not be equally
well-disposed towards itself. If you give it time to consider, it
will get out of your way. More than that; even if it has good
grounds for irritation, should it by any means come to the conclusion that you yourself have nothing to do with the matter, and
ought not to be held responsible, it will not attack you. I have
repeatedly, when a boy, aided in destroying wasps and bumble-
bees' nests with impunity by acting on this principle and standing
quiet in the swarm of enraged insects that rushed out to repel our
attacks, while my companions who ran away and endeavoured to

beat them off with branches, or pocket handkerchiefs, or anything that came handy, invariably got stung. It is true that the rule failed to work once or twice, but that I attribute to some wasp being more angry than the rest, and so incapacitated from using his judgment clearly, or one who was not so angry as the others, and so was enabled to judge only too clearly. The general rule, I think, is that no animal will attack a man, unless it believes that it will be attacked by him. Or, unless it is hungry; for the stomach overrules other considerations, and is like the lady of the poet :

"And when a stomach's in the case,
All other things, you know, give place."

However, this is only a theory of mine, and, while I hold to it myself, I do not insist on other people adopting it. "What is sauce for the goose," meaning myself, is not " sauce for the gander," meaning everybody else, and a theory which works well enough for one man may have very disastrous effects when acted on by another. It is a weapon, the value of which depends greatly on the skill and judgment of him who wields it. You recollect that tale told by " Sam Slick," of the man who had adopted the theory that the most savage animal could be cowed if you would turn your back to it, put your head between your legs, and bellow at it ; how he proceeded to give the assembled company an illustration of the modus operandi, and how, in so doing, he startled a bull-dog that had been quietly dozing under the table, and that flew out and pinned him by the nose. I dare say the theory was all right enough; it was the practice that was wrong. To " cow " a savage animal in this way, it is necessary that it should be to a certain extent prepared for what is coming : if it expects you to " do something," and that something turns out to be what it had never calculated on, the chances are that it will run away : but if you come on it suddenly, before it has time to reason that you are probably a harmless lunatic, the chances are that it won't retreat. A lady, it is said, once saved herself from a tiger about to spring on her by

opening her umbrella in his face : if she had gone up to that tiger
when he was asleep, and done the same thing, I would not have
given much for the umbrella, or her either. "Circumstances alter
cases," as politicians in power say when they are reminded of the
promises they made out of it.

To return to my Bloomahs : the desire for the slaughter of
perfectly innocuous creatures which they evince, arises from an
unreasoning fear of being in some mysterious manner, hurt by
them. It would puzzle them to tell you what mortal injury a
mouse, or a spider, or a harmless little grass snake could possibly
inflict; they only know that they are frightened, and will never
feel safe so long as the small monster is alive. You may call it a
natural repugnance if you like, but it is really fear : mere repugnance does not extend to the taking away of life. In man, the
case is different : he kills from a brutal desire of killing; brutal,
in fact, is not the word for it, for it is rare that a brute kills
aimlessly, and without reason. But man slays deliberately for
the slaughter's sake, and calls it "sport." I know that he endeavours
to conceal this, and alleges as the principal inducements the
healthy exercise, the excitement of pursuit, the attainment of skill
in the use of weapons, and other excuses of a similar nature, but
ask the hunter returning from a run with hounds that have failed
to kill, or the sportsman or angler coming home with empty game-
bag, or creel, what sport he has had, and he will tell you "none."
There is no sport without there is at least one death in it. I am
no sentimental humanitarian decrying these things as cruel and
senseless ; I am a philosopher, recognizing in this lust for blood
which has been implanted in the breast of man something which,
if it be not carried to excess, is wise, and necessary for the good
government of the world : and I am merely pointing out as a fact
that this thirst for slaughter is in itself a savage and barbarous
thing, and peculiar to man, as distinguished from woman.

And I point this out because in the younger members it
degenerates, or is very apt to degenerate, into the wanton killing
and maining of any thing that is weak and helpless. When this

is allowed to go on unchecked, the consequences are far more serious, and widely extended than we are apt to imagine. The boy that has no tenderness for the domestic animals, no pity for the wild ones, that does not recognize that the claim that every weaker thing than himself has on his consideration is a paramount one, grows up to be a man without chivalry, and without generosity; a man that knows no law but his own pleasure and interest, no restraint beyond the limitation of his power. He has no respect for the honor of women, or the peace of families; he will take to the last ounce the pound of flesh allotted him by law, and a slice over if he thinks he can do it with impunity. He is not generally a coward, but when he is, he is the meanest and most despicable of all cowards, a bully. It is this savage instinct in man that produces murder, adultery, fraud, and that is brought out in its fullest and most hideous form when the fumes of alcohol drive away the restraining power of reason. One of the most important first principles to be instilled into the young is the abstention of any form of abuse or illtreatment of the lower animals.

Now, as to my little friend, the snake, who is probably fast asleep by this time in the sun where he fancies I can't find him, let me say that he is a perfectly innocent and harmless reptile so far as you and I are concerned. What the field mice, and frogs, and ground birds think of him is an entirely different matter, with which we have nothing to do. For all his brave and threatening demonstrations when he was coiled up, he could not have done the least harm, however much he might have been willing. A bee is a far more serious antagonist, and a black hornet is a terror compared with him. Even a mosquito could hurt more, and he is really very pretty with those beautiful eyes of his, if you come to look at him, and very graceful in the undulations of his movements, and very swift in them when he is in a hurry. Does it not seem rather absurd that he should be viewed with such dread and abhorrence, and clubbed and pelted wherever he is caught? Surely God does not give life, and the enjoyment of life to a creature, even the meanest, that man should take them away without any reason.

Yes! I know that there are snakes, and snakes; that the bite of some is sudden death, and the embrace of others swift destruction; but they don't live here, and we have fortunately nothing to do with them. There may be, though I have not heard of any, a rattle-snake or two about; but a rattle-snake is a gentleman that always gives you fair warning that he is going to bite you if you stay; and if you don't run away after that he is clearly not responsible for the consequences. At any rate we have none of them in the clearing: take us altogether we are a very harmless, peaceable set of people—that is when the mosquitoes and sand flies are not round.

As We See "Ithers."

" Oh, wad some power the giftie gie us
To see ourselves as others see us,"

SANG Burns, and I dare say you have seen the lines quoted as conveying a deep moral truth. I am not quite sure that the aspiration is at all necessary, or even desirable to be granted. It is not the latter, because it would take a philosopher to bear the burden with equanimity, and philosophers are scarce outside of the clearing: inside we have plenty of them. It is not at all probable that the knowledge of the estimation in which we are each held by the general public would, if it were actively obtruded on our attention, conduce to that love for our neighbour which is the second great item of the moral law ; and it certainly would not render any of us a bit more comfortable. It is popularly believed that such an intimate acquaintance with other people's opinions of us would take down our self-conceit, remove all propensity to " blow," and render us meek and humble, but I very much doubt it. A man's conceit of himself is part and parcel of his very exist-ence which nothing that anybody else can say is able to abate one iota ; what they may do is a different matter which does not require the intervention of a " deus ex machina," to enable us to thoroughly understand and appreciate. Nor is a man's favorable self-estimate a thing that is a bad and injurious one in itself; it is one of his vital forces, and gives him the courage and energy to fight the battle of life, which would be wholly destroyed if he knew exactly in what light his powers and capacities were viewed by his neigh-bors and dearest friends. Take myself, for instance, (for there is nothing like giving a practical illustration) ; I have been, in the course of my life, singularly favoured with the candid expression of public opinion, so candid indeed that at times it has verged on what I may call a brutal frankness; if I was to attach any importance to what I hear, I should believe myself an "idiot," a "fool," and "escaped lunatic, a "dreary twaddler," an "abominable old fraud," and a great many other things besides, not less unflattering to ones self-love. All very true, no doubt; I am not going to put myself out of the way to contest the point; but if I were to allow myself to be in the slightest influenced by these opinions, generously and liberally furnished me free, gratis, and for nothing, I should be more dejected and spiritless that the most miserable tinker's donkey that picks up a scanty living from the thistles by the road side. As it is, I am perfectly serene and contented, because I know, philosophically speaking, that it is not what other people think of a man that is most important, but what he thinks of himself. "Be sure you are right, and then go ahead," is a very good maxim, but how are you to be sure you are right if you listen to people telling you every moment that you are wrong? That's what the farmer did who was taking his ass to market to sell, and the consequence was that the two asses, the biped and the quadruped, tumbled over the bridge into the river, and got a sound ducking for their pains. No! I don't believe that the private opinions of my neighbours and friends are of any more use to me when they happen to be publicly expressed; and I don't want any Power to give me more of them than I get now. I might be tempted to commit murder; in any case I could never drop in of an evening to tea, and eat doughnuts and pies until I am on the verge of dyspepsia.

Moreover, if a man cares to be honest and just with himself, it is not necessary for any special Providential dispensation to enable him to have a pretty accurate conception of the light in which he is regarded by others, and, what is more to the purpose, of the light in which he ought to be regarded. The motions of action are so complicated, and the circumstances giving rise to and directing it are so numerous, and frequently so obscure, that the judgment of outsiders is more likely to be an erroneous one than

that of the man himself, if he will only deal fairly.   I shall probably
be told that that "if" begs the whole question, but it does not, for
it exists equally on both sides of the equation, and may therefore be
eliminated.   There is just as much reason for supposing that his
neighbours will deal unfairly with a man as there is that he will
do so with himself.   What is that you say ?   The voice of the
majority ?   The voice of the majority is about as unreliable a thing
as you can find anywhere, and it is generally wrong, until it
becomes converted to the voice of the minority.   We have to
submit to it, it is true ; and we get in time to consider that it is
all right; but, nevertheless, all the persecutions and wars and
oppressions have come from the voice of the majority, and there
never yet has been a step taken in advance, or a beneficial reform
inaugurated, that the voice of the majority has not opposed.   And
necessarily so ; for it is the voice of the unthinking and ignorant.
You never catch a martyr in the ranks of the majority ; if you
want one, you have to hunt him up elsewhere.

But how we see ithers is a very different thing, and full of
useful, as well as of interesting speculation.   Useful in that the
enquiry is really a matter of self-research, and teaches us to be
cautious in the judgments that we form of others.   There is that
dirty, leather-cased, brown grasshopper, for instance, that dumped
himself down with a clatter of wing case and a whirr right in front
of me over ten minutes ago, and has been solemnly contemplating
me ever since, under the pretence that it is a very sunny spot, and
he must really rest and get back his breath before he goes any
further, whereas I am convinced that he is actually endeavoring to
make out what sort of a creature has got on that stump.   He does
not give me the impression that he is a particularly handsome
animal : he is what I should be inclined at first sight to call particularly ugly ; nothing like that little green beetle that is running
about just behind him, all aglow with fiery metallic lustre ; yet, if
he would let me catch him and put him under the microscope for
a tiny little moment, I should discover that his plain smooth wing-
cases were beautifully bossed and studded, and his dingy appearance would disappear, and make way for a lustre more subdued

and toned, but equally lovely with that of the beetle. His legs that I should have said were decidedly of the spindle variety, and ridiculously long, taper delicately, and have well-developed thighs, and even calves, through which you can see the blood coursing in the slender veins and arteries, and in which you can mark the graceful and delicate swell of the tiny muscles. His eyes are large and brilliant, though they looked dull and horny ; and altogether he is a fairly good-looking grasshopper. Or, he would be, if I took the trouble to examine him closely : as I don't, I take the liberty of saying that he is an ugly beast. In seeing ithers, we generally stick to first impressions ; and these, in nine cases out of ten, subordinate the good qualities to what appear to be the bad ones.

Now, there's that fly, that has been persistently trying to convert my nose into a promenade ground whilst I have been reflecting on the grasshopper, and which I have only just succeeded in finally persuading that it would be better for his health if he would take what exercise he requires some where else. I wonder, what, if I were that fly, would be my opinion of myself. How did he see me ? I don't know how many facets there may be in the eye of a fly ; there are 12,000 in that of a dragon fly, but then he is bigger ; and the peculiarity of these is that if an image be placed between a luminant body, and one of these sets of lenses, that image will be represented entirely in each individual facet. To make this clearer, I may mention a microscopic photograph which appeared in the September, 1896, number of the *Strand*, an English magazine, which showed a portrait in every facet of a portion of a beetle's eye, 198 in number. " The eye was first of all dissected and placed on the stage of the instrument. The portrait,—on glass, and, of course, exceedingly small—was then interposed, and the photograph taken through the microscope." The illustration gives, as I have said, 198 clear and distinct photographs of a man. Now, assuming a moderate estimate of only 6,000 facets in the eye of my pertinacious friend, he must have seen, and fancied that he was walking over, six thousand noses of six thousand philosophers at one and the same time !

What a stupendous notion of his own importance and agility such
a vision must have given that fly! Is it any wonder that he
laughed to scorn all my efforts to banish him, and was not a bit
frightened at seeing six thousand philosophic hands making a
united dash at his devoted head? You will observe from this
that an exaggerated estimate of the value of other people, does not
always tend to give us a lower opinion of ourselves, but just the
contrary. And the other people, after all, may not be quite so
important as we imagine them to be. It was only one philosopher
that the fly had to elude and evade, whereas he must have fancied
that he was sporting with six thousand; and if I had hit him, as
he richly deserved to have been hit, he would have said, "ah!
well! it's no great thing to kill a poor little fly, when the odds are
six thousand to one against him," and so would have died happy
and contented.

A great deal depends on the temper we happen to be in at the
time when looking at ithers, and this has to be taken into consideration in forming our judgment of them. What would pass as a
joke one day, may form a very serious insult the next; the stupid
conversation at one time, may, on subsequent recalling to mind,
appear a lively and interesting one; our dearest friend of a week
ago, a heartless and unfeeling monster seven days after. The
things themselves have not changed; only the manner in which
we see them. And in this sense the philosophy of William of
Ockham, which taught that the material world had no actual
existence further than as it is produced by the mental operations,
or in other words that all things are but thought, since without
thought they have no being so far at any rate as the individual is
concerned, has a very true meaning. "Ithers" are to us, not
necessarily what they really are, but what we conceive them to be;
just as the trainoil which takes the place of champagne to the
Laplander is a beverage which we certainly should not dream of
getting intoxicated on, or the curry of the Hindoo is an abomination
to the Indians of the far North-West. It would save us a great
deal of unnecessary heat in argument, and consequent heart
burnings, if we would remember this, and reflect that a man is not

necessarily either a fool or a knave if he disagrees with us; nay, more; that he may be perfectly right from his point of view, as we are from ours. Truth is many sided, and a great deal depends on how we take it in.

I do not pretend to treat of things in more than a desultory and rambling fashion, but I think I have said sufficient to suggest to my readers, who are more sober and sensible than myself, that a careful examination of how we see ithers may be more important and useful both to ourselves and them than too close an enquiry into how ithers see us. It is only a suggestion, but I think it is worth sleeping upon.

9

Christmas in the Clearing.

CHRISTMAS Day has been the subject of many writers, and viewed from many standpoints—Christmas in African wilds; in Australia; in the bush; in a lighthouse; in the mines; in prison; even in a balloon, though of this last I am not quite sure; but I don't think anybody yet has looked at Christmas Day in a clearing. At the very best of times, few go to the clearing unless they have business there; Bloomah and Nathan after the cows, or the children to pick berries; but in winter it is deserted. Even its usual residents shun it; the frogs are deep in the mud; the chipmunks are snugly ensconced under some tree root; the ants, and bees, and black wasps are either asleep or dead; and where the ground-birds have gone to, unless they have turned into chickadees and migrated to the woods, is a mystery only known to themselves. In winter time the whole interest of life appears to centre in the homestead in country parts, whether it be the home of man, of beast, or bird; there is very little travelling about, a sleigh or two on the roads; a rabbit, or a partridge track in the fields; now and then a hurried little delicate trail in the snow where Mrs. Field Mouse, or Mr. Chipmunk has braved the cold for a friendly call and a little gossip; and great wreaths of smoke rising from the farm house chimneys to tell of the warmth and energy within; these are the only signs of activity in the country. In the towns, it is different. There the full tide of life ebbs and flows through the noisy streets, noisier even than in summer by reason of the wrangle of the multitudinous sleigh bells; the snow has scarcely ceased falling, before on roadway and sidewalk it is trampled down into a hard dirty mass that might be some novel kind of patent pavement, only it is a deal too slippery; but in the country there is not enough life stirring out of doors to do this; and the whole landscape is covered with a glaring white sheet which obliterates all peculiarities, and removes all landmarks, so that the most practised agricultural lecturer could not distinguish between a stubble and a meadow, or tell which had been a patch of "garden sass," and which a potato field. Yet, the clearing still preserves its marked individuality, though its population has deserted it, and is reposing in its several beds, either temporary, or eternal, and its grasses and wild flowers have all withered away. It is still as aggressively assertive of its rank and position in rural society as are the middle classes amongst men. The fire-blackened, lichen-covered stumps rise defiantly out of the snow that threatens to cover them, but never fulfils its threat, for the wind takes care of that, and whirls it away in eddies from the stump roots. "There's the bush," it says; "I suppose you can see that: and there's the cultivated land: you can see that too. No! you can't either; for anything you know, it may be a lake, or a swamp, instead of meadow and ploughed fields. But at any rate, you can see me; for I come of a high lineage, and am descended from the great pines, and maples, and hemlocks, whose degenerate descendants form the bush behind me. Look at my stumps." There is a sturdy self-consciousness, and self-assertiveness about a clearing, as if it knew exactly what it was, and was not going to make any pretence about it, but was rather proud of it, that makes it not unworthy of a visit on a Christmas Day, especially if the sky be blue, and the sun bright, and the wind has gone off about his business elsewhere.

Such, however, is not the case to-day. The sky is a uniform grey; and the big snow flakes are falling fast, and softly. There is no wind at present, but he is not far off; for I hear him breathing among the bare tops of the deciduous trees in the bush, and whispering in the branches of the spruce and hemlock. Bye and bye he will wake up, and then if the big pines, on one of whose stumps I am sitting and meditating, had been still in existence, should have heard a roar that is like nothing so much as the beating of the ocean waves on the coast; but now all is quiet; so quiet that you might fancy you heard a silvery tinkle as each snow-crystal touches its sisters that have already fallen to the ground. It is very peaceful; and perhaps such a day as this is more fitting for that on which we commemorate the birthday of the Prince of Peace, than the glare on the cloudless sky of the winter sun, and the responsive glare of the snow fields lying below, and the keen nipping frost that is never still in the air.

Peace! That is what we all sigh for, (when we give ourselves time to think about it), and more frequently than not, we all fail to get. There is very little peace to be had for you, or for me, or for any animate thing in this world, for perfect peace here means stagnation, and stagnation is death. Transient glimpses of it we may have, rifts in the whirling storm-clouds of life, but long and continuous peace is not for us; we soon pass from under the eye of the cyclone, into the struggle of the tempest again. I speak of peace in what I believe to be the popular acceptation of the word, as signifying a state of complete rest and repose; what I conceive to be meant by the term is something very different, as I may show later on, but at present I am considering peace as meaning quiescence and rest. That is not attainable for any length of time by any animate being; it is only that which is dead that has it; dead temporarily, as are the trees in the bush with their pulses stilled in the winter cold; as are the dormice, and other hybernating animals, wrapt in their winter sleep; or dead actually, as is this stump on which I sit, or the bodies that are slowly mouldering into dust in their graves. But apart from this, there is no cessation of activity for any prolonged period: even the popular idea of the Heavenly rest pictures the blessed ones standing and continually singing hymns of praise, an idea which I do not hold to, any more than I hold to the conception of a life hereafter which is devoid of action, and the interest which attends upon action. And I think that He who was born as on this day meant to teach this among other things when He said "I came not to send peace upon earth, but a sword." Doubtless in these words He foretold the troubles and persecutions that should follow the acceptance of Him and His teaching, but I think that He also signified that He came not to bring rest and inactivity, but a very active and persistent strife during the earthly life, continuous with the evil that is in the world, and in ourselves.

Yet he is the Prince of peace, and His coming to men was heralded by the express declaration "Peace upon Earth." There was, then, a peace that He did bring, and that His Apostles prayed "might keep the hearts" of those who believe in him; not at intervals more or less prolonged, but continually. Strange paradox this, that peace should be coexistent with strife, or, if I may venture to use the term, co-equal to it. It seems to me that the paradox vanishes if we substitute another word for Peace and call it Love, without which it can have no existence. The heart that is filled with the love of its God can never be disturbed by pain, or sorrow, or care; the heart that is filled with the love of its neighbour, cannot be torn by envy, jealousy, or contention; and the heart that goes out to all creation, to the dumb animals, and to Nature in all her varied moods, has an exquisite sense of rest and enjoyment in them, which other hearts cannot attain to. "Peace, and good-will." And this is what I hold to be the peace of Heaven, which must be begun on earth—love to every created thing, and love to its Creator. I do not hold the future life to be one that is spent continually in praise, further than as all thankful and innocent enjoyment of God's gifts is praise, nor do I hold it to be one in which there is nothing to be done, and nothing to be learned, as I believe that He who is incomprehensible can be comprehended in no less a period than eternity; but I take it that the future life will be an active life of that love which He came to announce from the Father, to exemplify in Himself, and to enjoin on all His disciples—and such a life is peace.

"All this has been said before, and better." I know it; but the thrust of a raw hand may sometimes prove more efficacious than the efforts of a skilful master of fence, and an oft-told tale may recover the interest it has lost by being dressed in new phraseology, even though it be less refined, as the belle of some half-dozen seasons of futile dressing sometimes proves irresistible in the more homely garb of the country house; and this "oft-told tale" has been so spun out and travestied, that men are beginning to detect a false ring in it, and to mock at it. Amongst the Christmas cards this year and last I have noticed one as follows :—

WISHING YOU THE SAME OLD

MERRY CHRISTMAS.

Between the two lines was the representation of a chestnut, so that the card read, " wishing you the same old chestnut—Merry Christmas." A joke, indeed, and manufactured to create a smile ; but I am philosopher enough to know that there are things of deadly earnest that can only be safely mentioned under cover of a joke. The Christmas spirit has been lost sight of ; smothered under the weight of Christmas gifts, which so long as they were made to the poor and needy, to the children from the parents, and to the parents from the children, were good and healthful. In these days, instead of fostering the spirit of love, they foster greed, rivalry, discontent, and extravagance. People give now, not because it is their desire, but because it is expected from them ; and their gifts are accompanied with an anxious fear lest they should be thought too mean, or be less valuable than those sent by others. Year by year, Christmas presents are becoming more extended and more expensive ; more regarded for their value in dollars and cents than in the good will of the giver. Custom, or rather fashion, takes us by the throat, and calls on us to "stand and deliver" our money, or our time. No one dares express the feeling, unless it be such a one as I ; and then he must be out in the clearing and alone if he would do it ; but it is felt all the same, and finds vent in the bitter joke that calls the Christmas good wishes an old chestnut. As no doubt in too many instances it is

To be rid of this, it is necessary that we should get back to the old conception of " Peace upon earth ; good will toward men," or as it is more significantly translated, "Peace upon earth to men of good will," and understand that the celebration of the day is really a sacrament, whose outward and visible signs of gifts and the expression of good wishes, are valueless without the inward and spiritual grace of love ; nay! worse than valueless, for they are a desecration of it ; remembering, further, that when the pomp and vanity of the world enter in at the door, Charity flies out at the window.

How softly the snow is falling, and how gently the wind is stirring the little branchlets of the trees ! They are no great things, a small snow flake and a breath of wind. Yet the one keeps warm the tender rootlets of the grasses and wild flowers, as the other wards off the too deadly attacks of the frost from the otherwise motionless wood : and the quiet beauty of the one, and the gentle melody of the other, have spoken to the heart of the old man sitting on the stump, and made him forget that there is such a thing as cold, or that Polly and Bloomah are beginning to get fidgetty because he does not come in to supper.

A Christmas Carol.

I

Peace in the dreaming sky :
   Peace on the starry thrones
That are girt about with the melody
   Of the seraphs' joyous tones.
Peace, deep peace, in the Heavens above,
Where sits enthroned the Eternal Love ;
But the earth sent upward a bitter cry,
   The deadened inarticulate moans
Of those that are dazed with their agony,
And the sharp-rent sufferer's heavy groans ;
For violence covered her as a flood,
And the thick air reeked with the steam of blood.

II

Everywhere, sight and sounds of fear ;
Death lurked hid in each country glen,
And murder stalked through the cities of men ;
Clash of armour, and glint of spear,
Gleaming of sword, and catapult's rattle,
And the war horse neighing to snuff the battle —
   Woe to the widows and orphans then—
Fraud and deceit in the wares at the mart,
   Cruelty rampant where men were sold ;
While the princes and judges sat apart,
Or traded the innocent lives for gold.
The Halls of Justice were foul to the eaves ;
And the Holy place was a den of thieves.

III

Blood-red the sun rose up in the morn ;
   Blood-red he sank to his rest at night :
As was the promise of early dawn,
   So its fulfilment through the light ;
As was the threat of the Western wave,
So did night bring with her Death, and the Grave.

IV

" Lift up your heads, Everlasting gates,
And be thou lift up, Eternal door,
For the time hath come that the earth awaits,
And the Lord of Hosts is going to war.
    For the comfortless needy's sighing,
    For the widow and orphans' crying,
The Lord hath buckled His armour on ;
Lift up your heads, that He may be gone. "

V

    No trumpet's martial sound
    Echoed the skies around,
No angel cohorts mustered for the strife ;
    No glint of sword and spear,
    No hedge of arms drew near.
To compass, as He went, the Lord of life ;
    The everlasting portals
    Where dwell the blest immortals
Stood open that an army might march on,
    And lo ! a little sigh,
    Faint as an infant's cry,
Passed through them for an instant, and was gone.

VI

    A dreamy stillness reigns
    Upon the grassy plains
O'er which the crags of Bethlehem hold guard,
    And peaceful slumbers keep
    The lambs and mother sheep,
The while the simple shepherds keep true ward.
    The little laughing rills
    That babble down the hills
Grow silent, as they steal among the flowers ;
    The breeze, that all day long
    Swept by with murmured song,
Lies netted in vine-tendrils in the bowers.

VII

The song-birds dream 'mid leaves ;
The sparrow in the eaves
Chirps soft good night above the stable door ;
The full-fed kine within
Lie down before the bin,
Chewing the lazy cud upon the floor ;
And by the manger stands,
A mother with clasped hands,
And eyes all moist with happy dews and mild,
Watching his calm repose
Where, wrapt in swaddling clothes,
Lies the Desire of earth, the promised Child.

VIII

And overhead, the star,
Clear-shining from afar,
Summons the Eastern kings from distant coasts
To lay before his feet
The monarch's tribute, meet
For Him who goes to war, the Lord of Hosts ;
And lo ! the battle cry
Resounding through the sky ;
Startles the shepherds watching on the plain,
The shout of myriad voices,
As when a world rejoices,
Sending from Heaven to Earth the glad refrain.

IX

And this the song they sang
The while the welkin rang,
And the stars trembled in the blue profound ;
" To you this happy morn
The promised child is born
And in the stable manger may be found ;
Peace upon earth, goodwill ;
Peace upon earth : " and still
"Peace and goodwill with this, the Saviour's birth."
Nor changed the angelic lay,
As faint it died away,
" Hosannah in the highest : peace on earth ! "

X

Is there a lesson in this ; a lesson yet to be taught
Though the years have come and gone by centuries since that day ;
A lesson easy to learn, and not far off to be sought,
Though we shut our hearts to its teaching, and pass unheeding away ?

We set up race against race, and we set up creed against creed ;
Man arms himself against man, and friend against bosom friend ;
We listen to naught but our lusts, and the promptings of malice and greed,
And we struggle, and fight, and rend, from the cradle unto the end.

And the trader cheats in his wares, and justice is bought and sold,
And the cry of famine goes up from the helpless, and poor, and oppressed.
What matters ! We must have lands, and we must have houses and gold ;
Let each one fight for himself, and leave Heaven to care for the rest.

Lo ! Peace is a fair-seeming fraud, deep-set in the midst of alarms ;
Wars, and rumors of wars, from east and west, south and north ;
And the nations are hostile camps, bristling with horrible arms,
And ready to fly at each other's throats when the word has gone forth.

Not so does the Lord go to battle : He takes not the sword and spear,
When He comes forth to right the oppressed from the throne of glory above ;
Not His the shout of the warrior that strikes on the foeman's ear,
But peace, and the word of forgiveness, and proffer of infinite love.

*
* *

And these are His battle cries yet, till the whole wide world shall bow down,
Conquered and won at the last, by the tender touch of His hand ;
And so when that day shall come, it is love that shall wear the crown,
No longer a crown of thorns, in the midst of the ransomed band.

*
* *

Can we not learn the lesson, this Christmas time of the year,
And walk in the path it points out during all the days that we live,
That perfect love casteth out distrust, and malice, and fear,
And he has conquered his foe who has learned to say, "I forgive ? "

Felis Catus. The Cat.

FELIS Catus ; you may add, if you like, the specific " domesticus," to distinguish him from his cousin, who passes the whole of his life in the woods, and also to mark the general appreciation of his character conveyed in the final syllable, but felis catus, at any rate, is his proper designation when he makes his appearance in the clearing; for though we are not much to look at here, we know better than to treat visitors with undue familiarity by withholding from them their social titles, and felis catus does not often favour us with a visit; neither are we, that is the ground birds, field mice, and chipmunks, who form the upper crust of clearing society, at all anxious for him to give us a call. When f. c. is at home, he is a she, and is known by various names; " pussy," " kitty " when basking by the stove or in the sunshine, and under the ægis of feminine favour ; " the cat," whenever there is any breakage to be accounted for, or pie, or cream mysteriously disappears from the dairy.

There is another thing noticeable, too, in the subject of these remarks, who just at this moment is under the impression that the squirrel using the most offensive language to me from the next stump but three, and sitting with his back turned to him, hasn't seen him come into the clearing, and is not perfectly well aware that he is looking for a meal. He not only changes sex and name when he goes " foreign countries for to see," like a four footed Lord Lovell, but he changes character too. By the fireside, Pussy, the cat, is sweetness and light, dear to the women and the children, and purring all the time unless you accidentally tread on her tail, or a strange dog comes in; but directly she leaves the domestic precincts, he becomes quarrelsome and noisy, a rowdy, a thief and an assassin, with all the masculine vices, and with none of the feminine virtues except artfulness. The sudden change in the Jack Daw of Rheims after the Cardinal's curse was removed was not more complete and astounding than is that in the cat when he goes abroad. During the fall, winter, and spring, the theatrical and operatic season in fact, he generally chooses night for his per-ambulations, and from the company he then keeps, and the observations I have occasionally heard him make, I should, if I were a believer in the doctrine of metempsychosis, imagine that he was a former frequenter of the London music halls, and Bowery saloons, undergoing a purgation of his musical tastes. But in the summer time he chiefly affects the day for his peregrinations, and after repeated castigation coupled with threats of total extinction has convinced him that it is not lawful, (or rather, that it is not profitable) for him to take tithes of spring chickens and ducklings, he may be seen, as he is now, roving into the clearing in search of an unwary ground bird, or chipmunk, or even, if these are scarce, a meditative toad, or a philosophizing frog. He has no objection to a squirrel either, and will stalk him also if occasion serve, but you can gather from his looks that he has a very poor opinion of his chances of success; as, in truth, he may well have, for the bushy-tailed little fellow keeps a pretty sharp look out, and unless he is very indignant indeed about something or other, he is more than a match for F. C. Besides, he very seldom comes inside the clearing proper, and only haunts its fences as a rule.

At home, Thomas Cat, Esquire, dons petticoats, figuratively speaking, assumes the baptismal name of Tabitha, and the surname of Puss; Pusheen cat, as pretty little Norah O'Connor calls him. The word is, I am informed, derived from the Persians, and this again from the Egyptians, who deified Thomas; on what principle I cannot make out, unless as a deprecation of his powers of evil in the musical line; and called him Pasht. The Romans very probably had this name in mind, when they designated any wide-spread and terrible disease "pestis," for undoubtedly Pasht when he lifts up his voice in the yards, and on the house tops, is a most unmitigated pest, and I should not be at all surprised to learn that the Egyptians themselves had much the same opinion of him, for they not only deified him under the above name, but they mummified him also, thus evincing their stern determination that he should "dry up" some time or other, if it took a couple of thousand years, or more, to effect their purpose. And, if I am rightly informed, they took the precaution to store the mummified cats away in company with crocodiles, also mummified, so as to have the saurian handy in case the feline should wake up and begin to sing. We haven't got any crocodiles in Canada, and perhaps that is the reason why we don't go into the preserved cat business in the shape of mummies, but I am credibly informed that we do the next best thing, and when a cat, by some lucky chance, happens to die, he is immediately converted into sausages in the country, and mutton pies in the towns in summer, and into rabbits in winter. If this be a fact, it is one that is highly creditable to Thomas, as showing that he possesses what might be called a cosmopolitan flavour, ranging from the strong taste of pork, and the gamy soupcon of hare, to the delicate innocence of Mary's little lamb. I hope that it is true, for it is about the only thing I have ever heard of to his credit.

Of course, it may be urged that he has musical tastes, and possesses a voice unequalled in volume and compass by the best prima donna that ever appeared on the stage. Far be it from me to dispute this; but I may venture to observe that it is not a cultivated one. He does his best to cultivate it, and with such vigor that his hair, as well as that of his audience, stands upon end, and his tail swells to four times its ordinary size, which must be very uncomfortable for him. Oh, yes! He is conscientious enough about the matter of practice, I allow; far more conscientious than a great many young ladies when they are running over the scales; but he does not succeed. It is difficult to sing with melody when one's attention is partly diverted to dodging old boots, chunks of wood, spittoons, books, and other hard-hearted missiles, and a

finely sustained high note is apt to be suddenly converted into a
shriek when the performer is hit in the ribs by any one of these ;
but after making every allowance it must be confessed that the
voice of Mr. Cat is not capable of artistic cultivation. I have heard
that such an effort was once made, and that a genius conceived the
idea of a cat-piano.   It was a task requiring some time before it
could be accomplished, for the inventor had to search amongst
innumerable felines to get all the notes, and in the several octaves.
Then the piano had to be built expressly for the purpose, contain-
ing narrow compartments for the different cats, with their heads
turned from the player, and their tails brought up through little
round holes, and attached by pieces of cat-gut to the keys. When
one of these, say C, was struck, the C cat's tail was pulled, and the
required note at once produced. So far, the experiment justified
the expectations of the inventor, but when it came to playing a
piece it was found that the note could not be stopped by simply
removing the finger from the key, but was prolonged indefinitely,
and the patentee sadly turned his attention to pigs.   He might,
with patience, have ultimately succeeded in producing a cat organ,
or harmonium, but both these instruments were undreamed of in
those days, and all attempts at cultivating Thomas' voice were
thenceforward given up.

Yet, we must not be hasty in our judgments ; and an incident
occurred some two or three years ago which tends to show that,
under certain circumstances, Thomas is capable of harmony more
than earthly, and verging on the seraphic.   Of him it may be said
in the words of Moore,

> " The soul of music slumbers in its shell
> Till stirred and wakened by the master's spell ;
> And pious hearts, touch them but rightly, pour
> A thousand melodies unheard before."

For " pious hearts " read " wandering cats," and the lines are applicable to the Thomases whose experiences I am about to relate.

The story, as I read it, ran something in this way. "Once upon a time," namely three years ago, there was a very nice young man who boarded in a house in Montreal, whose yard was the nightly rendezvous for all the cats in the neighbourhood, and the scene of innumerable feline soirees musicales. Every morning the yard was heaped up with boots, slippers, broken bottles and crockery, bootjacks, etc., and once a tasseled nightcap was found amongst the spoils; but these practical tokens of disapprobation had no effect on the performers, and the human audience was driven to the verge of insanity. Now this young man was an ardent lover of canned salmon, and had accumulated a reserve fund of empty cans, which, one dark night, in a moment of peculiar exasperation, he gathered together, and hurled, like a volley of grape-shot, at the enemy. There was a fearful crash, and then a dead silence; so, after listening awhile to see if the defeated forces would return, the nice young man went off triumphantly to bed to dream of the nice young lady on the second flat, for whom he had long sighed in vain. Half an hour later he woke with a start, and sat up in bed, listening. All round him floated notes of exquisite melody; the tender strains of love; the pathetic outpourings of sorrow; the jubilant voice of martial music, with the clash of cymbals; all mixed together in wonderful harmony; rising and falling; from the yard; from the yard-walls; from the house-tops. Up went the windows on all sides, and heads, capped and uncapped, were thrust out drinking in those weird yet seraphic strains. When the sun rose, the maid of all-work rose with him, and went out into the yard, where the mystery was solved, for

" There in the morning cold and grey
Lifeless, yet beautiful, they lay,"

seventeen departed Thomas Cats, each with its head securely

fixed in a salmon-can. Their last song had been like the death song of the swan ;

> " The Tom cat's death hymn took the soul
> Of that waste yard with joy
> Hidden in sorrow ; at first to the ear
> The warble was low and soft and clear ;
> And floating about the under-sky,
> Prevailing in weakness, the coronach stole
> Sometimes afar, and sometimes anear :
> But anon his awful jubilant voice,
> ˙ With a music strange and manifold,
> Flow'd forth in a carol free and bold ;
> As when a mighty people rejoice
> With shawms and with cymbals, and harps of gold. '

And that day the nice young lady, with many blushes, thanked the nice young man for his lovely serenade, and there was a marriage just a month after.

10

Ferns and Fern Seed.

FERNS do not form a markedly prominent part of the clearing
vegetation. They like shade, and, as I had occasion to remark
once before, shade is an almost unattainable blessing here ; they
also, as a rule, like moisture, and the only moisture to be had is
in a little swampy bit near the edge of the bush, and that is too
much of a good thing ; or along the banks of the little stream that,
I was going to say, runs through it, but that would be an extreme
stretch of courtesy during the summer months at any rate, for then
it doesn't run, it only perspires like everything else about except
the grasshoppers. With the exception of the swamp and the
stream, the clearing is as dry in summer as an Arkansas Colonel
in a Prohibition State, than which I know of nothing drier, and it
is obviously no place for the moisture loving ferns. Still, there
are a few straggling clumps by the tree roots, and in the open,
which last are principally the fern known as the brake, or bracken
fern, which is not such a thirsty bit of vegetation as its congeners.
I have never felt quite certain in my own mind concerning the
bracken : I have an uneasy suspicion that he has a double, for I
recollect being told when a boy that if you cut him, not socially,
but literally, and transversely with a knife, you would find a very
good representation of a miniature oak tree inside him. I have
repeatedly tried the experiment, sometimes successfully, and sometimes just the contrary and quite the reverse, from which I am led
to one of two conclusions : either that there are brackens that have
not swallowed small oaks, or that there is another fern closely
resembling them, and not distinguishable from them by careless
and unbotanical eyes. I am rather inclined to the latter opinion

because I know that there is another member of the family, whose
tender shoots in the early spring form a delicious vegetable when
boiled, and another that almost exactly resembles it is a deadly
poison. I used to know how to distinguish them, and would give
the difference here in case any of my readers should be tempted to
make the experiment, but I have forgotten it. At any rate the
matter is of small importance. If this book should lead anyone
into making the trial and a mistake at the same time, the thought
that he has bought and paid for my essays will doubtless prove a
most consoling one, and cause him to bear with equanimity the
cramps in his stomach, and if he has not bought and paid for them,
poisoning is too good for him; which will also be a consoling
reflection for him. Still, I don't want to have the premature death
of a reader, even if he should not be a perfectly legitimate one, on
my conscience, so I will volunteer the advice not to eat of a dish
of ferns till somebody else has previously partaken of them and
shown no symptoms of approaching dissolution. This, I am aware,
is not good Christian doctrine, but it is sound nineteenth century
philosophy, and belongs to that branch of it which is popularly
known as the science of learning to shave on your neighbor's chin;
a science in which the promoters of useless railroads, bridges,
factories, etc., are adepts, as many a municipality knows to
its cost.

There are several species of ferns that are thus duplicated;
one is the pretty maidenhair fern, that is common enough if you
only know where to look for it if it has a black stem, and rare
if it has a green one; and a little mite of a fellow that we used to
call at school the oak fern which has the same peculiarity; the
green-stemmed one, I think, inhabiting only three places in England,
it was said, one of which was a good ten miles walk from our
school, and involved a trudge over heather-clad hills placed as near
to each other as possible, and divided only by brooks running in
slender threads between. They were about as steep as houseroofs,
and a great deal higher, so that when you got to the top of one
after much toil and perspiration, and the disturbance of the grouse

that haunted the heather and gorse, you had immediately to go down again; and as soon as ever you reached the bottom, you had to begin to go up. A twenty-mile walk under a blazing sun, and over ground like this, was no joke, yet the reputation of that horrid little fern induced three boys, myself among the number, to take advantage of a whole holiday given for a cricket match between the School and Lancaster, and to set off in search of it. When we found it, it was about three-quarters of the way up an almost precipitous cascade of over ninety feet, and if we had been anything else but boys, we should have infallibly broken our necks in getting down with our prizes. It is all very well to talk of the facilis descensus averni, but when the avernus in question happens to be the steep sides of a mountain waterfall it is a great deal easier to climb up than to climb down. However, we obtained our ferns; but having to make a forced march in order to be in time to answer our names at evening roll-call, and having rolled down several hills in the marching, the fellow who carried them lost them out of his cap on the way, and, as he was the smallest, received a good thrashing when we ascertained the loss. We were not philosophers in those days, but we were deeply imbued with Christian principles, and we argued that as we ourselves should have deserved a thrashing if we had done such a thing, so it was right that we should do to the third party as we should have been done to. Therefore we combined, and punched his head, and thereby prevented our expedition from being altogether without results; for we got satisfaction, and he got a licking; which was fair all round.

There was scarcely a boy that did not make a collection at our school; most of them, more than one; for the vicinity was rich in birds, plants, insects and fossils, of which latter there was an abundance in the limestone strata that prevailed all around. Some really good collections were made in this way, though I am afraid we did not set about it in the modern scientific spirit, and contented ourselves with the things themselves under their local names, instead of learning their Latin and Greek titles—of Latin and Greek we had enough and to spare indoors. But we knew to an individual how many specimens of egg, or fern, or fossil, or butterfly were attainable, and we also knew exactly where we might expect to lay our hands on any of them. Such knowledge was based on the common experience of the school, for there was no jealous hiding of secrets from each other, unless it might be an occasional nest of the kingfisher, water-ousel, or golden-crested wren, and was obtained by keen observation, patient watching, and many a long walk. But this last was only a part of the day's recreation, and I think there were very few of us that did not put in our six or eight miles in the twenty-four hours, though we worked hard too, going into school at seven in the morning for an hour before breakfast, and finishing nominally at nine in the evening, though the elder boys used to work with surreptitious candles at Greek and Latin prose, or verse, till close on midnight. We found time for fishing also, for the yellow Rother ran within a five minutes' walk of the school, and fell into the silvery Lune about a mile away, while there was a brook at every half-mile or so, and in it plenty of little brook-trout. We prided ourselves on our cricket also, and used to defeat with great rejoicing the old fellows that came up from Cambridge or Oxford, where they had fallen sadly off their play, we thought, in the great annual match. But collecting (with a little poaching now and then thrown in as a pleasurable excitement) was the great motive power that was supreme and above all these other minor employments. Even the Head Master used to collect. He had a great book into which were copied Greek Iambics, Latin Sapphics and Alcaics, Greek and Latin prose on different subjects, and even English, (though that seldom got in) all contributed by scholars, and touched up and corrected under his supervision. And we used to try and humour him in the matter, and feel great delight when any of our original compositions were thought worthy of being "booked." Yes! We worked hard, and we played hard; and I never heard any complaint of either. We asked nobody to "explain things" to us; did not find six hours a day in school, and a couple of hours preparing work in the evening, a very serious strain on our health, and never dreamed of question-

ing the capability or fairness of our masters. We had confidence
in them, and in ourselves. But all that is out of date now, and a
school teacher is just about as badly abused as a politician—the
only difference is that the latter makes his abuse pay, and the
former does not. But here have I been wandering off to the dear
old Yorkshire and Westmoreland hills, and forgetting all about the
ferns in the clearing. I wonder what it was that led to the old-
time fancy that fern seed rendered people invisible. No doubt, if
you eat enough of them, they will render you invisible by putting
you in a snug little coffin hid away underground; but that can
scarcely be what is meant, for it is not a thing that is likely to be
greatly desired by anybody; but apart from this I have discovered
no reason for assigning them this property, though several species
are minute enough to be almost invisible themselves. It is curious
into what vagaries the human imagination is led, and the utterly
unreasonable and preposterous things it will first invent, and then
end by believing in. Take for another instance that gruesome
conception of the Hand of Glory, which was akin to that of the
fern seed, in that though it did not make him that carried it really
invisible, it rendered him practically so by throwing the inhabitants
of the house into which it was carried into a state of catalepsy, thus
enabling its bearer to work his own will untrammelled by their
opposition, and unhindered by the bolts and locks that flew open
at his coming; the hand of a murderer, cut at midnight from the
body as it hung on the gallows, and having its fingers and thumb
tipped with tapers made of a dead man's fat. Compared with such
a horrible conception, the legend of the fern seed is beautiful and
harmless. There are occasions, too, in which the power of rendering oneself temporarily unseen would be very desirable. I
suggested to Bloomah that she and Nathan should try the experiment the next time he wanted to snatch a kiss behind the buttery
door when I was about ; but she scouted the suggestion—said that
he never did it, which I know to be a fib; and hinted her opinion
that I was a scandalous old reprobate for ever dreaming of such a
thing. But of that charge I am totally guiltless. I never dreamed

of Nathan's kissing her, any more than I dreamed of myself doing so. I know it to be a very wide-awake fact—Nathan's kissing, I mean—don't make any mistake here. Anyway, I am not so sure that she did not try the experiment, and find it successful, for I have several times since heard noises in the buttery as if ginger-beer bottles were blowing out their corks, and have never succeeded in accounting for it. I don't keep ginger-beer in the buttery, so it could not be that; and moreover, when I have investigated the place, I have found nobody there but the cat. Nathan says it must have been the cat; but though pussy crackles when stroked the wrong way, she does not make a report like a Martini-Henry—at least I've never heard her do it, and I don't think she is big enough.

To Let. A Stump.

M Y wife has of late evinced a more than usual interest in my state both physical and mental. She overheard Nathan telling Bloomah that "the old man was kinder off his feed," and Bloomah replying that she had noticed I was not so "perky" as usual, so Polly, like the good little soul that she is, has been what she would call "worriting" herself about me, and I have several times of late detected her surreptitiously criticizing my appearance, and endeavoring to ascertain how nearly I was reduced to a skeleton. Finally, the storm burst. "You are not looking at all well," she commenced, one morning at breakfast, "and I'm sure you need rest, and a change of air." "Rest!" I said in some astonishment, "change of air! Why, you yourself have been complaining that I do nothing but go out in the clearing and sit there all day, coming back so sleepy that you can't get a chance to talk to me." "That is just it," she replied. "You go and sit blinking like an owl on that horrid old stump, and think, and think, till you muddle up what little brains you have got, and lose your appetite, and come home all "crocked" with the black from the charred wood, and your hair like a wild man of the woods; while your clothes are getting positively indecent. You have forgotten how to dress, and the scare-crow in the corn field is the pink of fashion compared with you. What you need is travel to enlarge your mind, and introduce you to civilized society; so I shall just pack up your white shirt, and your Sunday clothes, and off you go!" "Go where?" I feebly enquired. "Any where you like, but go you must; and don't dare to come back for a month. If you do, I'll pour kerosene on the stump and set fire to it." "Don't do that," I said; "you'd hurt the centipedes and spiders, and cremate a whole colony of ants." "Much I care if I do, the nasty things," she made answer, "but it all depends on yourself. Will you go?" "And

who's to look after you and Bloomah?" "I'll look after myself, and
Bloomah too,—and you," she added, pursing up her lips significantly.
So I thought it best to give in. When a woman closes up her
lips tight, you may depend upon it she is going to bite, and the
sooner you get out of her way the better for your health. Thus it
came about that at this present time of writing there is a piece of
paper pinned on my stump, signifying that it is to let, ready
furnished and stocked for the space of one calendar month, and I
have been losing myself in the labyrinths, and breaking my shins
down the precipices which they call streets, in a little place you
may have heard of, and if you haven't it is no fault of its inhabitants,
named Quebec.

Quebec is an oasis in the great Canadian Wilderness, which
is known to a few Americans as a pleasant summer halting place
on their way to the seaside resorts of the Lower St. Lawrence, or

> The pathless woods where sporting men do go
> To hunt the moose, and shoot the bounding roe,
> And sand-fly haunted lakes where anglers fish
> For " land-locked salmon," alias ouananiche.

Nobody dreams of going to Quebec on business, but a great
many visit it for pleasure, and, to give the little city its due, they
generally get it; for the Quebecers are a genial and hospitable
tribe, and nothing rejoices their hearts more than to get hold of a
posse of American strangers, show them all the sights that can
be seen from Wolfe's Monument on the Plains of Abraham, to the
Montmorency Falls, and entertain them royally in their comfortable mansions. So long as the Americans are in Quebec, it is all
sunshine, and when they go away it begins to freeze, and the
snow comes down.

But, summer or winter, Quebec has peculiar attractions of its
own. It is perfectly wonderful what an amount of interesting
matter is stowed away in such a little city. In the first place, it
is very old; how old, nobody knows exactly. The school books

say it was founded by Champlain in 1608, and the Quebecers so
far condescend to humour the popular delusion as to be on the
point of erecting a monument to that illustrious man in his alleged
capacity of founder of the city, but in their hearts they know
better. If you can get hold of one of the local antiquaries in a
confiding moment, he will tell you that this is undoubtedly the
city spoken of in Scripture which is " set on a rock, and cannot be
hid ;" and, as a proof, he will whisk you down the Elevator from
Dufferin Terrace, *and show you the rock.* If you are wise, you
will refrain from hinting that the passage in question was written
many years before America was discovered by Columbus, for if
you do, you will be told that Columbus was a fraud, and so were
the Vikings, and the Welshmen ; that it is a well-known fact that
the Carthaginians used to trade here ; and that certain decaying
timbers have been dug up on the Plains of Abraham which would
seem to render it not improbable that Mount Ararat was the
ancient name for Quebec, and that Noah's ark rested here after the
deluge. The theory does not seem so wild after you have caught
sight of some of the *habitants* that come in to sell their produce,
especially on a wet day. They look very much as if they had
just come out of the ark, and I know one old market woman in
particular, who bears a strong family resemblance to the wooden
Mrs. Noah whose paint I sucked off, and nearly poisoned myself
with, in my days of youthful innocence. Moreover she is accompanied by her son, who is as much like Mr. Ham as one pea is
like another.

But without insisting on this extreme antiquity, there is no
doubt that Quebec is a very ancient place. The very rocks are so
old that they fall out of sheer decrepitude, and go crashing through
the houses of the confiding inhabitants who have built underneath
them. Nobody thinks much about the occurrence unless some
one is hurt, and then the Government gets abused for not having
had that particular rock clamped, or plastered, or done something
or other to. The fortifications, too, are old, and want a deal of
repairing ; so the people say, especially in winter time when there
is no other work to be had ; and the gates were old—once on a

time—they are new ones now, very handsome and imposing, and more in accordance with modern ideas. There are quaint old houses in unsuspected nooks, and queer little streets like those of the Ile de Paris in the time of Nostradamus, scarcely broad enough for two carts to pass, and altogether too narrow for a couple of modern belles to walk abreast. Some of them go nowhere, and others go anywhere; it does not make much matter which to the unattended stranger that happens to get into one of them, and finds it an exceedingly interesting matter to discover how he is going to get out, and where he will be, if he ever does.

Besides her antiquity, another strong point of Quebec is her history. From time immemorial she has been a battle-ground of races; of the red man, and the white, the savage and the civilized. The arrow and the scalping knife have done their work here equally with the musket and the bayonet, down from the time when the Six Nations swept like a devouring flame all along the country from the Ottawa to the St. Charles, and drove the shattered remnants of the Hurons to take shelter beneath the walls of Quebec, where their descendants may still be seen at La Jeune Lorette, some seven miles off. A quiet people they are now, dwelling in what Umslopogaas would have called "a place of stinks" in the summer, owing to the drying of the hides of the deer they kill in their winter's hunting, which they convert into mocassins, and beaded purses, and other knick-knacks for the curious. As civilization has divested them of many of the characteristics of the "untutored Indian," so intermarriage with the habitants has effaced in most nearly all the distinguishing lineaments, yet here and there, especially amongst the children, specimens may be met with of the pure racial type. They have a reservation of their own, and a church, together with a small cannon presented them by George III., of which they are immensely proud. It is the last lingering relic of martial days, and the very sites of their ancient battlefields are forgotten.

Not so with the rock-fortress that sheltered them of yore. There, are cannon enough, of all sizes and all ages, grimly looking out from embrasure and bastion, or quietly reposing in the grass where the boys play football and lacrosse. And there are battle-fields, and reminiscences of battle enough, from the Dufferin Terrace, where Frontenac defied Phipps, and the Church of Notre Dame des Victoires, where the captured flag of an English battle-ship hung, to the Plains of Abraham, where Wolfe was married to Fame by Death, and those of Ste. Foye where de Levis threw a last ray of glory on the French cause. All these will be shown the visitor, as well as the place where, still later on, the gallant Montgomery met a soldier's death in his daring but unsuccessful attempt at a coup de main. Quebec knows the value of her history, and is careful not to let the interest in it cease. She is perpetually digging up all sorts of gruesome things, and now and then, for variety, she pulls them down out of walls, as she did lately when making a new entrance to the Archbishop's Palace. If you want a cannon ball or two, or a bullet, she will root them out of the grounds of the Q. A. A. A.; if you wish for a skull or a rib, you have nothing to do but to "prospect" on the Plains, only you must be careful not to let the governor of the gaol, which overlooks them, see you; if you are ambitious, and nothing less than a whole skeleton will satisfy you, you can get them by the half-dozen on the Ste. Foye road: that is, if you happen to hit on a burial-trench. Not long ago, she discovered the remains of a dozen or more of Montgomery's soldiers, and buried them decently, putting up a slab to mark the place of discovery. All these stories are interesting to the visitor, and properly so—what is the good of one's ancestors' bones if they can't be utilized? We are a peaceful and civilized people now, and don't want to fight any longer, but that is no reason why we should not get what we can out of those who did fight. We no longer scalp our enemies; we fleece our friends, and there are some of these latter who think they would infinitely prefer reverting to the older custom.

COWS, in their relationship to the clearing, come under the head of day-boarders, and they are as much harder to keep in their proper places, and in good behaviour, than the rest of its living inmates, as a day scholar is than the one who boards with the Principal of an institution, or with an assistant teacher. They are always pretending that they do not get enough to eat, and breaking down the fences to wander off into the bush, where they get less. When they are at home, and under the supervision of their titular Papa and Mamma, by which I mean when they are in the farm-yard under the conjoint authority of Nathan and Bloomah, they are on the very best of good behaviour; they have nothing to say against the hay, and they always have enough; in fact they are so thoroughly content that they lie down, and it is very difficult to get them to stand up and be milked; but they don't lie down when they are put under my charge in the clearing; they are restless and dissatisfied; turn up their noses at good dry grass, and burdocks, and roam in a melancholy discontented manner all over the place till I get tired of watching them, and turn my eyes away. About five, or at the most ten, minutes after I have done so, there is an awful crash in the distance, and "good-bye, John." At this stage of the proceedings I get up, and go off home, for it would never do for any of the household to come up to the clearing and find me cow-less; and as for going after the truants and bringing them back, I know by sad experience that it would be half a hot day's work to do so, and that even then I should have to sit in the gap to prevent fresh lapses from bovine virtue. Now a philosopher with his back propped up by a friendly stump is a reasonable and reasoning being, dignified in his appearance, and comfortable in his position, but a philosopher sitting in the debris of a cow-gap, like Marius in the ruins of Carthage, is a preposterous animal that I decline to recognize. So I saunter off home unconcernedly, as if nothing had happened, and at milking time Bloomah will go to the bars and shout till she gets a "frog in her throat," and then come back and start Nathan off, just as he is washing his hands and face at the pump in anticipation of supper. "Drat them cows!" says Bloomah, who never gets farther than breaking the commandments of grammar; I wish I could say the same thing of Nathan; but then it must be considered that he has to go farther after the cows.

The cow is a ruminant animal; the philosopher is a ruminating one. This is a very important distinction which we are led to overlook entirely from a too careless use of words, and a too hasty jumping at conclusions. The cow, being a ruminant animal, may be said to ruminate, but the philosopher, though he ruminates, is not a ruminant animal. This is the essential distinction between the two. There are minor and more obvious ones, of course; for instance, a cow has horns, and hoofs, and a tail, and a philosopher, —a good philosopher, I mean—has not. There are certain beings that are popularly supposed to have all these, but they are not cows; and the distinction is that they, too, ruminate. I mention this to show you where the real difference between a cow and a philosopher lies, and prevent you from mixing up the two together. Now a cow is a ruminant animal because she possesses more than one stomach, and a philosopher is a ruminating one because he does not. There are no philosophers in the city; they are only to be found in the country: and to be endowed with more than one stomach to cultivate dyspepsia in, where the staple food of the aborigines is home made bread, hot soda biscuits, pumpkin and squash pies, and fat pork, would utterly destroy all a man's mental faculties; his whole thought would be concentrated on the pains in his several stomachs, two or more, as the case might be. The philosopher chews, and reflects; the cow chews without reflecting, because the one operation is so constant that it leaves no time for the other. I don't say that the cow would not think if she had time; but she never has. All her energies are directed to chewing, and this is the real reason for the defective state of education in some of the very remote elementary schools where the scholars can easily obtain spruce gum. There, they are likewise always chewing, and when the little school marm confiscates one chunk of gum, and puts it in her own mouth, they have another ready for use. The consequence is that they spell " water " with two t. s, and " very " with two r. s ; forget the multiplication table as fast as they learn it ; say " Be you going to skule " ; and grow up into school commissioners who are very critical of the school marm's intellectual attainments, and sign her report of how the school acquitted itself when they visited it with

JAMES
His × mark
BLOBBS.

Before, however, they have achieved this high and responsible educational position, they will have changed the gum of boyhood for the black tobacco plug of manhood. Thus, through the act of chewing there is established a sort of evolutionary link between the lower and higher grades of non-intellectual animals, incapable of ruminating : the cow chews grass ; the boy chews gum, and the man chews tobacco. The cow has an extra stomach to keep her supply of fodder in ; the boy has his trouser's pocket ; and the man that of his coat ; and herein we again see the trace of evolution from the inside and invisible, to the outward and visible.

" And in these lineaments I trace
What time shall strengthen, not efface."

There is a calf-like appearance in the physiognomy of the juvenile gum chewer that develops into the more sedate and heavy aspect of the cow in the mature tobacco chewer.

The daily denouement has not yet occurred, and there is one of the "milky mothers of the herd" standing a few yards away, and quietly chewing the cud with an appearance of deep thought. She does not lie down ; no cow of good breeding, and moving in the first circles of bovine society, ever thinks of lying down in the clearing unless she fancies that somebody is looking for her, or wants to delude her watcher into the belief that she is going to

behave herself to-day, and does not intend to smash through the
fence into the bush at the very first opportunity. She makes a
pretty picture as she stands there, with her glossy sides shining in
the sun, her ears pricked forward inquiringly in unison with the
direction of her large patient eyes, and motionless, save for the
action of the jaws, and an occasional switch of the tail at some
impertinent fly. Both of these movements seem purely mechanical,
almost independent of the volition of the animal, which, but for
them, is the perfect picture of contented repose. I hold very
strongly to the belief in the doctrine of compensation ; by which I
mean that matters are not so unevenly divided as we fancy, and
that if we only knew enough to enable us to strike the average, we
should find that there was a pretty even balance maintained
between the debit and credit sides of happiness and unhappiness,
advantages and disadvantages. Now at the beginning of this
chapter I touched half in jest, and with what you will doubtless
think a great deal of nonsense, on the distinction between a
ruminant, and a ruminating being. One has to talk a great deal
of nonsense if one wishes to get the attention of the public directed
to a little sense ; to sugar-coat the pill, as it were, if it is intended
to be swallowed ; we used to act on this principle when I was at
school. I think I said elsewhere, that we were obliged to go into
school for an hour before breakfast ; and this was, especially in
winter time, uncomfortable, and sometimes, as we always had to
have a lesson and exercise prepared, inconvenient. Then we used
to "fox ;" that is to say, lie in bed, and excuse our non-appearance
by a headache. I fancy the Doctor had his own private theory
about these headaches ; at any rate, the result was invariable : an
examination of our tongues ; orders to swallow two pills which the
housekeeper would bring us, and a recommendation to be in school
at 9 a.m. This last injunction we kept religiously ;——and the
pills also ; and every month we made a general collection of them ;
bought several gingerbread horses from the village confectioner ;
studded them all over with pills ; and gave them to the doctor's
pigs, which swallowed them. There was a great deal of squealing
and commotion in the pig stye that day, but it did them good, I

am convinced. Occasional opening medicine is as necessary to a pig's health as it is to a boy's. But it would not have been swallowed, had it not been for the ginger-bread. Similarly, though not in the slightest degree comparing you with those very respectable and useful members of the community who furnish us with smoked hams and flitches of bacon, if I did not talk a great deal of nonsense I should despair of getting you to swallow any sense. The parsons can't do it, and their congregations go to sleep.

Now, what I want you to notice in this fanciful distinction of mine between a cow and a philosopher, is what is taught by the attitude of the animal I am contemplating. The intellectual pleasures are denied to the lower animals; they have not the reasoning faculty in that full extent which confers the power of sustained and connected thought; and the same thing may be said in a less degree of certain men and classes of men. That, you will readily admit, is a very great diminution of the happiness of life; or rather, it would be, if it were not compensated by a greater enjoyment of absolute repose. I might refer to the almost unlimited capacity of dogs and cats for sleep; to the evident pleasure which a horse takes when standing still; and to numberless other instances in the brute creation; to the Italian lazzaroni, who bask in the sun in the streets of Rome and Naples; to men whom we have known ourselves, and whom we call lazy, but who are not lazy, but simply non-intellectual. The most remarkable, and the most beautiful instance however that I know of is given by the butterfly; and who that has seen the pretty thing settle on a leaf, and sit motionless for a time, till its wings begin to quiver with the exquisite delight of its quiet can doubt for a moment of the extent of its pleasure, so much greater than when it was on the wing, and flitting from flower to flower. There is, and always must be activity and unrest where there is the intellectual faculty; and in proportion as it is wanting there is inactivity and repose. The pleasure derived from the one, is not unequal to the pleasure derived from the other, and I see a proof of Creation by design in this balancing of the possibility of the happiness of life to all things living by Him whose tender mercy is over all His works.

11

The Gender of a Wet Day.

IF I recollect right, there is some such a rule as this in the Latin grammar of early youth: "Substantives of the Fifth Declension are Feminine, except dies, a day, which in the singular is sometimes Masculine, and sometimes Feminine, and in the plural always Masculine." If the announcement excited any passing emotion at the time it was simply that of satisfaction to find that there was any of the five declensions that was so reasonable in the matter of gender, and had not a host of exceptions to the general rules that were always tripping a fellow up unexpectedly when he began to parse, and bringing down the wrath of the teacher on his unwary head. Looking out to the clearing to-day, and seeing my accustomed roosting place dimly through a drizzling mist of rain, the old rule comes back to my mind, and seems worthy of careful investigation. How was it that the Latins, who were so certain of the gender of all the other words in the fifth declension, were puzzled and uncertain about this one? How was it that this uncertainty only lasted whilst considering the individual day, and disappeared when they were taken in the aggregate? And how was it that the old Latins decided that days were certainly masculine, while one day might be either masculine or feminine? I am thankful to say that these questions did not occur to me when I was painfully studying my Latin grammar as a boy. I bolted it whole, as an owl does a mouse, without stopping to trouble myself with inconvenient speculations; and even if I had not, I doubt whether I should have been able to solve the enigma satisfactorily.

Philologists would probably put the enquirer on a course of roots, and just as evolutionists would derive the whole of the visible created world from a stupid little blob of jelly dignified with the high-sounding title of Protoplasm, so philologists would present to me some particular one of the grunts or squeaks, which, I understand, formed the method by which primeval man publicly expressed his private opinions, and would tell me that the said grunt or squeak signified Light, which, as it was the great fructifying principle of all things living, might be said to be their parent, and hence might be regarded as l'apa or Mama, according to the fancy of the moment; and they would talk about Dis, and Diospiter, (from pater a father), and bring in the worship of the sun, and the myths allegorical of the seasons. It is sufficient to say in refutation of this theory that when men conveyed their ideas to each other by differently modulated grunts, and groans, and squeaks, (if they ever did), the feminine gender was a thing absolutely unknown. Directly Eve was introduced into Paradise she began to talk, and we may be very sure that she did not confine herself to inarticulate sounds; in proof of which we find Adam quite advanced enough to give names to the different animals within a very short time after he was married; probably before the end of the honey-moon. It makes one tremble to think of the flood of words that must have been poured into Adam's ears when Eve first got at him, to enable him to talk fluently in such a brief period; but it is evident that he had made progress enough in the art of language to enable him to master the science of zoology. It is highly probable that he did nothing but grunt or squeak until Eve came, for we do not hear of him speaking before that event; and, no doubt, he often grunted after she came; but no language before the advent of woman could have the idea of the feminine gender, and any language after it was composed of words, not dubious roots.

⋅ The grammarians, while they do not absolutely scout the science of philology, get along very well without it, and will not allow that gender comes within its sphere of action. They will refer this ambiguity about the sex of the Latin day, to the comparative ignorance of those times, when there was not a fresh grammar published every six months for the benefit of the author and the publishers, and there were no elementary or model schools, no Teachers' associations, no Inspectors' reports, no Government examinations, and no diplomas. Under such circumstances there must naturally have been a deplorable ignorance of grammar even

in the educated classes, as anybody may see that has pored over
the choruses of Æschylus, and the lower classes must have had
very confused ideas on the subject. Hence local idioms crept in,
and solecisms abounded; and while, in latter days, the Principal
of the Model School at Rome was teaching his scholars that dies
was masculine, and the Elementary schoolmarm at Brindisium
was impressing on the tender minds of the infants under her
charge that it was feminine, the great mass of the ratepayers came
to the conclusion of the Yorkshireman who was asked to decide
whether e, i, t, h, e, r, spelt eether or ither, and declared that other
would do. And when the ratepayers say a thing, it is useless for
the teacher to protest that he, or she, knows better, as witness the
general use of such expressions as "that's him"; "I seen him done
it"; "between you and I," in spite of all the grammars to the
contrary thereto made and provided. Hence the grammarians
made the best of a bad job, and compromised matters that dies
might be either masculine or feminine according to taste. The
theory is a very plausible one, but as it does not account for the
word dropping its femininity in the plural, and becoming sternly
masculine, it is very evident that it cannot be regarded as tenable.

You see that there is really a very interesting question here,
and a mystery of which neither the philologist, nor the grammarian,
is able to give a solution which will commend itself to the general
acceptance on investigation. Looking at the matter, however,
from a philosophical point of view, I conceive that the subject
presents little, or no difficulty, and that the key to the secret lies
in the state of the weather. The state of the weather has a deal
to do with a great many things where we are least inclined to
suspect its interference. If it is bad, it makes a man a "perfect
brute" when he comes home and finds his dinner not ready; it
neutralizes the effects of the patent remedies that cure every known
ill if taken in bottles varying in number from half-a-dozen to six
hundred; it paralyzes the beneficent influence of the potato or old
chestnut that we carry in our breeches' pocket to ward off the
malignant attacks of rheumatism; it even affects our religion, and
keeps us in bed on Sundays when we ought to be getting ready

for church ; if, on the contrary it should be good, our temper is
serene, and undisturbed by trifles ; our morals are unimpeachable ;
and the general state of our health is most fitly expressed by the
word "jolly." It is this potent magician whom I conceive to have
tampered with the grammar of the ancient Romans.

You have doubtless observed that nobody has a good word
for a wet day. Even the lower animals appear depressed by it.
You will see the horses and cows in the pasture, if there is no
friendly tree to shelter them, (and there generally isn't), standing
with their backs to the driving rain, heads down, ears thrown back,
and looking altogether washed out; the impudent little sparrow
sits up in the tree a round ball of wet feathers, with all his
liveliness gone, and the rooster in the farm-yard beneath gets
under the hay cart with all his tail draggling on the ground. The
farmer has no patience with a wet day. When it was fine he
might have wanted it, but he has no use for it now. If it is doing
good to his seed crops and causing them to sprout, it is also
swelling the brooks and rivers, and making them flood his fields
and carry off his bridges ; if it is benefitting his wheat and oats, it
is ruining his hay, or making his potatoes rot. Whatever a wet
day does, it is sure to do it wrong, and to be found fault with by
everybody. Therein it is just like a man. He never does anything
right, and if he wants any praise he has got to furnish it for
himself. Therefore the ancients said that " dies " was masculine
—when it was wet.

Now, on the other hand, take a fine day. Everybody likes a
fine day. No matter how hot it may be, you just wipe the
perspiration from your manly brow and exclaim "Beautiful
weather." It cannot go wrong. If the oats begin to look a little
parched and yellow, the silken tassels of the corn are drinking in
the heat ; if the potato bug is vivacious, the potatoes themselves
are safe from rot; if the wells are a little low, the first wet day
will cure all that, and in the meantime everything is bright and
cheerful, and man goes whistling to his work in the morning and
kisses his wife and tells her he would just as " lief " have the pork

burned as not, when he comes home to dinner.   If it happens to be Sunday,

> " Oh then he's drest all in his best
> To take a walk with Sally,"

.

and as he knows that he will find Sally ready on coming out of church to take the said walk, he attends Divine Service most religiously twice a day.   And in all this, a fine day is just like a woman.   Whatever she does or says, or whatever she doesn't do or say, she is sure to be right, and he would be a bold man that would venture to dispute the proposition.   Therefore the ancient Romans, who were keen observers, said that " dies " was feminine —when it was fine.

So far the solution of the mystery seems easy, and the diversity of gender in the singular number is duly accounted for on philosophical grounds.   Nor is it any more difficult to explain the sole use of the masculine gender in the plural.   This is done by the law of averages, and the doctrine of chances.   In speaking of a number of days, it was manifestly impossible to divide them into the two classes of wet and fine, and to determine accurately which side was in the majority ; so the ancients took them all in a lump, and taking the doctrine of chances into consideration decided that these were in favor of the period being an average wet one. They were the more induced to do this from the principle that any unpleasant thing, as, for instance, a rap on the head, is apt to make a deeper impression than a pleasant one.   Hence, although the majority of days in the period under consideration might have been fine, yet the wet ones would always be sufficient in number to more than counter balance the pleasure received from them. Therefore the period was, by common consent, allowed to have been rainy, and in accordance with the rules for the singular number which I have given "dies " in the plural was masculine.

You see what it is to be a philosopher.   Don't you wish you were one ?

Rather Mixed; Mud.

THE intelligent reader will probably have guessed from the subject of the preceding chapter that it was written on a wet day when I could not get to the clearing, or rather, could not have stayed there to write if I had gone. And the intelligent reader would have guessed right. It was a wet day, with what I may term a dry rain falling, and not a wet one. You never heard of a dry rain before? Probably not, but that does not prevent its actual existence; and probably there are a great many things in the world that neither you nor I ever heard of, or ever will hear, but they are there, all the same. It is a very fortunate thing that the existence of persons or things does not absolutely depend on their recognition by other persons: if it were otherwise I know a great many women, who, so far as my wife was concerned, would have been dead long ago, and to even matters, my wife would have been in the same lamented case, had it depended on her recognition by other women. So, though you never heard of a dry rain, there was one yesterday; to-day there is a wet one, by way of variety. Perhaps, however, I had better explain. A dry rain, then, is one that you may be out in for three or four hours, if you have an over coat, without getting much more than uncomfortably damp: if you have a waterproof, you may brave it all day. It is divided into two classes; the first, a sort of overgrown fog or drizzle which can with difficulty be called rain; which obliterates all but the very near features of the landscape, and which renders it desirable to chew up the atmosphere a little bit before you venture on the experiment of admitting it to your lungs. The second is a more pronounced rain; it allows you to see a little further, and you can draw in your breath without a feeling of suffocation. It comes down gently, but persistently, like your wife's efforts to get the money out of you for a new

bonnet, or set of furs, or anything else she ought not to have, and
therefore has set her heart on having.   The peculiarity about these
two classes is that they do not wet you through as fast as you
have reason to expect they will if you go out in them, and therefore
I call them dry rains.   They come with due notice, and after a
long preparation of quiet gathering of clouds.   The wet rain differs
entirely from them.   It comes suddenly with a swirl and roar of
wind, and with big drops that you can see and fancy you can
dodge between, and before you have been out in it three minutes
you might just as well have jumped into the river.   That is a wet
rain ; and that is what we are having here to-day.   Yesterday
there was a dry rain that laid the dust in the clearing, a thing
that was very much needed ; to-day there is a wet rain that is
rapidly converting the consolidated dust into mud ; a thing that,
in my opinion, wasn't wanted at all.

Mud, in chemical notation may be designated as H O D-n.,
H.O. signifying water which is, as everybody knows, a compound of
hydrogen and oxygen, and D signifying Dust, with the index " n "
added to show that the number of parts of it taken is indefinite.
Some carping critic may urge that dust does not appear on the list
of elementary substances in any work on chemistry ; but his
ignorance will be apparent in this, since it serves to show that he
is not up-to-date with modern scientific discoveries, and has not
made himself master of my new book on chemistry which will be
published as soon as I have time to write it.   There is not the
slightest room to dispute that dust is an elementary object.   Man
was made of dust ; and that, I should hope, is a sufficient proof of
itself.   But, after all, I do not wish to insist too strongly on a
point which is not material to the purpose.   I am writing for
people whose notions of chemistry are probably confined to the
comparative merits of cough mixtures, hair-restorers, and pain-
killers, and care very little about scientific terms.   That is, they
like to hear them, and be able to quote and talk about them,
without wishing to know anything further.   So if the chemists
find fault with my notation of mud, all I can say is that they are
welcome to find a better or more concise one, if they can.   I waive

the point. In the meantime, everybody knows mud when he sees it.

The mud in our clearing is argillaceous, saponaceous, contumacious, and anything but gracious. It is a friend indeed, for "it sticketh closer than a brother." A man travelling all day up and down the clearing with a basket on his back into which to scrape the mud that adheres to his feet every five minutes, might gather together in the twelve or fourteen hours a big enough slice of the superficial area of the field to make him a comfortable farm if he could only get a place to spread it out on. And it has a very insinuating and caressing way of its own. From the boots it creeps up to the bottom of the pants; from there it twines lovingly round the ankles; from the ankles it steals up to the calves of the legs; and from them sends out foraging parties to the knees. Did you ever try the experiment of putting an ear of bearded wheat or barley on the shirt cuff, between it and the coat, and then leaving the cereal to its own devices? If you have, you will know that the probabilities are that in less than ten minutes you will find it tickling the back of your neck. Well, mud is a still greater automatic traveller than the ear of bearded wheat or barley. If it once gets on you it is not content to stay quiet where it is; it is as restless as the deep sea itself, and its motto is ever that of Longfellow's young man—"Excelsior." You may observe the same thing also of metaphorical mud; though that is generally thrown at a man, and he does not willingly walk in it. It sticks; and if there is only a little bit that hits you, unless you brush it off quickly it will grow and spread, until the whole person is covered with it and becomes a disreputable moral scarecrow. People aware of this characteristic should be cautious how they throw metaphorical mud at their neighbour. A chance word, a shrug, or a sneer is a very little thing; scarcely a decent handful; but if it hits him it is apt to have very disastrous effects: and people should also be careful how they put themselves in the way of having this mud thrown at them.

For mud is easy to acquire, but it is very difficult to get rid of. It cakes and dries, and requires a scraper to remove the outside layers, and the diligent application of the brush to efface the inside ones, and the resulting stains. And here again there is a marked similarity between literal and metaphorical mud. If it is hard to get rid of the thing itself, it is equally hard to remove the traces of it : if it is difficult to hunt down the slanderer, to disprove the calumny, to silence the gossip, it is still more difficult after all this is done to eradicate the rankling soreness of the mind that is the result. There is another resemblance, also, which may be noted, and that is in the effect of the mud on the temper of the person to whom it is, pro tem, attached. If a man has got himself all be-mired in his walk, he does not feel half so annoyed as he does by a splash or two of mud from a runaway horse, or a careless driver of waggon or cart, because, as I take it, the first damage has been done as it were by his own consent, himself virtually aiding and abetting; whereas in the second case he has in no wise contributed to the position he finds himself in. It is the same thing with metaphorical·mud; when a person has been injured by the petty gossip, (not always meant to be illnatured), which we are all of us prone to indulge in respecting even our dearest friends, behind their backs, he is a great deal less angry with the disparaging remarks made on him when he happens to hear of them, as he is pretty certain to do, if he knows that they were in some measure well-founded, than if his conscience acquitted him of all blame. I am aware that the opposite view is the one most generally held, and the epigrammatic legal dictum "The greater the truth, the greater the libel" may be held to lay down the principle that the bigger scoundrel a man is, the less justified you are in calling him one, but in saying this, the law is, I fancy, considering the case of libel more from a pecuniary than a moral point of view, and that by the words "the greater the libel" all that is meant is that the damage done by proclaiming the delinquencies of the individual is commensurate with the enormity of them. Now, what I am contending for is that it is easier to forgive a thing to which we have ourselves partly contributed, than one to which we have not. The mud that we get on our clothes ourselves, is tolerated with more equanimity than that which others put on them.

The father of Ham, (I don't mean Noah, though he too had a great deal to do with mud in his day, but the domestic pig) has been generally set down as an unclean beast, on account of the enjoyment he takes out of a good roll in a mud wallow, provided it be stiff enough. His big cousin, Chuckuroo, as some of the African tribes term the rhinosceros, is just as fond of his roll, if not fonder, but I have never heard him stigmatized as dirty on that account ; probably because Chuckuroo is a very bad tempered individual, and has sometimes one, and sometimes two horns, which he uses pretty effectually when anything puts him out, whereas you can't get anything out of piggy but a grunt. All animals as a rule are extremely cleanly and neat in their habits, and piggy is no exception in a wild state : when domesticated, he is dirty per force. Before you condemn him, just consider what you would be yourself in his place, cooped up all the days of your life in a little pig pen, with perhaps half a dozen other pigs as big as yourself cooped up with you. Now don't take offence, and fling the book to the other side of the room, because if you do, you'll be sure to spoil the most important part of it, the binding, without discomposing me in the least. I don't mean to say that you are an actual, or even a metaphorical pig, but am only treating you, for the time being, as a pig hypothetical ; given the same conditions, you would be dirty yourself, though I grant that you might not like it. And indeed, when you come to think of it there are plenty of human beings in the great cities living under conditions not dissimilar to those which surround piggy in his stye, and held thus for the profit of the owners of the tenements they inhabit, just as pigs are kept by the farmers ; and who are looked on with the same disgust by the daughters of the said owners as they pass them in the streets, as that with which the city-educated farmer's daughter contemplates her father's pigs. There is, however, one important difference between the biped and the quadruped : the farmer feeds *his* pigs, and the landlord doesn't feed his.

And, after all, I do not see why mud should necessarily be looked upon as dirty and unclean. If it happens to be of an

argillacious nature, and has been consolidated by time into the
consistency of clay, there are tribes in South America I am told
who make their meals off it, and consider it very delicate eating;
and it is a well known fact that in Quebec the natives at certain
seasons of the year drink it in a more or less diluted form, and
appear to thrive on it. The number of unlicensed stills, and the
large amount of smuggled whiskey annually seized by the Customs
officials in the city and the vicinity would seem to show that
there is a minority which objects to taking its liquid in a semi-
solid form though it is colored a delicately beautiful red-brick
color, and is driven to anti-prohibitionist absorptions much against
its will; but that the majority is absolutely content with its mud
and water is plain from the fact that the City Council, though
repeatedly urged, has persistently neglected to build a filter for
the liquid with which it supplies the town. Even the sentiments
of the minority on the subject are doubtful, for I have heard it
maintained that the abnormal consumption of excommunicated
spirits is due to the fact that such whiskey is much cheaper than
water at the present water-rates.

There are some things which rather go to support this
contention, though I must do Quebec the justice to say that they
are not to be found there. In the sister city of Montreal, the
authorities cut off the supply of water altogether from those who
are unable or unwilling to pay for it. There are always people
to be found who will find fault, and this proceeding has from time
to time been stigmatized as harsh and cruel, and prejudicial to the
sanitary state of the city, but it has been altogether overlooked
that though the authorities have been economical, even to the
verge of severity, in the matter of water, they have been very
liberal, on the other hand, in the granting of licenses for saloons
for the retailing of whiskey. They are evidently of opinion that
whiskey in its natural state is more easily obtainable than water,
and that the man who cannot afford to pay his rates can easily
spare money for his whiskey. Men must drink something, and
the less the water imbibed, the more the whiskey. Moreover, the
more whiskey a man drinks, the dirtier he gets.

OW much longer I should have made the preceding chapter had I not been interrupted, it is impossible to say. My subject was, as I stated, rather mixed, and I shouldn't wonder if I was getting rather mixed myself. Not that that is a thing to be ashamed of; we take everything mixed in this world, from our religion down to our whiskey; and though, doubtless, it would be a very good thing for us in many instances if we didn't, if for instance we took our religion without our worldliness, and our water without our whiskey, yet the general law is mixture, and there is no evading it. "Simplex munditiis" is a poet's ideal to which no woman now dreams of paying attention; the nineteenth century femininity is not simplex but complex; and where woman leads we have all of us got to follow. So I am rather proud of being a little mixed at times, and the day was the very thing for a long and rambling meditation. It was raining heavily, and I could not get out to the clearing. Now, though the clearing is productive of thought, yet it is not favorable to the lengthy exercise of it. It is soon either too hot, or too cold; too windy, or too still; though it is never lonesome or uninteresting, for there are plenty of ants and mosquitoes about; but at home, in an easy chair, with an equable temperature, the rain beating steadily on the window-panes, and Polly and Bloomah deep in the mysteries of household enjoyments, and consequently forgetful for the time being that I was comfortably doing nothing, there was every reasonable prospect of my prosing away till I fell asleep, when the door suddenly opened, and one of my oldest and dearest friends walked in. When I say oldest, I refer to the time I have known him, which is ever since I used to stand him on the form for improving himself in the art of conversation, and neglecting the study of his Latin rudiments. He is still young, comparatively speaking, and green, though he won't allow it, with the bump of reverence for his elders almost entirely undeveloped, and what, when a boy, he would have called "altogether too cheeky" in anybody else. As a proof of his irreverence, I may mention that instead of addressing me by my proper title of Philosopher, he abbreviates it into Flossie, a name which is usually applied only to girls and pet poodle-dogs. "Hello! Flossie," he exclaimed as he entered, "in the dumps, old man? Look about as cheerful as an owl in an ivy-bush, and not half as wise. What have you been after?" "Bob!" I replied with dignity, shaking hands with him as I spoke; "Bob! I have been excogitating." "Oh! ah! I see! thinking, you mean. Why on earth can't you use plain words? I should think you might; you are plain enough yourself." "That's what my wife tells me, but you had better not let her hear you say so. Her opinion of me, privately expressed, is just the one thing on which she will not allow the general public to agree with her; she makes up for it by insisting that they should share her ideas on everything else." "Oh! Mrs. P.! I have no fears on that score. Bloomah is going off to a ball, or concert, or something of that sort; and she has just got a paper pattern for a dress. So the two have wheeled the dining-room table into a corner, and are sitting on the floor with the different pieces laid out between them, debating which goes where, and trying, with tears in their eyes, to make the piece for the sleeve fit in as a collar for the neck, and if not, why not? just as I looked in. So we're safe for a good couple of hours." "What do you know about women's dresses!" I enquired severely, "You are not a married man." "You call yourself a philosopher," he returned with a shade of contempt in his tone, "and don't know that an unmarried man is more up in the subject of ladies' dresses than even the dear creatures themselves, to say nothing of a stupid hum-drum married man who has lost all interest in the matter except when he is called on to foot the bills. 'The proper study of mankind' may be, as the poet says 'man'; no doubt it is for the married portion of mankind, though I have noticed that you occasionally evince symptoms of studying Bloomah. Oh, yes! unconsciously of course; it's a habit of yours to study, and you're not always very particular as to the objects—but the proper study of the unmarried portion is woman ; how else can it guide its steps aright, and ultimately evolve into Philosophers ? " It is not at all a proper study." " How do you know ? Did you ever try it ? " " And, besides " I said, ignoring the question with disdain, " that does not explain how you come to be so well acquainted with the mysteries of ladies' dresses." " Heaven send you more wit, Flossie," he replied : " dress is the more important part of a woman ; it is the greater part of her, just as, if you take the feathers from a humming bird there is nothing left but the beak and claws. If you want to get an accurate idea of a woman, *study her dress.* You forget, I think, that if I haven't got a wife, I'm plagued with three sisters. " So I did ; ' the three Graces '." " Hum ! you may call them so if you like, but there are times when I should rather say ' the three Furies '." " Yes ? When you have been more than ordinarily saucy, I suppose. I don't blame them." " Neither do I, to tell you the truth," said Bob ; " they are dear, good girls, but there are times "—" when you would provoke a Saint." " May be ; but that is no excuse ; they're not saints. But come ; I am ashamed of your frivolous conversation, Flossie. You have been writing, I see. It's to be hoped that you write more sense than you talk."

With that, he seized on my unfortunate M.S.S. which were lying on the table, sank into a chair, and proceeded coolly to peruse them without evincing any recognition of my presence, more than if I had been a wooden block. The rain descended, and the wind began to rise, and still he read on. I was beginning to feel flattered with the interest that kept him so absorbed, when he threw the papers on the table, lighted a pipe, and opened fire. " Going to publish ! " " Yes." " Got your life insured ? " " No." " Then your wife will have some reason, at any rate, to be sorry when you're hung." " Shouldn't wonder ; it isn't everybody that will be regretted after his death ; eh, Bob ? But what is all this about ? " " Nothing ; only that your theology is heterodox ; your science a fraud ; your moralizing a set of old platitudes ; and your originality *nil.*" " That all ? It wasn't worth while making a fuss about; only observe that I ain't got no theology; I ain't got no science; and I ain't got no originality; (I think you said that last, yourself); the old platitudes I confess to, and am proud of them."

"Now, look here, Bob. If you want to get along in the world, don't set yourself up for an original: people don't like it. It startles them, and they take their revenge by saying, 'Bob? oh, yes! a clever fellow, but a little eccentric; a kind of a crank, you know, in some things;' the said things being precisely those on which you plumed yourself for your originality. And you are lucky if you escape thus easily, and are let off with a passive good-natured contempt. The general public is apt to be more severe with original men; it used to burn them; assassinate them; imprison them; fine them; at present it either ostracises them, or sucks their blood. It is rarely the inventor that makes any profit out of his inventions, and when he does, the chances are that he has simply improved on some other fellow's ideas, and is not the original Simon Pure himself. The father of printing is to this day represented as having sold his soul to the arch-enemy; the discoverer of the motive power of steam died in a lunatic asylum. Men do not like originality; they are afraid and suspicious of it; and the only original that they will tolerate is original sin, because that is so handy to lay the blame of all subsequently acquired sin on. But they like worn-out old platitudes that they have been accustomed to, and when they come across them in a book say 'Ha! that is just what I always thought myself; an uncommonly sensible fellow that writer is." Authors are like the planets and satellites; they shine with the light of the sun, alias the reader, pro. tem., and not with any inherent light of their own; they are witty or stupid, geniuses or cranks, just as they happen to coincide with the opinions of the public, or to disagree with them. Now, if you want to please the great mass of mankind you must talk platitudes: when you can't do that, the next best thing to do is to talk nonsense. Why is it that oyster patties, and Charlotte Russes are such general favorites with dainty palates? Because, though they are quite large to look at, there is nothing in them when they are once in the mouth. Don't despise common places, my boy. A goose feather is a very common and insignificant trifle, but you can tickle a man to death with it."

The rings of meditative smoke rose lazily from his pipe. You can always tell when a smoker is thinking seriously by that; at other times the incense from his clay or briar-root rises in formless puffs, or, if a ring occurs, it is plainly by accident. But when a man is debating a vexed question with himself, he "draws it mild," and ring after ring ascends into the circumambient air. At last he thought he had found out a weak point. "But if you are not original, you are a plagiarist, Flossie; a regular fraud, trading on other men's ideas, though you may not, perhaps, use exactly the same language." "And what of that? If plagiarism is really the wicked thing that some people, (generally jealous authors), make it out to be, don't you think that I deserve some credit for not giving anybody else an opportunity of plagiarizing from me? Next to the man who does nothing wrong himself, the best man is he who prevents others from doing wrong, as far as he is able. When you were a boy, and used occasionally to go out plundering orchards at night, did not you strip all the best trees in order that other boys might not be tempted to follow your bad example? At least, that's what I overheard you telling Joe Benson, (you recollect Joe?) the day after my magnum bonum plums had mysteriously migrated during the night. You two were up in my hay-mow, if you remember, and saying what fine ones they were, and how blank the old governor looked when he found them all gone. I was so struck with the soundness of the reason you assigned, that I would not listen to Polly when she wanted me to put the matter in the hands of the village constable, and I kept your secret religiously till now; but I took it out of you all the same. You both had headaches next day, and couldn't go to school. There was my opportunity, and I seized it. I think it is Shakespeare that says 'For this be sure thou shalt have cramps.' Eh, Bob? Do you recollect that dose of six big Ayer's pills? Yes! I see you do." He laughed; "so that was the reason why you doubled the ordinary dose? You designing old villain! I'd rather have

12

taken half a dozen canings." "No doubt, Bob! no doubt. But, you see, it wasn't what you'd rather, but what I'd rather. It was far less trouble to tell you to swallow half a dozen pills than it was to cane two boys even once; and, besides, you wanted the bile taken out of your system."

"Plagiarize? What is everybody but a confirmed plagiarist, in the sense that very little he possesses is due to his own exertions? You nourish your body with the bodies of other animals, you clothe it with their skins, and you ornament it, at least the women do, with their feathers; why should you not nourish your intellect with the intellects of other people?" "That's all right enough, Flossie, but it is not the nourishment of our own intellects that is in question, but the trying to feed other people's." "Nonsense! When you have got anything peculiarly nice to eat, I suppose you may give a dinner, and invite your friends. And you don't say 'this is turkey, and it came from Mr. Jones; this is ham from one of Mr. Brown's pigs.' You make believe that it is all your own. "Yes! but I pay for it." "Does that alter the fact of original possession? You did not think it necessary to inform Joe that you had stolen my plums, did you?" "Of course not: that was a self-evident fact." "Well! a plagiarism is generally an easily recognizable one, and when it is not, what saith the law? 'Inscienti non fit injuria;' a man is not injured if he doesn't know it."

He meditated again. "I am shot if I can ever make out when you are in earnest, and when you are not, Flossie. You will drop into a bit of dry moralizing, or wander out into the sentimental and pathetic in the midst of a joke; and just as you have got one in a serious or melting mood, you will turn it all off with a laugh. Do you ever know what you mean yourself? I can never quite understand you." "It is not worth while trying, old friend: grave and gay, laughter and tears are inextricably mingled together in this life; the sweetest waltzes are those that have an under-harmony of sadness running through them, and, strange as it may seem, there is often a sensation of pleasure in the very sharpness of a pain. And so, a joke may possibly cover something more serious than a sermon does, and a highly moral discourse be nothing more than a huge joke. If a man sugar-coats his intellectual pills, the chances are that he pills his sugar-coats, if I may use the expression. The effect on the swallower depends not so much on what he swallows as on the assimilative powers inside him. There! there's a pretty bit of plagiarism for you." He looked up enquiringly, and I laughed. "Oh! if you can't detect it, I am not going to tell you. Look up your Dickens, old boy, and study Captain Cuttle. But come! we've talked nonsense long enough, let us think of more serious things and see if the womenkind are going to give us anything for dinner." And so we went into the dining room, where we found the pair of amateur dressmakers with the pattern neatly spread out on the table restored to its former position of dignity, and

"The sun of sweet content
Re-risen in Polly's eyes, and all things well."

Old Logs.

THE amount of old logs to be found in a clearing depends very much on its age. If it is in its infancy, the number is a tolerably large one; there are felled trees that have been valueless for the lumber market, or, for some cause or other, have not been cut up for fire-wood, lying about in every direction, with sharp spikes of truncated branches projecting, and with a wealth of rank vegetation growing under their sheltering sides, and overmounting them in a tangled maze of fern, blackberry, raspberry, and perchance, nettle. As the clearing grows older, these are gradually removed; the smaller ones are built round a large one; the scattered branches are heaped over them, and the bush fires leave a mass of charcoal and ashes in their place. Some of the best and soundest are also chopped up at odd times by the boys on the farm, and carried off to the wood pile. By-and-by there only remain one or two of the largest, eaten to the core with dry rot, and ready to crumble away at the touch; the rest are covered over with vegetable mould and grass, and form their own graves. Then the plough comes along and buckwheat, or it may be oats are sown; and the next year there will probably be potatoes and potato-bugs, and the clearing has gone for ever. The stumps have been pulled out and burned; the stones gathered together in heaps for carting away; the old-make-believe fence that was the scorn and contempt of the cows has been replaced by a newer and better one; and the field of civilization has been evolved. My clearing has not yet arrived at the final catastrophe: there are still stumps throwing out sinuous roots to clasp the ground, and still a few old logs visible, and presenting an appearance of solidity which I know by sad experience to be illusory and deceptive.

Unsightly and dead as they look to the careless eye, it is wonderful what a world of beauty, and what an amount of variety of life they present to a more critical examination. Their bark is stained with the grey and green lichens, amid which rise the crimson tipped chalices of the cup-mosses. Other mosses there are, too, soft, and of varying shades of green, and an occasional little fern, but these last do not seem to me half so beautiful as their sisters with the blood-rimmed goblets, or half so mysterious, and when I see clumps of them growing, I always recall to mind Jules Verne's fanciful description of the strange world in the interior of the earth where the explorers, amongst other adventures, walked in the shade of a forest of gigantic toad-stools. I imagine that these cup-mosses must be looked upon in much the same light by the minute insects that run to and fro under their shade, and by whom the small red spider must be considered as an outrageous and formidable giant. Underneath the bark the red-brown centipede, and the iron-clad millipede work their devious ways; the carpenter wasp, and one of the ichneumon flies bore holes for their eggs in the sounder parts; beetles there are innumerable, and of all sizes; and ants! but it's no use talking about ants; they are everywhere in the clearing, except where it happens to be damp; and there are wood lice. There are other tribes besides of which I know nothing beyond the fact shown by the microscope that they do exist; and, taken altogether, the population of a good sized log that is not too dead may be calculated at about that of the United States.

Of course, this wealth of life and beauty, at which I have scarcely done more than hint, is not peculiar to the log as a log, and would have equally attached itself to it, if the tree had perished while yet standing. What I see, and what I want you to see with me, is that there is no waste in the scheme of the Creator. Man wastes and destroys. He has exterminated the buffalo that formerly used to range the western plains till only a few scattered remnants are left of the mighty herds that once fed there, and their skeletons lie by the hundreds to mark the places when they have been slaughtered for the sake of their hides, and left to rot on the prairie. The beavers and the seals are sharing the same fate; there is scarcely anything left of the wild pigeons, whose cloudy cohorts darkened the sky, and broke down the branches of the trees at their roosting places with the weight of the birds that settled on them; nothing but a tradition.   Our brooks and streams are troutless; our lakes depleted of their fish; and all this because these things have been abused, even in the using of them, and the season of their abundance has also been the season of their wanton, I had almost said deliberate, waste.   These logs that lie before me as I muse, are only a chapter in the universal tale.   At the time that they were felled they were allowed to lie, because there were others that were better and would command a higher price close by, and to be had for the chopping; if they were standing now, they would be looked on as a prize; but it is too late.   So far as man is concerned they are perfectly useless : worse than useless, for they only cumber the ground.

But in the plan of the Maker and Creator there is nothing wasted.   It seems to me that there is a hint of this, as well as a moral lesson conveyed, in the instruction of the Saviour to His disciples after the miraculous feeding of the five thousand on the five barley loaves and two small fishes ; " gather up the fragments that remain, that nothing be lost."   Here is the Divine mind ; the principle on which He acts, that of all He gives there should be nothing lost or wasted.   And we may be assured that there is nothing so wasted.   We can never see this with a perfectly clear eye ; though we see traces of it continually, if we will look carefully, as in the instance of these decaying trunks of trees, which, even in decay, are ministers to beauty and life, and the enjoyment of life : but generally the very opposite to this seems to hold good, and we fancy we see a great waste in the natural world, and in the life of man.   The seeds of a maple or poplar would, if they were all allowed to grow, cover hundreds of acres with forest; the eggs of a generation of fishes, if they all came to maturity would fill a lake ; the fruitfulness of nature is so great that if it were not checked, and rendered to some extent useless, would result in an over population of all living things.   So great is this apparent waste that it raised a quasi-doubt in the mind of England's dead laureate which he thus expresses :

" Are God and Nature then at strife
    That Nature lends such evil dreams ?
    So careful of the type she seems,
So careless of the single life.

That I, considering everywhere
    Her secret meaning in her deeds,
    And finding that of fifty seeds
She often brings but one to bear,

I falter where I firmly trod,
    And falling with my weight of cares
    Upon the great world's altar-stairs
That slope through darkness unto God,

I stretch lame hands of faith, and grope,
    And gather dust and chaff, and call
    To what I feel is Lord of all, '
And faintly trust the larger hope."

He sees an apparent disregard of the individual life, while clinging to the belief that the type of which it is a member is held in more consideration; but even this is dispelled on further reflection.

" 'So careful of the type ?" but no.
        From scarped cliff and quarried stone
        She cries 'a thousand types have gone :
    I care for nothing, all shall go.' "

Yes! Destruction with a purpose we can understand, but this apparently purposeless destruction is a riddle that has puzzled men in all ages, and in all countries. Now, it is obviously impossible for the finite to understand the purposes of the infinite mind, or to grasp even an infinitesimal part of the great web of infinity and eternity. Yet what we cannot understand, we may at least have

the assurance of, and I think that assurance is given in the
command "gather up the fragments that remain." It is not the
purpose of the Most High that any, the smallest crumb, should be
lost. Life and death ; joy and sorrow ; labour and ease ; all are to
be utilized. Nay, further : if I may say it with all reverence, when
the world was ruined by the introduction of sin, He came to it to
seek and to save that wasted and lost creation. Man wastes and
destroys ; but not God.

And when man wastes, is there no remedy ; nothing that can
be done but to lament ? Each one of us, looking back over what
has already past of his life, cannot fail to recall wasted opportunities,
wasted friendships, wasted love, wasted enjoyments, ay ! and wasted
grief. Are all these to remain so wasted ? You will tell me that
they must ; that nothing can recall the past, or undo what has been
done. To this assertion I answer, " In one sense, yes ! in another
sense, no ! There is a promise, as well as a reason given in those
words 'that nothing be lost.'" Do you understand ? *Nothing :*
not even that which has long ago been wasted and destroyed, if
only you gather up the fragments that remain. Then, and only
then, your past will revive and be utilized. I think that was what
the poet—Alice Carey, I think it was,—meant when she said she
thanked God, even for her sins. It sounded harsh and out of
tune, if not irreverent, but I fancy that she meant that the
knowledge—that knowledge of good and evil which is so dangerous,
and often so fatal—gained from them had been utilized for the
support of a better life growing up in her. Gather up the fragments
that remain, and you may depend upon it that nothing will have
been utterly wasted. You cannot bring this about, any more than
I can utilize this rotting log which is nevertheless not without its
uses—another must do that ; and will.

I once embodied some such thoughts as these in a few lines
written for a New Year's Ode. It is not New Year's Day now,
but what of that. Every day sees a new year commencing, and
an old one dying; so I add the verses here.

The snow lies white as a shroud on the plain,
  And steely-blue is the passionless sky ;
The rivers are dumb in their icy chain,
  And the chill wind shivers past with a sigh.
The music of laughter and talk is still,
From the farm in the vale to the cot on the hill,
For the day has come, and the day has gone,
And the hours of night are speeding on :
Night, that bends o'er the infant's bed ;
Night that wakes o'er the sleeping dead.
And night shall come, and night shall go
As the time-waves down to the great sea flow ;
The Sea of Eternity, lying in wait
For the lives that shall sink in it, soon or late ;
And the old year hastens to its embrace
With its work all finished. It dies apace.
What does it leave wherewith to greet
The coming on earth of the New Year's feet ?
Laughter and Sorrow,—Hope and Fear,
Are the heritage left to the coming year.
No more ? Ah, yes ! When the old years die
They leave behind them Memory.

* *
*

      Where stoops the grassy plain,
Gemmed with star-flowrets, scented with wild thyme,
    To where the waves of blue Gennesaret
    With many a lapping kiss and foamy fret
Curve, and recurve, and mount again, and climb
      Upon the sounding shore
With ring of pebble and deserted shells,
That makes faint music in the distant dells
Which dimple all the land-slope, there He fed,
From scanty store of fishes and of bread,
The multitude that came from all around
To hear him. Faint with hunger, on the ground
By companies arranged, they eat, and saw,
With wonder ever growing into awe,
The lad's few loaves and fishes furnish food
For all the needs of that vast multitude,
And still consumed, and still again supplied.
Till at the last, when all were satisfied,

And that strange feast, so free of cost,
　　So ample and so bountiful, was o'er,
He spake, who spake as never man before :
" That nought of what was given may be lost,
　　　Gather ye up the fragments that remain.

　　　　　　＊ ＊
　　　　　　　＊

So, hour by hour, and day by day,
As pass the seasons of the year away,
　　As to the greatest, so unto the least,
He spreads for each the appointed feast,
　　　The bread of Time and Life.
Strange feast it is of mingled joy and pain,
Of laughter and of tears, of dull despair
Changed into hope, and hopes dispersed in air :
Of friendship's sweet communings, and of strife ;
Of meetings and of partings, toil and rest ;
Of straitened means, of sudden gleams of wealth ;
Of all the lusty glow and pride of health,
And of the Shadow of the Unwelcome Guest ;
But when the feast is done, and by and by
The fu l-orbed year has come at length to die,
　　　And of the now past days
Time leaves us nothing but the memory,
He brings our life before our eyes, and says,
　　　' Gather ye up the fragments that remain.'

　　　　　　＊ ＊
　　　　　　　＊

Oh ! sweet were the hours when Hope was young,
And sweet were the songs her mating birds sung :
'We have found a place in the old elm tree
Where the nest on the branch shall swing safe and free,
And the eggs of promise shall be unstirred
Neath the sof· warm breast of the mother-bird,
And the father beside her the whole day long
Shall pour out his treasures of happy song.'
　　　Though the storm swept down on the elm tree's crown
　　　　　And the branch was cleft by the lightning's stroke,
　　　And though torn the nest from its place of rest,
　　　　　And the brooded eggs lay shattered and broke,
The storm has passed, and I hear the strain
Alone of the mating-birds again,
　　Treasured up in the memory,
As my heart once treasured them up for me,
And I gather the fragments that remain.

Oh ! sadly and slowly the days went by
    When Pain and Anguish stood by the bed,
And sleep fled far from the straining eye,
    And a weary wakefulness watched instead ;
When the clock was a burden through the night ;
    And the silence was full of whispered ill ;
And the longed-for reign of the busy light
    Was but a weight and an agony still.
But dear were the friends, and the sympathy,
    As Love bent over the couch of pain,
And their looks and their words live in memory,
    As I gather the fragments that remain.

* *
*

Oft from the beaten path I strayed
    In the yearly stage of the journey of life,
In pleasure's bowers a halting made
    Where the sensuous flowers of sin grew rife ;
And often I wandered apart, alone
    Into the wilderness, bleak and bare,
Quagmire planted, and strewn with stone,
    That lies in the realm of Faithless Care.
O love unfaltering, constant, deep !
    That sought, and brought again to the way,
Each time that it wandered, the truant sheep,
    And fed and tended it day by day.
What shall I garner in Memory ?
    The cleansing love, and the cleansed stain,
As, of the life that is left, for Thee
    I gather the fragments that remain.
The midnight bells ring out to the earth
The cradle song of the New Year's birth,
The blessing-grace for the feast that is near,
The thanksgiving grace of the past old year
With its joy and sorrow, its pleasure and pain.
Gather its fragments that remain ;
Gather them up that there be no loss,
And lay them down at the foot of the Cross.

Toad-Stools.

" Five little white heads peeped out of the mold,
When the dew was damp, and the night was cold ;
And they crowded their way through the soil with pride,
' Hurrah ! we are going to be mushrooms ! ' they cried.

Bu· the sun came up, and the sun shone down,
And the little white heads were shrivelled and brown ;
Long were their faces, their pride had a fall—
They were nothing but toad-stools, after all."

THUS sang Walter Learned in St. Nicholas, dear to children,
and I am debating what useful lesson either in morals or in
botany could be intended to be conveyed in these apparently
simple rhymes. It will not do to pretend that nothing further
was meant than the mere delectation of children, because this is a
practical age that scorns amusement *per se* as something
altogether unworthy of regard ; it must be of some practical
benefit either to the intellect, the body, or the purse, to be acceptable.
As for the soul, that does not so much matter ; we have really
very little time to spare to look after that ; but the other three
things are important, the most important being the last, to which
the two former are subsidiary. So our children must be taught
something, even in their nursery rhymes of modern days, and the
dear old nonsensical ones of respected Mother Goose have been
fitted up with divers meanings, until pungent political satires have
been discovered in some of them. Therefore I take it for granted
that Mr. Learned had a deep meaning in view in his tale of the
five little mushrooms that turned out to be toad-stools eventually,
and I am a loss to decide whether he wished to warn children of
the difficulty of discriminating between *the* edible fungus par
excellence, and its congeners; or wished to inculcate the lesson

that " Pride goeth before destruction, and a haughty spirit before a fall "; or to moralize on the futility of human hopes, and the deceptiveness of youthful expectations. I incline to the latter; I think he wished to say, (guardedly, of course), " My dear young friends ! Don't imagine that you are going to turn out anything very remarkable in after life, presidents, or premiers, or judges, or savants in different branches, or merchant princes, or bloated monopolists ; the chances are a hundred to one that after the fierce sun of the struggle for life has had an opportunity of causing you to " dry up," your beautiful little white mushrooms will turn out to be shrivelled up toad-stools, after all.

Well ! and if they do, are we any the worse for having indulged for a time in a pleasing illusion ? Are we not rather the better ? Granted that the awakening is all the more bitter for the previous dreaming, what saith the poet in his wonderful tribute to the memory of his dead friend ?

> " I hold it true, whate'er befall ;
> I feel it, when I sorrow most ;
> 'Tis better to have loved and lost
> Than never to have loved at all."

And so the day-dreams of our childhood, castles in the air though they were, to be shivered into fragments in the contact with actual life, were a real pleasure, so long as they lasted, and, it may be, helped to ennoble and invigorate the future manhood. There is a great deal of comfort to be got out of blowing soap-bubbles ; and it is none the less, because the bubble soon breaks, and leaves nothing but a little stain of soapy water that might represent a tear. The child's philosophy is the true one. He does not despise the bubble because it burst ; and he immediately sets to work to blow another. There are some of us that are children all our lives in this respect, and I don't think they are the least happy and contented of mankind. I question whether they are the least useful.

However what Mr. Learned meant is, as the village folks say,

" neither here nor there," and I only mentioned him because the sight of what appeared to be a "truly truly" mushroom greeted me to-day as I was rambling about in the clearing, and reminded me of his rhymes. A mushroom in a clearing is an incredible fungus. I don't go so far as to say that it is an impossible one, but there are many things which may be conceded as possible, and of which the actual existence is, nevertheless, rejected as incredible. This was one of them. There are, indeed, certain infallible tests for deciding on the true inwardness of what pretends to be a mushroom, and no one need have any doubt on the subject so far as the tests go : the trouble is that you have to reckon with the fallibility of the tester. The proofs are all right enough ; it is the application of them that is apt to be wrong ; and the consequences of a wrong application vary from considerable internal incon- venience up to the qualification for a lot in the cemetery. I remember a case in point which was brought before my notice when I was staying with a friend at Rawdon, a little village at that time, in Montcalm County, many years ago. One day, my friend called my attention to a strapping young fellow, six feet three inches in his stockings, and I am afraid to say how many inches across his shoulders, quick as a flash in all his movements, and I think one of the most splendid specimens of muscular manhood I have ever seen ; and I have seen a great many, for I have been up in Megantic County where the descendants of the antediluvian giants still live ; at least they would have been their descendants, if the said giants had not all got drowned. Of whom I then and there heard the following tale, which I have every reason to believe a true one. Some year or so before, Dan, (that was his name) having undergone the common lot of young men, and fallen an easy prey to the bright eyes of a young girl who lived a couple of miles out of the village, set out one evening à la froggie, that is to say, a-wooing. It was a dark night, with barely light enough to pick his way, and the road was a lonely one after the village was left behind. A mile and a half out, it descends down a moderately steep incline to a brook whose waters turned a saw-mill a few yards above, and at the top of the incline stands, or stood at that time, a particularly large elm tree with a particularly large bole. As Dan approached this, two black animals ran out from behind it, and, thinking that they were the two dogs of the brother of the young lady he was going to visit, he stooped down to caress them. As he did so a tall form rushed out and approached him in a menacing fashion, but without causing him much apprehension, and he called out to the supposed owner of the dogs, "It's no use, Jim; you can't scare me!" Dan was, however, considerably scared the next minute, when he discovered that "Jim" was a remarkably healthy she-bear, whose cubs he had been taking liberties with without having been previously introduced, and who was bent on taking liberties with him in return. He was alone and unarmed; the next house was half a mile off, and it was no use shouting for aid; so Dan faced the music like a man. As Mrs. Bruin approached to give him a friendly hug, he shot out his right arm, caught her by the throat and forced her back, holding her at arm's length despite of her struggles and clawings, till she was choked. Then he let her fall on the ground, and made the best of time to his friend's house where he told his story to the inmates. Guns and a lantern were soon in requisition, and the old farmer, his son, and Dan returned to the scene of the late action, only to reenact the experience of the lamented, but popular, Mother Hubbard:

> "When they got there
> The cupboard was bare,"

or rather, it wasn't bare, for there was no bear there, and no anticipated bear steaks. Mrs. Bruin had recovered from her faint as speedily as other ladies do when there are no gentlemen round, and departed with her family to regions where the social convenances are more ceremoniously observed. There was nothing left but her tracks, and the lair behind the elm tree where she had proposed to put her babies to bed for the night. I did not see the tracks myself, for I only came a year after the occurrence, but I

saw Dan, and I saw the elm-tree, and the road, which was the
next best thing.   Moreover, I have no reason to doubt the accuracy
of the tale, almost incredible as it may seem.

Now, a man that can hold a she-bear off at arm's length, and
choke her into a state of temporary insensibility, is one that, it will
readily be allowed, is by no means deficient in courage and strength ;
yet I learned two years later that Dan had become a perfect
wreck, as weak and as nervous as any young girl ; and this change
was brought about by a relation of my friend, the toad-stool.   In
one of his wanderings in the woods, Dan had found what he
thought looked like some very fine and large mushrooms, and
being ignorant of the fact that mushrooms never grow in the woods,
and very seldom in the clearings unless they have gone into the
transition-state of sheep pastures, he took them home, and had them
cooked.   He not only did that, but since the whole family had a
taste of the *soi-disant* mushrooms, he made his father, mother,sisters
and little brother very sick for a week, and all but succeeded in poisoning himself fatally.   His youth, and magnificent constitution
pulled him through eventually, but only after a severe and protracted
illness, and when he was at last able to get about, his nerves and
strength were gone.   I never heard whether he ever recovered them.

A toad-stool, (for after all, mushrooms are only edible toad-
stools) is not a thing to be treated with disrespect, if you are
thinking of eating him.   There are some, I am told, which are
delicious if you venture on them, and it is a wonder that such an
abundant and tasty article of food should be so much neglected.
Remembering Dan, I don't participate in that wonder.   We can't
all study botany, and if we could, it would not help us much ; the
toad-stool is a fungus, *per se,* and totally independent of botanical
rules, when he is treated as an *article de cuisine.*   He may be
very nice, but the culinary rules concerning him are capricious ;
one is harmless eaten raw ; another, if he is fried ; another, if he is
boiled ; a fourth, if you eat enough salt and pepper with him ; a
fifth, if you don't eat any ; but one and all will poison you if you
neglect the especial rule.   They may not all kill you ; they vary
in deleterious effects, but, at the very best, an hour's cramp in the

stomach, and a dose of emetics is not a very alluring prospect to contemplate. Mushrooms, and the substitutes for mushrooms, are what the Scotch call " Kittle cattle to shoe " for the inexperienced, and the safest plan is to fight shy of them altogether, unless you can buy them from the market gardener, or grocer, or some other responsible person whom you can sue for damages if he happens to kill you by mistake. At any rate, your heirs can, if that is any satisfaction. The only reliable fungus is the truffle, who is a negro, lives underground, and has to be hunted by pigs, or dogs trained for the purpose. But I never heard of his being a native of Canada, and though my pigs root about in the clearing whenever they can get in, they have never informed me of having come across any truffles. I don't think they have.

There are no mushrooms, however, in the clearing, though there is a toad-stool that marvellously resembles them when it is young, even simulating the peculiar color of the tender flesh, and only distinguishable from the mushroom by the difficulty of peeling. It may be harmless, for anything I know, but I would rather see somebody else dine of it first ; and I may say the same thing with respect to that very appetizing looking sphere commonly called the "puff ball," which I am told is delicious, cut into slices, and fried in butter. I shouldn't wonder if it was—for some people, but I have my doubts about it myself, remembering the old saw that " What is one man's meat is another man's poison." Probably it never struck you that there might be a deeper and more literal meaning in this proverb than the one generally assigned to it, and that it need not be taken as simply referring to the likes and dislikes of different individuals. The word poison is an indeterminate one, if I may use the expression. It means in common parlance something that produces deleterious, if not fatal, effects on the human system. Now it is very doubtful to me whether there is anything on which we support life that does not do this to a greater or lesser extent. We breathe poison ; we drink poison ; and we eat poison. Very likely you will exclaim at this, and as I am not engaged in writing a scientific treatise, I'm not going to defend my position ; but, allow me to point out to you

13

that there is not a more inveterate destroyer of all matter than
this same oxygen without which you could not live an instant,
and which compels you to look sharp after your meals in order to
replace in your bodies that portion of them which it is incessantly
burning up. Death is the great nurse and nourisher of life; by
which I do not mean that all living beings are nourished at the
expense of the existence of others, but that those things which in
themselves are the inveterate enemies of life are compelled to
support and maintain it; a curious material foreshadowing of the
higher spiritual idea expressed in the words "Death is swallowed
up in victory." Our bodies are as much nourished by poison as
was that of the legendary sorcerer's daughter whose kiss was fatal.

Now on the hypothesis that everything we eat and drink is
naturally a poison, deleterious or otherwise according to the
amount of it consumed, and, also, according to the constitutions of
the consumers, it is easily seen how I can assent to the statement
that some people can get a great deal of gastronomical enjoyment
out of toad-stools, whilst I decline to make the experiment in my
own proper person, or to advise others to make it. Man should
always be distrustful of himself; that is, of the different parts that
go to make himself up; and of all these, there is not one to be
more suspicious of than the stomach. You can never be too
cautious of what you confide to its keeping, because you can never
be certain of what it is going to do with it. I once knew a boy who
had only eaten for supper half-a-dozen innocent buckwheat pancakes, (each the size of a dinner-plate, and proportionately thick),
who woke up at two a.m. to see the ghost of his great-grandfather
sitting by his bed side, and preparing to extract the pancakes from
their depository with the ghost of a carving-knife. He was so
alarmed at the sight that he jumped out of bed, and ran to the
bottom of the hall stairs, where he seated himself, and where I
found him scantily arrayed, and shivering, (it was a morning in
January) when I came down at seven o'clock. If it had not been
for the hall stove, he would have been frozen so hard that even
the knife of his lamented great-grandfather would have made no
impression on him. Perhaps he reckoned dimly on this.

The Flowers of the Clearing.

J wish to be as truthful as original sin, and the contemplation of the example set me by my fellow-men, will allow me to be, and therefore I may at once confess that the clearing is not a pretty thing to look at. I look upon it as a friend, it is true; but what's the use of having a friend if you may not candidly acknowledge and bewail his little failings when you are in confidential intercourse with other people? "So-and-so is a very good fellow, but I must allow that he is a little hasty at times;" "Maude is a sweet girl, and she would be positively lovely, but then, poor thing, she has no taste in dress." We don't tell So-and-so, or Maude, of these drawbacks to their perfection: we tell our friends, and we say how sorry we are that there should be these "spots in the sun;" but then...etc., etc. So I am willing to confess that the clearing is not pretty to look at; and that the more readily, because any one who has seen it knows it for himself without my telling him. In its earlier stages it is suggestive of snakes, and bears, and babes in the wood; later on it has an untidy, frowsy look; and still later on it seems a desolate waste. My own peculiar clearing that I am talking about has arrived at this last stage; it is not inviting; and most people would hesitate to believe that it is really a garden of Eden, a garden in perpetual blossom from early spring before the snows have all gone away to swell the brooks and rivers, and carry off the country bridges, till after the frosts have nipped the phlox and asters before the house door, and the great Virginia creeper that mantles above it has turned a dusky red.

"Oh, yes! wild flowers!" Well! why should you look down on a flower because it does not grow in a garden? When it does try to do so, poor thing, you pull it up and call it a weed. You have got an idea in your head that your own are better because they are larger, and more "perfect;" married flowers, so to speak, that is to say, double instead of single. You may be right. Man is large in his views; he loves size, and he likes complexity rather than simplicity; the only instance in which I have known him to deviate from this, is when he has been invited to partake of hash in a boarding house : then he prefers a leg of mutton. It is not a healthy taste that leads us to set made dishes above plain ones, and plum-pudding above apple pie; and it is not a healthy taste that induces us to have a low opinion of Nature as compared with Art. I am not saying, mind, that made dishes, and plum-pudding and art, are not good things; but I think the other things are also worthy of respectful, and even loving, consideration— especially apple-pie, when it is well made. And as for size, man is a very small animal compared with the earth on which he walks; still smaller viewed in relation to the planetary system; and an utterly insignificant atom when you get beyond that. He has good reason not to "despise the day of small things," being so small himself. What does Victor Hugo call him? "An ant, cursing God from the top of a blade of grass"? He is not very far wrong; but he is not complimentary to the ant, which, though conceited enough, as I well know, is not half so conceited as man, and which has never seemed to me at all dissatisfied with his condition in life, as man, too generally, is.

The wild flowers have a beauty all their own, and a subtle essence of loveliness which we search for in vain in their civilized sisters. I think there is nothing more exquisitely delicate than the buds of the wild rose that blooms in the English hedge rows; the tender pink blush is only equalled by that which you see sometimes in the interior of sea-shells. We don't have them in Canada, but we have the little speedwell with its pretty blue flowers, and another more "deeply, beautifully blue" plant, which I don't know the name of—to my own satisfaction at least. I am told it is the Blue-eyed grass, a plant of the Iris family and described as being rather common in wet meadows amongst the grass, which so far corresponds with the one I am talking about, but Sir James LeMoine, in "Maple leaves," says that "it has an umbel of very pretty blue flowers which open and wither in a day, succeeding each other for some time in the same umbel," which my plant certainly has not. It has one star of vivid blue springing from the middle of the lance-shaped leaf. That's not a very scientific description ; but, perhaps it will be the easier understood. There is no blue in the garden flowers that in richness and brilliancy of colour surpasses, or even equals these two that I have mentioned, as there is no white so pure as that of the bloodroot, or so rich as that of the wind flower, the anemone that haunts Canadian woods. No doubt, the garden flowers are very hand-some ; they are the society belles of the floral world, but in a clearing they would be as much out of place as our violets, may-flowers, and buttercups would be in a garden. *Chacun à son goût ;* which I once heard a boy translate " Every one has got the gout ;" for my part, I admire the garden flowers, and I love the wild ones. That is, when they are in their proper places, the meadows and the marshes, the clearings and the woods. When they are adopted into civilized haunts, and begin to undergo the process of evolution, my interest in them ceases.

Experiments of this sort have been often tried, and generally resulted disastrously ; possibly, owing to the want of skill in the experimenters. The usual result has been that the transplanted ones have obstinately refused to be transplanted, and died off; just in the same manner that a wild bird will die, if caught and caged. There are some plants, however, that you can't kill, however much you may want to' do it; and the best thing you can do is to keep them as far as possible off your premises. The Marguerite, or ox-eyed daisy, is one of these, and a curious tale was once told me of the fatal results that attended an effort to settle this really pretty flower in a garden. Many years ago, I was passing along the Craig's Road from the station of that name on the line of the Grand Trunk up to Leeds, and I noticed with some astonishment, for the sight was new to me then, that the hay fields looked more like snow fields from the number of daisies that were growing in them. I was told that, a few years previously,

the plant was unknown ; but that a young lady who had gone on
a visit had seen it blooming elsewhere, and fancying it would
make a pretty addition to her garden, brought home a few roots
and planted them in it. From this centre of operation Madame
Marguerite had worked her way, and at the time that I was there
had colonized and possessed every farm for miles round. Once in
a while she shows herself in my clearing, and when she does, is
instantly rooted up and burned. The American alien law is
strictly enforced in our floral world.

We want no interlopers ; we have flowers enough of our own,
though you have to search carefully before you find them ; not
because there are few of them, but because they are, with the
exception of the buttercup, modest and retiring, and reluctant to
obtrude themselves on the notice of the public. At the far end of
the clearing the woods keep up a sort of connection by supplying
us with the anemone, May flowers, and an occasional trillium ;
at the other end the cultivated fields supply us with buckwheat,
thistles, and the burdock, for which last we are not particularly
grateful ; and we ourselves possess the violets, white, blue and
yellow ; the dog violet, wild oats, strawberry, and partridge berry.
"Not very much to boast of," you say. Well ! that depends. If
you took an interest in them, watched for the earliest appearance
of each as it came into bloom, and hunted for the last survivor ; if
you could say with almost absolutely certainty "that fallen tree
will shelter the first white violets ; and that other one, the first
blue ones ; the earliest ripe strawberries will be found on that
mound, and the latest strawberry bloom on that," you would
perhaps think differently. Men talk of the intrinsic value of
things ; the intrinsic value of anything is that which each individual
assigns to it for himself. The little toy-horse that runs on wheels
is as precious to the child as the animal with a long pedigree and
a record is to the man. The politician does not attach more
importance to the premiership, or the lawyer to a seat on the bench,
th in ho di l long ago to the stocking which he hung up for Santa
Claus to fill.

" For not to desire or admire, if a man could but learn it, were more
Than to walk all day, like the Sultan of old, in a garden of spice."

Thus Tennyson sings in Maud ; but the philosophy is not that of
the poet himself, but of the morbid man whom he represents as
speaking—and being so, is a false one. Yet, if a man could learn
neither to desire nor admire, it would doubtless conduce more to
his peace of mind than the possession of great wealth and luxury,
and power. But a man cannot learn this ; he cannot refrain from
admiring something or other, and to admire implies desire. And
if he could do these things there is scarcely a conceivable state of
more utter wretchedness than that in which the eyes are closed to
all excellence, of whatever sort it may be, and view the outside
world with the passionless gaze of the sphinx looking out over the
dreary waste of the Egyptian sands. It is well that man should
admire, and in so doing desire; ay ! and that both admiration and
longing should ever attach themselves to higher and higher things,
and things more and more unattainable ; that in this respect there
should be a spirit of unrest in him which ever impels him onward,
as " his own thought " drove Sir Bedivere, " like a goad." It is
well, too, that man should not content himself with small things
and those that are easily attainable : it is well, also, that he should
recognize that these are the sources from which alone he can draw
the purer and best part of his enjoyment of life.

And, therefore, if in my laudation of the wild flowers of the
clearing as compared with their cultivated sisters of the garden,
of the child's rocking-horse as compared with the racer, of the
Christmas stocking as compared with the direction of a people or
the administration of the law, I have seemed to decry the higher
and nobler things for the elevation of the smaller and ignoble, I
have not succeeded in conveying to you my real meaning, which I
faintly hinted at when I said that man had good reason not to
" despise the day of small things." The most really precious
things are the most common ; those from which pleasure is most
easily obtained are, at the same time, most easily attainable. Light

and air, the society of our friends, the colors and perfume of the
flowers, the beauty of the starry skies, these, and a hundred other
things, are in the power of the poor as well as the rich ; can be
understood by the least intelligent, and felt by the most apathetic :
all that is required is a loving heart, and, thank God, there is no
heart incapable of love.   If there were such a thing, it would be
that of a devil.

There is nothing so coarse that love cannot beautify ; nothing
so low and common that it cannot ennoble ; more than this ; like
the quality of mercy, which is but one form of it, love beautifies
both the giver and the receiver.   Nor is it to natural objects that
this alone applies, but to our dealings with each other, and our
estimates of human souls.   He is the wisest and happiest man
who can search out patiently for good in even the most unpromising subjects ; he is also the most successful, for the good is
there for him to find.   Not without deep meaning did the Master
call all the works of His creation good, nor does His word perish,
or change with time.   The ore of the gold is there, though it lie
deep under superimposed rock, and be covered over with earth
and vegetable refuse ; there, for each one of us to dig out.

The Striped Ones.

THE Striped one is a náme which, if I recollect right, Rudyard
Kipling bestows on the great cat of the Indian jungles : we
have got two varieties of them here, of " Striped ones " I mean,
not of cats, big or little, which generally affect the barn yard and
house.   One variety is to the manor born, and lives under ground
in snug family mansions excavated beneath the stump roots, and
is known to zoologists as Tamias Striatus, alias the ground squirrel,
alias the chipmunk ; the other, I am happy to say is not a native ;
I don't know where he resides when he is at home, and I am not
anxious to know, either.   He visits the clearing during the summer
season, and stands in the same relation to it as the summer girl
does to the seaside ; both frequent their respective resorts for the
purpose of preying on the unwary ; and both have airs and graces
peculiarly their own.   " Native airs and native graces " do well
enough for us in the clearing ; and we do not tolerate perfumes,
even in our wild flowers.   Now mephitis mephitica always carries
a scent bottle with him, and he is very liberal in the bestowal of
its contents if you come too near him.   Mephitis mephitica is the
zoological name for the other striped one that may be seen very
early in the morning, and very late in the evening in summer at
the edge of the clearing nearest the bush ; as for his common or
vulgar name I decline giving it, it is so very vulgar.   I don't
mind saying " Chipmunk," but when it comes to dropping the
" Chip," and substituting " sk," for the " m," why, I really can't
do it.   In the observations I have to make concerning the
gentleman, we will call him, if you please, Mephitis, or for the
sake of brevity, Meph.
     I never had the pleasure of a tiger's acquaintance, and thus,
not knowing him intimately, can only judge from hearsay, but I am
led to believe that he is a great deal more honest and truthful an

animal than Meph. A tiger does not take you in with false
pretences; when you see him, you want to run away from him. If
you can't run away from him fast enough, and consequently get
caught and eaten, that is not the tiger's fault; it is your own. You
can run away from Meph fast enough, and he is equally willing to
accelerate his speed in a contrary direction, but here the villainous
deceit of the animal comes in, and brings strangers to him to grief.
He is to all appearance a very innocent gentleman, in a lovely fur
coat with beautiful black and white stripes, and such a tail ! It is
as long as his body, and so broad and bushy that he can cover
himself with it, and use it as an umbrella in case of a shower ; but
when he does put it up, the shower doesn't come from the clouds,
by any means. To those who do not know him by sad experience,
Meph seems so sweet and guileless that, instead of wanting to run
away from him, they want to catch and pet him. If you were
to come suddenly on a tiger in an Indian jungle, and were to
attempt to pet him, the chances are you would only do it once ; the
same remark may be made in the case of any one attempting to
interview Meph. They don't try it again. Not long after I came
to reside at Slab City, I was out walking one evening with a couple
of young ladies, the daughters of my host, when suddenly we
perceived a youthful scion of the house of Meph standing in the road
about thirty yards before us, and looking enquiringly in our direction.
There were two simultaneous feminine cries of admiration, " Oh !
what a dear little cat ! " and the couple started off enthusiastically
in chase, bent on capturing and fondling it. I followed more
soberly, not being at all aware of the true state of the case, and
making a mental memorandum that the Canadian cat was a totally
new species to me, as I had never before seen a black and white
striped one with a large bushy tail that it carried over its back.
" The dear little cat " gazed for a moment at the advancing ladies ;
ran a little way ; halted ; ran a little way again ; then made up
its mind to stand the consequences. The ladies came within a few
paces of it, and then—Well ! I can't exactly say what happened
then. I know they suddenly lost all interest in the cat, but I
don't know where the cat went to. In fact when I got close to

them, I had reason to believe that there had not been a cat there at all; only Meph.

Not that Meph is a bad fellow in his way if he is not put out : the trouble is that a very little thing puts him out, and then everybody about gets put out too. My bedroom at that time looked on a little narrow bit of garden separated from the high road that ran through the village by a low stone wall surmounted by an iron fencing; and during the summer time I used to have my windows open all night. Soon after the incident I have related, Meph, or one of Meph's brothers, sisters, or cousins, used to select that stone wall just underneath my open window as a favorable spot for astronomical studies, and come punctually to sit there every night about eleven o'clock. Cats would occasionally try the same place ; but they are not contemplative. When a cat gets on a fence or a roof, he always wants to sing. Meph does not. What he likes, is to be quiet and think. There can be no objection to that, and would not have been on my part if Meph had not been gifted with a singularly nervous temperament. He starts at the slightest noise, and becomes hysterical ; not noisily hysterical, you understand ; he is not obtrusive ; but what I might term a silent cry comes from him that is magnetic, and you sniff the air and say "Poor dear Meph! What a sensitive creature that is." At least, that's what you ought to say, if you have any Christian feeling in you ; that, however, is not what I said ; but, after about a week's nightly ministrations, I filled all my pockets with stones before I went to bed, and when Meph made his appearance I stoned him off the wall ; and ran down stairs and stoned him up the road to the turn; and up the turn to the old school house ; and from the old school house half way up the hill. Every now and then, he would stop and prepare to make a remark as soon as I got near enough, and then I would stop too, and lay in a fresh supply of ammunition. So I engaged him at long range and defeated him gloriously. "And he never came back any more."

It is not a general thing, however, that anybody having, either of malice prepense or involuntarily, a difference of opinion with Meph comes off so jubilantly as I did on the above occasion.

I have had several little disputes with him myself, and have had good reason to remember most of them, not altogether without a lingering feeling of regret. He never attempted to what I may call serenade me but once; his conduct, however, in after years was still more objectionable to me, and brought the Meph of that day to a lamentable, and I think very uncomfortable end in consequence. You see, Meph is cosmopolitan in his ideas: he does not confine himself to the bush where he was brought up, or to occasional visits to the clearings where he hunts frogs and young birds and such like small deer for his breakfast or supper, but he also comes into the barn yard by night, and breaks the eighth commandment. He is very fond of eggs, and also of chickens; but these latter are unattainable without serious trouble being raised by their mamma, and so Meph is reduced to taking them, like oysters, in the shell. If he can catch an old hen sitting on a dozen or fifteen eggs, he is sure of a good supper. He waits till it is very late, and the old lady is fast asleep, and then he "snuggles up to her," and gives her a little shove. She thinks it is another old hen, and makes a bit of room, not without a grumble, and a sleepy peck or two, and the mischief is done. After a few minutes, Meph insinuates his nose under the old lady, gets out the eggs and eats them; or rather, some of them; for, of course, such villainy cannot be expected to be altogether overlooked, and by and by Biddy wakes up to the perception of what is going on, and gives the alarm. I was sitting up late one night when one of these disturbances occurred, and rushing out to the hen-house, arrived just in time to see Meph's tail disappearing up a sort of covered burrow formed by some boxes and the wall. There was a long iron rod in the place and a hoe, and I pinned Meph to the wall with the one, and punched him in the ribs with the other, until I punched all the breath out of him. I was very nearly in the same condition, myself, by the time that I effected this, for the atmosphere in the shed might possibly have been eaten, but it was a deal too thick to be taken into the lungs. That night I had scarcely been back in my study five minutes, when all my household woke up and began to cough and sneeze as if they were laboring under a violent

attack of la grippe, and presently a voice from up stairs called out
"Philosopher! Philosopher! I'm sure Meph has got into the
kitchen. Don't you smell him?" "Meph, my dear," I replied,
"is, I regret to say, at this moment lying an unconsidered corpse
in the hen-house; 'none so poor as do him reverence,' and no
one to 'kiss him for his mother';" and then I explained.
"Well!" said the voice as soon as it had got through a fresh fit of
sneezing, "of all the old—wait! I'm going to throw you down
a complete change of everything, and you'll go out into the porch
this minute and put it on. Afterwards you may go and bury
what you've taken off, and don't you come back to the house for half
an hour." Heigh—ho! Long before I heard the last of that night's
work I was willing, nay ! anxious, to change places with poor dear
Meph. Still ! there were compensations : if you never get the fat
of this world without the lean, you also never get the lean without
a streak of fat. The hoe handle with which I punched Meph was
of great service to me for years after. I used to lay it for two or
three days at a time amongst my early cabbages, or tomatoes, or
wherever I though it was needed at the moment. The plants
used to think that there was a top dressing of guano just put on,
and the vigorous way in which they would grow astonished everybody who was not in the secret. "I really don't see how it is,"
they would say, "that your plants look so healthy and vigorous.
Your soil must be much better than mine." And then I used to
smile gently, and think tenderly of poor Meph.

Tamias Striatus is no relation of Meph, who belongs to the
weasel tribe, while Tammy belongs to the shade-tail, or squirrel
tribe. He is an energetic, busy little fellow, and I'm always glad
to see him, which is more than I can truthfully say of Meph. A
trifle peppery ; at times, I fancy, a little given to unnecessary fault-
finding, as your energetic fellows generally are, for I hear him
scolding away at a great rate sometimes, when there is really no
reason for it that I can discover. He generally looks as if he were
suffering from the malady known as "the mumps," or else an
excessively bad toothache, owing to his habit of packing away a
large quantity of eatables in pouches inside his cheeks. I have

known boys do the same sort of thing at oyster suppers, so-called, and bring home a vast amount of cakes and candies in their trouser's pockets in addition to what they had laid in by way of supper. Tammy's pockets are inside his cheeks, and very funny he looks when the buckwheat is ripe, and he has made a successful raid on it. Sometimes I see him when he has only got half through, and looks one-sided about the head, and then I am tempted to forget what's the matter, and shout out "Try a linseed poultice, Tammy." But this is very rarely the case; more often, he has got both sides of his head swollen almost to bursting.

He is a great friend of mine, and therefore I would not for a moment have you think him greedy. Tammy is simply doing what it is thought to be the duty of a man to do, that is laying up a sufficiency for his maintenance when he can't work any longer. He is carrying that buckwheat, or those nuts, or whatever else it may be, to a snug little burrow of his where he expects to pass the winter, and where he is laying up Christmas and New Year's dinners for himself and Mrs. Tammy. If I remember my Greek right, though it is so long since I learned it that it would be no wonder if I had forgotten it, he gets the first part of his learned name from this propensity, tamias signifying steward, or house provider; his second name being Latin, and signifying striped— "the striped house-provider," alias chipmunk. "*Si non e vero, e bene trovato*;" anyway, that's what he does; and very tantalizing it must be to carry home a lot of good things in your mouth, and have Bloomah take them out and store them in the pantry, telling you to look sharp and bring in another load before supper. But I suppose he takes the precaution to make a good square meal before he sets to serious business. I know I should in his place.

Robert of Lincoln.

ROBERT of Lincoln, called affectionately Bob-o' link, sometimes takes a look into the clearing—but that is because it is next door to a meadow patch where he has his summer residence, and where Mrs. Robert is hatching out and bringing up a progeny of Masters and Misses Lincoln. Mrs. Robert never favors us with the pleasure of her company ; she is too much engaged elsewhere, but Bob will occasionally tumble in upon us out of the skies as he is finishing some unusually rollicking song, and he always does it as if he had intended to light on the fence and finish his tune there, but had changed his mind all of a sudden because he was afraid Mrs. Robert might see him. He's a wild dissipated bird, is Bob, and whether he belongs to the family of Larks, as I am told he does, or not, he's always up to larks, and ought to be ashamed of himself. He never is. He does not care for public opinion in the least, and is as supremely indifferent as to what his audience may think as any prima donna. In fact, he is very like a prima donna in some respects : he will stop in the middle of his song, and pretend he is not well ; and when he does sing you can only hear the notes, and can make nothing of the words, though I once knew a man who said he could, and on being pressed to state them produced the following : gorgaly worgaly ; swiggle-waggle ; wiggle-waggle, wiggle-waggle ; splitter-splatter, splutter-splitter ; zip, zip ; chee, chee, chee ; sloom, sloom ! " But you can't make any sense out of that. This is what Steele says : " The grotesque, though charming song of the Bobolink is a curious medley of jingling, incomprehensible notes, uttered with a volubility and earnestness that borders on the ludicrous ; but when the listener is just beginning to be enraptured, the music ceases as suddenly as if an organ bellows had burst." It is just at these times that he comes tumbling down amongst us on our side of the fence, and after looking round to see that none of us are watching him, makes a little run under it, and so, under cover of the grass gets quietly home, and persuades Mrs. Robert that he had only gone a little way off because he thought he saw a nice juicy caterpillar that he was sure she would like.

For Robert and his wife, when they come to Canada, confine themselves almost entirely, if not quite, to an insect diet; which is probably the reason why they have such good times, and are heartily welcomed, instead of being molested. "Way down south in Dixie," they have a different reputation, and a different name, being termed the Rice-eaters, or rice birds, because there they give up animal food, and take to grain, becoming the pests of the wheat fields in spring, and the rice plantations in autumn. Partly on account of their misdoings, and partly because in consequence, they become as fat as butter, and a very great delicacy for the table, they lead very precarious lives, and come to the conclusion that the United States is a very unfit place to bring young people up in, so they migrate to Canada for that purpose, and instantly become moral, and cease to break the eighth commandment. I suppose that there must be something in the air of the Dominion that conduces to moral and law abiding habits, and something in the air of the United States that has the very opposite effect; for it is a curious fact that however blameless a life Robert has led during his summer vacation, directly he begins to go south on the approach of cold weather, he suffers a relapse into bad habits, and by the time he gets as far as Pennsylvania is an utterly reprobate and abandoned marauder, who gets lynched accordingly.

"It takes all sorts of people to make up the world," says the old saw, and one of the sorts is an animal that goes by the name of vegetarian. His principal doctrine is that flesh, if not injurious to the human body is, at any rate, not necessary to its proper maintenance. I know papers that furnish medical advice to their subscribers, gratis; a very proper proceeding, considering the nature of the advice, which mainly consist in an injunction to refrain from meat, and adhere strictly to a vegetable and farinaceous diet. The prescription is like a patent medicine, and applicable to all cases.

If you are suffering from Canadian cholera, eat porridge and abstain
from meat; if you are just the reverse, abstain from meat and eat
porridge : if you are dyspeptic, a steady adherence to an oatmeal
diet, and as steady an avoidance of flesh will set you all right,
especially if you swallow a tumbler full of boiling water before
meals; if your appetite is abnormally ravenous, you can cure
yourself by steadily avoiding flesh, and adhering to a farinaceous
diet, and the cure will be more rapid if you preface each meal by
taking a good drink from the spout of a boiling kettle. There is
no evil under the sun that cannot be cured in this way, except,
perhaps that which is caused by the guillotine, and that is only
irremediable because, when the head is cut off, there is no possibility
of eating porridge and cornstarch.

"What has all this got to do with the Bob-o' link ? " Wait a
bit, and I'll tell you. Vegetarianism is frequently defended on
the ground that it was universally practised by man before the
deluge, when the average time of human life was much longer than
it is now, and that the permission to eat flesh, which was given
after that event, marked the commencement of an earlier mortality,
and the ultimate fixing of the span of the average man's existence
at seventy years. Hence it is argued that if man had stuck to his
potatoes and porridge, and eschewed canvas-backed ducks and
oysters on the half shell, he would still be only just approaching
maturity after he had numbered five centuries, and would have
been a baby when he was a hundred years old, and going to school
when he was two hundred. If you come to look into the matter
closely, the prospect of spending a hundred years in the cradle at
home, and in the perambulator abroad, is not an alluring one, and
the further prospect of a couple of hundred years more at school is
perfectly maddening; but I suppose we should become accustomed
to it in time; and I may concede at once that a strictly vegetable
diet is shown to have been eminently conducive to longevity. It
does not follow that it is desirable. However good an influence it
may have on the body, it has a very bad one on the morals, and I
have only to adduce as a proof of this the fact that the world which

14

was drowned for its excessive wickedness was a vegetarian, and not a carnivorous world. You asked me just now what Robert of Lincoln had to do with all this, and I am ready to answer you. He is a living corroboration of what I have just said. When he eats wheat and rice, for of course he can't get porridge and starch, he becomes greedy and a thief; he is trapped, and shot, and eaten himself: when he comes to Canada and devours insects, he is a respectable householder, and the father of a family. You may depend upon it that one of the main essentials of a virtuous life is a good supply of beef-steak, and legs of mutton; and one of the greatest provocatives to a vicious one is the want of them. The principle is one that is acted upon by government, perhaps unconsciously; it feeds its criminal classes, when it catches them, on the food most congenial to them; bread and water gruel; but it nourishes its Jack Tars on salt beef and pork: even the ship biscuits, I am told, are often full of weevils.

"Robert of Lincoln," says Bryant in his charming little poem on our friend,

> " Robert of Lincoln is gaily drest,
> 　　Wearing a bright black wedding coat ;
> White are his shoulders and white his crest,
> 　　Hear him call in his merry note.
> .. ..
> Robert of Lincoln's Quaker wife,
> 　　Pretty and quiet, with plain brown wings,
> Passing at home a patient life,
> 　　Broods in the grass while her husband sings."

I never could get a very distinct idea of Bob's dress myself, though I once brought up a whole family of young Lincolns, but I have no doubt Bryant accurately describes it. The contrast between him and his wife, Mrs. Bob, is very striking, and is common to a great many birds, and insects, the male being by far the most brilliant and ornate. In birds the distinction has been accounted for by the protection afforded by her quieter colours to the female when brooding on her nest, but I have some doubts as to whether this be really the reason, for it must be remembered that the male bird has to do his share of the sitting as well as the female—Mrs. Bird takes good care of that. She provides the capital for the firm in the shape of eggs, but the husband has to help in the carrying on of the business, as well as in the construction and furnishing of the store. The lady allows no shirking, and that is why Master Bob, when he has been a little more riotous than usual, and has stayed out singing " We won't go home till morning " till he has exceeded his time, cuts his song short abruptly, and drops down on our side of the fence, intending to sneak home through the grass quietly. I once had a little canary who came to me one day as I was sitting on the verandah sand-papering a wooden paper knife, perched on the knife, and said in what appears to be the universal bird language, " cheep." I called to my wife, and she brought out a large breeding cage which a morning or two before had contained a couple of birds, but which contained them no longer, thanks to our cat. This she set on the floor of the verandah, and sprinkled a few seeds at the bottom of it, " Dot," as I afterwards called him, watching her very closely from the blade of the knife which I was holding all the time, and when she withdrew, flying down and taking possession of it at once. I never could find his owner, though I made enquiries all through the village; but he had evidently been a great pet, and as such he had generally the run of the sitting room, his cage being regarded by him merely in the light of a bedroom. He breakfasted, dined, and supped with us, sampling the loaf and cakes, and making occasional raids on the sugar bowl, but his great delight was to get on the top of an old fashioned rocking chair in which I used to sit, and sidle along from one end to the other to get a hempseed from between my finger and thumb. I provided him with a wife, and in due time a snug little nest was built in Dot's bedroom, five little eggs were laid, and Dot and Dorothy settled down to the serious business of life. Dot, however, soon found the proceeding monotonous, not to say stupid, and he never wanted to come back and take his turn at sitting. The programme that followed was very amusing. When Dot's time came, Dorothy would call to him from the nest, and instead

of answering like a good little bird, he would fly down on the floor,
and make for the door of an adjoining bedroom. Then Dorothy
would call again; this time, more emphatically; and Dot, having
got behind the door, would answer faintly, as if he were a long
way off. Finally Dorothy would leave her nest to hunt up the
delinquent, and when she found him, would try and drive him up
to his duty, scolding vigorously all the while. It took quite a
little time to do this, for, as I knew by my own experience, it was
very hard to make Dot go where he didn't want to go, but when
she succeeded, Dot went to stay, and don't you forget it. There
was no more coming off that nest for him till it was time to go to
bed: he would plead very earnestly for just a minute to stretch
his wings, but Dorothy was relentless, and never went near the
nest again till she went for the night. Poor Dot! I would give
him a hempseed now and then, when Dorothy wasn't looking,
which comforted him a little, and he would try to wink as if it was
all a joke—but it was a very mournful wink.

So, you see, I am able to say from my own personal observation that the gentleman has to take equal turns with the lady
during the day time in the business of hatching, and thus the
protection theory to account for the sober colours of the latter can
scarcely hold good. It is difficult to assign any reason that is
perfectly satisfactory: possibly the possession of song, and the
more brilliant plumage of the male are intended to mark the vast
superiority of that sex over the feminine one. There are a great
many truths dimly hinted at in the works of creation, and this is
one of them. Polly says that it is no such thing, and that the
true reason is that the masculine sex is so deficient in good
qualities that a little extraneous adornment is necessary to make
it at all tolerable. That is a new view of the case, and is well
worth careful consideration, without which I am not prepared
wholly to reject it. If the principle is true, and is to be held good
with the lower animals, it will also hold good with man, and will
explain why it is that brilliant apparel belongs, by common consent,
to the " Woman's Kingdom," and why it is that she does the most,
not only of the singing, but of the talking too.

Violets.

When beechen buds begin to swell
And woods the blue-bird's warble know.
The yellow violet's modest bell
Peeps from the last year's leaves below.

Of all her train, the hands of spring
First plant thee in the watery mould,
And I have seen thee blossoming
Beside the snow bank's edges cold.

IN "The wild flowers of Canada" published by the Montreal
Star, from which I take these lines, I find this assertion of
Bryant's criticized on the ground that the yellow violet "blossoms
in April in the South, but further northward in May, long after
the last 'snow bank' has disappeared." *C'est selon;* there are
violets in plenty, yellow, white, blue, and dog in the clearing, and
I have myself found the former, and, indeed, all of them in April,
and whilst there were plenty of patches of snow left. In fact, so
far as my experience goes, the violets are the earliest spring
flowers to blossom in the open; the dog-tooth, which is not a
violet at all by the way, but belongs to the lily family, is much
later, and somewhere about contemporaneous with the Mayflower. I think, however, that the difference between my own
experience and that of the critics of Mr. Bryant is easily explained,
and that while they are talking of the different flowers in question
as they put forth their buds on the outskirts of the bush where
they have been snugly blanketed all winter by the dead leaves, I
am talking of them as they make their appearance in the clearing
beneath the sheltering sides of fallen logs, or on the more or less
moss covered hillocks which mark the place of a decayed and
buried stump. In hunting up the earliest spring flowers I go to

the clearing for the violets, and to the outskirts of the bush for the Mayflower, and dog-tooth, and I generally find the first two or three days before the last begin to open out. Which of the three violets is first to be found depends a great deal on the season, and on the place where you look for them; they make their appearance about the same time, but I have a faint impression that the yellow violet generally comes first; at any rate, I recollect, having very good reason for doing so, that in 1858 I gathered a few yellow violets on the day before Easter Day, which in that year fell on April 4, and that these and a stray white one were the only flowers I could find.

However, that is "neither here nor there," as the old women say. I don't set up for an authority on botany, or anything else, and aim rather at a little, quiet, informal chat with my reader, than at scientific or any other discussions. "Then I had no business to contradict other people." Well! perhaps not; but if they don't mind it, as they probably won't, you need not trouble yourself about that. "Inscienti non fit injuria," those who do not read this book will not be offended; and this class embraces everybody deeply versed in scientific studies, botany among them. What you have to see, my son, is that in the remarks I have just been making I wished to impress upon you the fact that we have got all the three colours of violets in our clearing. If you did not understand that, you would not understand how I came to write about them: now that you do, it is a matter of perfect indifference whether there is any snow left when they begin to flower, or whether there is not; whether they can be found in April, or are undiscoverable till May. They are here, and that is quite enough.

I don't say this in a vain-glorious spirit: it is not so much to boast of as you may think, though the poets have glorified the violet, and affixed the epithet of "modest" to it. Next to the politician and newspaper man, who may be bracketed equal in the class-list of consummate humbugs, is the poet; (I do a little in that line myself, so I ought to know). "Modest" quotha! I have caught the blue violet absolutely winking out of the moss, or round the corner of an old root, hundreds of times, and no modest flower

does that. In fact it is not a flower at all, but simply the eye of
one of the old pagan divinities that haunted the woods, who got
himself into trouble on account of this very peculiarity of hiding,
and peeping out at you from unexpected places, making you jump
when you caught a glimpse of him. His name was Pan; and to
this day the violet, when it gets into the gardens and obtains a
floral normal school certificate of first-class education, is called the
pansy; Pan's eye, that is; and not a corruption of *pensee* as ·
sentimental lady botanists make out. But here is the truth, the
whole truth, and a great deal more than the truth, for you in verse,
being

THE LEGEND OF THE PANSY.

In olden times, as the poets sing,
When there dwelt a spirit in every thing,
    When every stick and stone
And every breeze, and every beam,
And every valley, and every stream,
    Had at least one soul of its own,

*
* *
*

A spirit there was that haunted the bowers,
(See Tennyson), hid in the leaves and the flowers,
    But his home was not merely there :
He dwelt wherever water ran,
Or breezes blew, and they called him Pan,
    For the rascal was everywhere.

*
* *
*

A strange and antic spirit was he,
Full of what we call diablerie,
    And all sorts of quips and quirks ;
With a leering face and a shaggy coat,
And legs like the hinder legs of a goat,
    And beard as long as a Turk's,

But the strangest thing was his eyes.   Their hue
Was the sweetest tenderest violet-blue,
    Full of deep thought, and weird.
Who ever saw them, his pulses stirred
Like the passionate heart of a handled bird,
    Loving, although it feared.

       * *
        *

The laborer, wending his homeward way
Through the scented fields at the close of day
    Would start with a sudden fear,
Silence his whistling, and turn to fly
With Parthian glances he knew not why,
    But was sure that Pan was near.

       * *
        *

And the youth that, deep in some forest glade,
Wooed with soft whispers some half-coy maid,
    Would drown her shriek with his shout
As they saw a stealthy tremor and beat
In the velvet mosses beneath their feet,
    And the eye of Pan peep out.

       * *
        *

Nay, more ! when the battle was all but won,
The victors themselves would turn and run
    As fast as the vanquished ran,
Seized with a sudden and vague alarm,
For sheltered beneath some dead man's arm
    Were the violet eyes of Pan.

       * *
        *

But the children, hunting the flowers that hide
In sunny nooks by the burnie's side,
    Would utter a joyous cry,
And rush to secure the elusive prize
With tremulous hands and rounded eyes,
    Whenever the rogue was nigh.

Till one day, Jove, who had set out to court
In a manner no decent immortal ought,
　　Stopped short in his naughty ways,
For there, (it gave even him a shock),
He spied, half-hidden behind a rock,
　　That mischievous, twinkling gaze.

* *
*

He shook for a second or two—no more—
Then, vexed at his terror, Jupiter swore
　　As only that heathen can,
And the twinkling suddenly changed to a stare,
For the angry god had fixed it there,
　　The beautiful eye of Pan.

* *
*

Alas, poor Pan ! Has not Milton said
That a voice cried out "great Pan is dead " ?
　　As indeed he was from that hour,
When the catcher of others himself got caught,
And naught was left of the wood-god—naught
　　But his eye in a woodland flower.

* *
*

But the pansy knoweth the name it bore
In the good old-fashioned ages no more,
　　And, in our elegant way,
The flower that typifies hidden thought,
And sudden fancies that come unsought,
　　We have re-baptized " pensée."

* *
*

I cling to the old name. Methinks I see
In the uncouth heathen fantasy
　　A meaning more deep and rare ;
A hint of Love with his searching eyes
Love, masking itself under many a guise,
　　The Pan that is everywhere ;

The mischievous Love with his groundless fears ;
The frolicsome Love with his quips and jeers,
　　The torment of man and maid ;
Love staying the blow of the upraised arm ;
Love, of whose witchery and charm.
　　The children are never afraid.

*_**

Then, turning my eyes to the heavens above,
I think of the Everything, truest Love,
　　That came upon Earth to die ;
I think of His tender humility,
And the violet carries my fancies free
　　Beyond the violet sky.

"I'd be a Butterfly."

BEING a dry sunny spot, the clearing, at the proper season of the year, abounds in butterflies. The cabbage and tortoise-shell pay us visits from the grass fields and ploughed lands at one end, and the swallow-tail, emperor, and other larger and more gorgeous butterflies drop in at the other when they are tired of sailing about the branches of the overhanging maples. These are our visitors; summer-girls of the butterfly world that come from the aristocratic mansions of the forest, and common tramps from the cultivated lands; but besides these we have butterflies of our own, and quite as pretty as any that come to see us. There is one before me just now; a multitudinous butterfly, if I may be allowed to call him so; a jolly little yellow fellow who is immensely social, and is never seen alone if he can help it. Directly one settles down he is joined by another, and then by a third, until finally there is collected a whole congregation, which resembles a human one in this that it seems to settle itself down to a quiet sleep. I should not be at all surprised to learn that this was really a butterfly church meeting, and that one of them was preaching a sermon, though, of course, I can't hear what he says, and can only guess that he occasionally grows emphatic by seeing a pair of yellow wings lazily opening and closing, here and there, as if their owners were just half awake. Bye and bye, the address will be finished, and then the whole assembly will rise, not to disperse and go about the several business of the individual members, but to settle down somewhere else in a comfortable nook, and enjoy another sermon and sleep. My little friends do not, however, always affect dry places, and dry discourses; sometimes I come upon them gathered together on the sand which the brook heaped up when it *was* a brook, that is to say, when the melting snows of the spring furnished it with a supply of water, and which is even now damp, as if it were perspiring. Here, they are much more lively and restless; the wing quiverings are more frequent and general; the stay is shorter in one sense, and longer in another, for though the meeting rises, it settles down again immediately in almost the same spot, like a committee of the Legislature reporting progress and asking leave to sit again.

There was a song, very popular in my youthful days, and, perhaps, not quite forgotten even now, which expressed a desire for the lot of a butterfly, not, apparently, because it was, or seemed to be, a joyous life, free from all care and anxiety, but because it ended abruptly.

> " I'd be a butterfly, born in a bower, ..
> What though you tell me each gay little rover
> Fades as the leaves that in autumn decay ?
> Better, far better, when summer is over,
> To die when all fair things are fading away.

Well! I don't know about being "born in a bower." Some butterflies are, no doubt, but the general lot falls almost anywhere else; wherever, in fact the caterpillar has been taken suddenly ill, and strung himself up just in time to await his "transmogrification." But, granting the bower, I don't see, myself, what particular advantage there is being "born" in one, and I should decidedly object to the manner of the "birth." How would you like to be packed in a tight-fitting oilskin case with your arms close to your sides, hung up by a stout rope, head downwards, and left to kick and struggle till you burst open your covering and were able to crawl out at where your shoulders had been ? If a butterfly seems to have an easy time after he is "born," he deserves it, for he had a mighty hard time of it before. As a matter of fact, no butterfly ever is born, he is simply an evolved caterpillar. The latter is born, but not the former.

We have most of us heard, though it is probable that com- paratively few of us know, the old pagan legend of Cupid and Psyche. The English of Psyche is "the soul," and her emblem was the butterfly. If the old girls, (I mean the young girls of the old time), were as gorgeous as those of the present generation, and as volatile and hard to catch, one can easily see why the ancients should represent Psyche, considered as a mere woman, by a butterfly : there may have been, also, some hazy idea of a connection between the two from the habit of entomologists of sticking pins into butterflies, and the habit of women of sticking them all over themselves ; one which has considerably startled ingenuous young men before now when the pins happened to be in the region of the waist ; but it is not so easy at first sight to perceive the propriety of emblematizing the human soul by so fragile a thing as a butterfly, however lovely it may be. I sometimes wonder if the fancy was not an inspiration, for if it be true, as I have somewhere read, that the perfect butterfly exists in the body of the caterpillar from which it springs, no more fitting emblem of the soul could well be imagined ; the larva itself representing the body concealing the soul within, which passes through the death like trance of the chrysalis into its final and perfect state. Hence, as I said just now, there is no birth of a butterfly ; it is a resurrection.

"Fanciful!" Perhaps so : and yet the world gets a great deal more out of pure fancies than we are willing to believe, and "castles in the air" have their own particular usefulness, if we only know how to set about extracting it; whether we know, or not, in fact. After all, it is not worth debating much about whether a butterfly is "born in a bower," or resurrected on the inside of a cabbage leaf. Speculations concerning the place and manner of the nativity of a butterfly are, like other speculations, very interesting, even if of doubtful profit, but the solid fact of its existence is independent of all these. You recollect the story of Dan Murphy, and the widow Mulrooney's pig? Perhaps you never heard it though. Dan had confided to the priest under the seal of confession that the disappearance of the widow's pig which she was lamenting was due to his ardent attachment to that animal, which was by this time converted by him into hams and flitches of bacon, and the reverend gentleman was in vain exhorting

him to make restitution. "What will ye do, Dan," he enquired
"when the widow and the pig rise up against ye in judgment, and
ye're asked, 'Dan Murphy! where's the widow Mulrooney's pig?'
What will ye say, Dan?" The culprit was rather taken aback at
the prospect thus held out, and moved uneasily from one foot to
the other, till a happy thought struck him. "Did yer riverence
say that the pig would be there, too?" he enquired. "Yes, Dan!"
was the answer, "the pig will be there to bear witness against you
unless you make restitution." "Thin, yer riverence, I'll say,
'Widdy Mulrooney, there's yer pig!'" Whenever, and wherever
it was born, there's the butterfly.

> " Better, far better, when summer is over,
>   To die when all fair things are fading away."

Well, now! I don't hold to that philosophy; I don't believe that
it is better for man, woman, or child, to have all the good things of
this life, and none of its evils, than to take the fat with the lean,
and to have the inner peace that comes from the patient endurance
of pains and griefs nobly and courageously borne with. It is a
selfish thought, and a coward's shirking of the common lot of man:
a distempered view of life which often leads to the madness of
suicide. For to most of us who live long enough there come times
when to our thinking all fair things are fading away, and there is
no longer joy, or prospect of joy, in life. What then? Are we
to hold that, when these occasions come to us, it would be better
for us to die, and have done with it, as the prophet Jonah held,
when the gourd had withered and there was no shelter for him
from the glare of the sun and the buffeting of the east wind? I
trow not: for after the storm came the calm, and clear shining
after rain: other fair things blossomed out to take the place of
those that had faded away; other interests rose from the graves of
the dead ones.

And yet, as a matter of fact, we do, all of us, die when all
fair things are fading away, or, to put it more clearly and accurately,

the fair things of life, be they few or many, gorgeous or humble, continue with us until its end. The pleasures of childhood vanish as youth comes on; the dreams of youth give place to the aspirations of manhood; and these in turn are merged in the quietude and rest of old age. And as there is no season of life that has not its own distinctive enjoyments, so there is no life so utterly desolate and miserable from which no sort of happiness can be extracted; not even that of the scantily clad little waifs that appease their hunger from the garbage picked out of the gutters of city streets, or of the pallid seamstress toiling over shirts at twenty-five cents a dozen. There are lives dreary and desolate enough, Heaven knows; and Heaven forgive us whose selfishness and thoughtlessness helps to make them so; but there is none of unadulterated misery and despair. The gold-seeker washes bucket after bucket of sand, content if he finds in each after his hard toil only a few grains of the precious metal. His is the true philosophy of life that disregards the great mass of worthless matter for the little good that it holds concealed in it. We should all of us be much happier and better if we would only persistently look out for the good in the persons and things around us, and in the various happenings that befall ourselves. I don't mean to say that we should ignore the evil, the pain, the sorrow, or the loss: there is not much danger of that; but that we should not dwell upon them. It is a hard thing to do, but it may be done, if we will only try earnestly enough, and the results will be well worth all the trouble taken.

Now, if I were disposed to be fault finding, I should say that the butterfly, regarded from a feminine point of view, was a decidedly objectionable insect. It looks pretty enough, I grant, but it must be very dirty. You never saw a butterfly washing itself, and I don't believe it ever does. Flies do: they spit on their feet and then rub it all over their backs. It's not what you might call a refined kind of washing, but it is the best they can do, and they ought to be respected for it, just as his constituents respect a member of the Legislature for making a long speech about nothing. But a butterfly does not even spit on its feet, and when you consider that the colors on its wings that come off on your hands when you catch it are really a mass of fine feathers, and further reflect on the amount of dust that the insect flies through in the course of even one day, you will easily see that it must be very dirty indeed. I will venture to say, however, that nobody entertains the conception of a dirty butterfly; any more than a society belle with paint and powder on her face is usually regarded as a very dirty girl. And it is as well that it should be so in both cases, otherwise what pleasure should we take, as we undoubtedly do, in looking at either. If we were pinned down to the solid facts, we should have to confess that they were both dirty things; but what of that? They are pretty: and in admiring them, to the extent of wanting to catch them and have them for our "ownest own," we are acting on the principle that I have been trying to impress upon you of always looking at the bright side of things.

Wanted,--A Donkey.

EXCUSE me! I know exactly what you are going to say, so you needn't put yourself to any trouble. You are about to remark that you don't see what particular need there is of a donkey in the clearing since I am there myself. It is the old tale of the unphilosophic mind, hasty as usual, and jumping rashly at conclusions because it either will not, or cannot, view things in more than one, or at the most two lights. There are donkeys,— and donkeys : the intelligent ass like myself, and the stupid ass like—well! somebody you and I know. Then there is the two-legged ass, and the four-legged ass ; and it is one of these latter that is wanted in the clearing ; so long as you and I are in it, it is well supplied with the two-legged ones, as you very kindly prepared to observe before I anticipated you. But the asinine biped cannot eat thistles, and the quadruped can ; so as, I am sorry to say, there are several of these prickly children of Nature in the clearing, and about half-a-dozen of them in unpleasant proximity to my stump, I want an ass to eat them up. I can't do it ; and you can't ; the only resource is to endeavour to get somebody or something that can.

I have a great respect for a thistle, whether it be the common or Canada one ; the Scotch variety I do not remember to have seen in a wild state in Canada, though I have two or three times met with them in gardens, where they were much petted, and regarded as sacred plants. Needless to say that the owners of the said gardens were Scotch either by virtue of birth, or virtue of descent. Sentiment plays curious tricks sometimes. Had these gentlemen been in Scotland and found thistles growing in their gardens there, they would have called them nasty weeds, and have taken prompt measures to get rid of them, but, being in Canada,

15

nothing is too good for these same thistles, and they are shown to the visitor with a pride scarcely inferior to that with which a young mother shows her first born baby. I think we, who seem to need all our energies and all our thoughts for the present in this ever increasing struggle of life, who can barely find time to give even a few hours of the week to the momentous issues of the future, have but little idea of how much we unconsciously live in the past; not the past of our lives, but in that of those who preceded us, so that we are in very truth "heir of all the ages." The thistle represents to the Scotchman the long and brilliant roll of warriors and statesmen, sages and poets, the equals of any that the world can show, and the less showy, though not less noble, examples of that national characteristic which placed Duty and Honour at the head of all earthly things, and which clave to it amid the storms of persecution, the presence of poverty, and the loneliness of adventure in foreign lands. All this is his heritage from his forefathers, and the thistle is the sign of it. It is not the most imposing, or the most valuable things of the world that touch the deepest chords in our heart, or even can touch them: it is the unconsidered trifles of life; a bit of ribbon, or a strand of hair, more than a bracelet or a diamond ring; the tone of a chance word, or the glance of an eye, that are more tenderly remembered afterwards than greater and more practical testimonies of good will. These may win gratitude; the former win love.

Not being a Scotchman myself, the Scotch thistle does not affect me; and besides, as I said, I very seldom see one. It is the English, or common thistle that I have the most veneration for, and this sentiment was instilled into me by my father when I was a boy. He didn't waste any words about it either, but did it in that English practical way which is very effective, but peculiarly irritating to those who are exposed to it against their will. He armed me with a long pole at the end of which was fixed a sort of broad sharp chisel some two inches wide, and sent me out into a field which was over run with the beasts to stub thistles in the summer holidays, when I had other views of amusement. My instructions were to drive my stabbing spear into the earth at the root of each individual thistle in that field, cut it off underground, and then pull it up and throw it away : and I was also informed, as an inducement to thoroughness on my part, that if I omitted any they would be sure to seed, and the work would all have to be done over again next summer vacation. I believe my respected parent quite endorsed the maxim that

" Satan finds some mischief still
For idle hands to do, '

and was resolved to get ahead of Satan so far as I was concerned by keeping me fully employed when I came home for the holidays; considering that I had quite enough to do at school to keep me out of mischief, and was only in danger of falling when under the parental roof-tree. Between the two of them, my father and headmaster, I had as much trouble to go wrong as most boys have to go right, which was very depressing to the spirits, and stubbing thistles in a hot July sun, when I wanted to go riding or fishing, was not calculated to elevate them. But this was not the worst of it. Unenticing as the occupation of thistle-stubbing might be, there was at any rate the satisfaction of taking vengeance on the unconscious authors of my discomfort, but when it came to laying hold of the tops and pulling them up, the vengeance was transferred to the other side of the account, and I pricked my fingers dreadfully. They tingle even now at the remembrance, and I have ever since retained the highest respect for a thistle and give it as wide a berth as I conveniently can. It would have been well for me had I been philosopher enough then to have seen and profited by the lesson that was there ready to be learned. The rooting up of thistles is a necessary operation, whether they grow in the ground or in the heart, and it is also a painful one ; but it is better than letting them grow up and run to seed. If that is done, the field, whether it be a literal or a metaphorical one, is a pasturage only fit for asses.

Since I had such experience in managing English thistles,

perhaps you wonder why I do not avail myself of it at present, instead of wanting to call in the assistance of a quadrupedal donkey. The reason is that the Canada thistle is an utterly irrepressible bit of vegetation, and like the Canadian lord of the soil, obstinately refuses to give in. Nothing short of subsoil ploughing for five square yards around him will have any effect on a Canadian thistle, and even then, if you don't pick him out of the ground and burn him, the chances are a hundred to one that you have only succeeded in subdividing him into numberless other thistles. "Roots extensively creeping" is the description given of him in botanical treatises, and you can't stub him up as you would an innocent English one. Now, a donkey will nibble him off just as fast as he grows up, and it becomes simply a trial of which will get tired first; the donkey of eating, or the thistle of growing. I'll back the quadruped against the vegetable every time. There are a great many uses to which a donkey may be put, and thistle-eating is one of them.

Strictly speaking, a donkey is not a donkey at all. I fancy that we should all of us be very much astonished to find out how many things there are in this world that are "not at all what they are cracked up to be," when we come to examine into them closely. Even a ghost, which in virtue of its belonging to another world might be supposed to be exempt from the rules which govern material objects in this one, always turns out to be something else when it is investigated. You recollect the story of the countryman returning home late one night from the village tavern and astounding his wife with the declaration that, as he had passed by the church-yard, he had been frightened nearly to death by seeing a ghost in it. "What was the ghost like, John?" she enquired. "It was like a great big ass," he replied. "Get thee to bed, thou fool!" was the disappointed commentary; "it was only thy own shadow thou saw'st." There was a great general principle at the bottom of the remark, and ghosts are not the only things which are simply the shadows of our own imaginations. It is this that makes actual life one continued series of disappointments, in which we are perpetually clutching after objects that when attained do not yield us the pleasure and satisfaction that we anticipated from them. Wealth, honors, powers, luxury and ease, on the possession of which we have set our hearts, and for which we have toiled so earnestly and painfully, and have sacrificed so much, what are they when gained, but incentives to fresh desires and fresh struggles, or apples of Sodom whose taste is bitter, and whose contents, dust? " I might be expected to say this," you think, and imagine that it is the part of a philosophical mind to despise and belittle " the pomps and vanities " as the catechism has it, "of this wicked world." No! it is no true philosophy that despises, or affects to despise, anything; no true philosophy that refuses to recognize the good that is in everything created or ordained, even though it be latent, and hid in a superincumbent mass of evil. All these things that I have mentioned are good things in themselves, but they fail to satisfy us because we have not pictured them to ourselves as what they really are, but as something different which we expect them to be; they are not ghosts, but the shadows of ourselves.

The donkey is, strictly speaking, not a donkey at all; he is a horse : "equus asinus;" an ass of a horse. I should not at all wonder if he were an evolution of a balky horse, for a more perfect ass than such a quadruped it is difficult to conceive. Did you ever happen to be driving one with a deep ditch on either side of the road? And did you ever find him take advantage of the situation to balk and refuse to proceed? If you did, you will know that any application of the whip results in the backing of the waggon towards the nearest ditch; and if you get out and try to lead the brute along, the only change in the situation is that the probabilities are that, if you persist, you will go into the ditch on the top of the horse, instead of having him fall on the top of you. Lucky for you, if this takes place on a by-road where there is not much danger of interruption, and you can possess your soul in patience, seated in the waggon till such time as it pleases your gallant steed to move on. In the meanwhile you can relieve your feelings by calling him an ass, with as many opprobrious adjectives tacked on to the noun as you can recollect, and your conscience will allow you to use ; but you need not make any mistake about the real thing.   It is not the horse that is an ass, but yourself.   At any rate, that was the conclusion I came to when I got served as I have just described.   After I had succeeded in getting half the circumference of the hind wheels over the brink of the ditch, I concluded that discretion was the better part of valour, and, desisting from any further efforts, contented myself with thinking disrespectful things of my enemy for fully ten minutes.   At the expiration of that time I remarked aloud, " Philosopher! you look like a confounded ass."   The horse turned his head, nodded, sneezed, and went on.   It was as if he had said " I thought you would see things in their proper light, if you only had time to consider the matter."

The Drum-Major.

RAP-RAP! Rap, rap, rap! Rap! The sound breaks with a startling effect upon the ear in the clearing, when a grasshopper or two are the only living things *en evidence*, and the air is full of the drowsy droning of unseen insects in the grass. In the woods you know you may expect to hear it any minute, but in the clearing it is a different thing, and makes you give a little half-jump when you first hear it. However, it proceeds from a very innocent source, our drum-major, called by country folks the sap-sucker, and mentioned by poets as

" The woodpecker tapping the hollow elm-tree."

There are no elm-trees, hollow or otherwise for him to tap here, but he is an accommodating bird, and doesn't turn up his beak because we are not quite up to his requirements in high art. For want of a tree he will take a stump—that is, provided there are plenty of grubs in it—just as a country constituency will take anybody that comes along for its representative, doctor, lawyer, merchant, even an old resident farmer who has to get his campaign speeches written out for him that he may learn them by heart, provided that he has plenty of money to spend on his election. The constituents regard the candidates much as the woodpecker looks on trees and stumps, the grubbier they are, the better. And, indeed, this is a weakness that we all have in more matters than politics : we value persons and things, not so much for what they have in them, but for what we ourselves can get out of them. I have taken politics as an illustration of the reason why the woodpecker will sometimes desert the trees of the forest for the stumps of the clearing, because the principle is, perhaps, more easily discerned here than in other matters, and because it explains why our Legislatures are, if anything, a little more stupid than other assemblages, and have got our laws into such a muddle that even the lawyers themselves don't understand them, and they require to be revised and codified afresh about as often as it is necessary to take a census. Given the candidate that the constituency believes, or is led to believe, that it can get most out of, and he will be returned though his name were Dogberry, and that of his opponent, Solomon.

The gentleman who so noisily announced his presence, previously unsuspected, a little while ago, is the commonest of all the woodpecker tribe, and the plainest, though he is really a handsome bird if you examine him closely. In the far corner of the clearing, where there is a bit of swampy ground, you will sometimes come across several of the golden-winged woodpeckers, larger, and more gorgeous, but these do not haunt the stumps at any time, and are seldom, if ever, met with beyond their little bit of marsh. They seem to me to be gregarious, whereas the drum-major only hunts in couples, and not always that. He is a bird with the bump of cautiousness strongly developed, and unless you come upon him suddenly, and he is so interested in his business as not to notice your approach for the moment, you won't get much chance of seeing him at work. But he is not what I should call a timid bird. If he flies off directly he perceives you, you may understand that it is because he has nearly finished where he is, and does not think that there is any prospect of advantage sufficient to make it worth his while to stay. This, indeed, is what generally takes place in the clearing, where there is but a limited field of operation on each stump, and where the stump itself has been exploited again and again, and the larvæ are few and far between. On the standing trees in the bush the case is different, and the only sign that he gives of his being aware of your presence is the extreme care with which he keeps the trunk of the tree between you and him. That done, the rap-rapping will go on as loudly and merrily as ever, till, all of a sudden, it will stop, and you think he has gone off to parts unknown. Then, in another minute or two, it will begin again, apparently in the same tree. During the interval, if you have been watching carefully, you would have seen a little head with a dab of red on it pop suddenly round the trunk, and a pair of little black eyes looking inquisitively at you. He had just stopped work to have a peep at you and see what you were doing, and having satisfied himself on that point, had resumed operations with fresh vigour. It is his way of "going out to see a man" between the acts ; and a very pretty and graceful little way it is.

So pretty and graceful that it is impossible to feel offended at what seems to imply a considerable distrust on his part of your peaceful intentions; and, indeed, I am sometimes in doubt whether to set his behaviour down to timidity, or to a certain shy playfulness which you may observe showing itself in much the same manner in young children, especially girls. I often think when I see my friend, the drum-major, doing this, that he is wanting to have a little game at hide and seek, but, having arrived at bird's estate, and being probably a householder, with a wife and family, he thinks it necessary to combine business with pleasure, and attend to the grub on hand, or, rather, in the tree, at the same time that he has a little fun with me. I dare say you have noticed a squirrel doing much the same sort of thing. I mean, keeping himself persistently out of view on the other side of the trunk of a tree, except when he occasionally runs round to have a squint at you. Now, whatever may be said of the woodpecker, this similar behaviour on the part of the squirrel cannot be fairly put down to the score of cautiousness. Skug, as we used to call him at school, is as bold as brass, and his moral cheek is as much developed as his physical tail. If he is disposed to regard you as an unprincipled and bloodthirsty villain, he will not stand upon any ceremony in giving you his candid opinion of you, and the only precaution he will take will be to get up on the highest branch, as far as possible out of the reach of stick or stone, and deliver his remarks from that coign of vantage. Afraid of you ? Not a bit of it ! In however bad a light he may regard you, he knows better than to be afraid of a great clumsy animal that can't climb trees and jump down from them at need.   So when, instead of sitting in high places and swearing at you, he condescends to keep quiet and peep round the tree at you, you may feel flattered, and consider that he thinks you are not such a bad sort after all, and a person whose acquaintance it might be worth cultivating.   At any rate, I like to fancy that it is so.   I like to trace in such little things as these, a faint vestige of the times when man and the brute creation were on friendly and confiding terms, and when no wanton and repeated slaughter on the one side had raised up an insuperable distrust on the other.   We call the animals that we have not subjugated to our uses, and domesticated "wild," for they have good reason to be so; and yet wherever we can persuade them that they have not anything to fear from us, nothing can be more graceful or more touching than the affectionate confidence they bestow on us.

That the drum-major has his failings, I must confess.   In the first place he has an awfully long tongue.   Where he puts it to when it is not in use, I can't make out: a butterfly keeps his coiled up in a sort of spiral, but I don't think the woodpecker does. He must draw it back into his stomach, or crop, or whatever he calls the receptacle for food inside him, and yet I should think that that was calculated to interfere materially with his digestion. Any way, he has a tongue as long as that of a village gossip, and he uses it much for the same purpose, to wit, to destroy helpless and unoffending creatures.   If he could talk with it, he would be an eligible candidate for membership in the association that meets nightly at the village store and post office, or at the teafights of the village matrons.   Also, his tongue is barbed, and when once he gets it into a victim any contortions and wrigglings that may be made might just as well be dispensed with at once for all the good they are; a proposition that holds good with the subject of gossip, whether it be in country and town.   So far there is a resemblance between the long-tongued feathered biped, and the long-tongued featherless ones, but here the resemblance ceases, and the difference begins, much to the advantage of the drum-major.

I don't mean in the matter of toes, of which he has only three, while his human confreres have five, which is a decided advantage when we consider what pain and trouble corns are ; I am referring to his character. For the drum-major is a candid bird ; he does not pretend that he impales the grubs and swallows them afterwards for any other reason than his own personal interest, and the gratification of his own personal appetite, whereas the gossip will maintain that he, or she, is actuated solely by a sense of duty, and a concern for the morals and respectability of society, and so far from deriving any enjoyment from it, is absolutely pained to say anything at all.

The Fences of the Clearing.

WHEN I say "the fences of the clearing," I speak advisedly. If it had been circular in shape it would, of course, have had only one; not being so, it has more. As a matter of fact, it has three, and may be geographically described as being bounded on the north by the bush; on the east, by the meadow; on the west, by the potato field, and on the south, where it comes to a point, by Nathan and Bloomah's lane. Thus it is hemmed in on three sides, and each of these has a distinctive fence of its own. That which separates it from the bush I have referred to before; it is a fraud and an imposture, a weariness to the soul of man and maid, and the laughing stock of cows and calves; the potato, (vice buckwheat) field is separated from the clearing by a low wall composed of all the stones picked up and ploughed up in it, and surmounted by old roots and dozy logs from the clearing itself, while that which guards the meadow from bovine incursions is commonly known as a snake fence. It is a similar one to that referred to by a gentleman in his eloquent and picturesque description of the misfortune that befell him while making the best of his way out of the reach of a bull that was philanthropically desirous of giving him a lift in the world. "The bull roared like thunder," said he afterwards, "and I ran like lightning; and getting over a zig-zag fence, I split my br—— pants, as if Heaven and Earth were coming together." I shouldn't wonder if he did. The zig-zag fence is composed of rails and trunks of young trees, generally hemlock or balsam, laid over one another at an oblique angle, and kept from separating and tumbling down by posts driven into the ground on each side at the apex of the angle; and when the top rail happens to be a young tree, on which there are left the projections of topped off branches, getting over requires more circumspection than a hurried flight will allow of. A young friend of mine once came to grief on this very clearing fence that I am talking about, owing to this peculiarity of it. He had been picking raspberries at the edge near the bush, and coming home had varied his occupation by chasing and stoning the cows, in which pursuit he was detected by Bloomah. She immediately assumed the offensive, and my young friend found it advisable to change his base, but unfortunately selected the wrong line of retreat, and instead of making for the gate, which he could easily have passed through, or the potato fence, over which he could have escaped without scathe, directed his forced march on the zig-zag, and scaled it with great celerity and success. On proceeding, however, to evacuate his conquest, his rear guard became involved with a sharp projecting splinter of the hemlock trunk which formed the fence's *tête du pont*, and overlooking this circumstance, or neglecting in his hurry to extricate his rear guard from its entanglement, it was pierced, and the whole *corps d'armée* was involuntarily compelled to pivot on it, in which condition it was surprised and captured by Bloomah, and got its ears well cuffed. It was very merciless on Bloomah's part, for the spectacle of a small boy suspended between Heaven and Earth by the seat of his trousers from a knot in the topmost rail of a snake fence might draw tears from the eyes of a potato, but the feminine heart is hard towards masculine urchins. When they get larger it is a different thing, and then the bigger and wilder scamps they are, the more soft and tender does the said heart grow to them. If it had been Nathan, now, that had been caught that way! But it's no use speculating on any such thing: the cloth is not woven that would have held Nathan up long enough.

The clearing fence is offensive and defensive. Its primary uses are to keep the cattle out, and also to keep them in; that is, out of the potatoes and hay grass, and in with the ferns, thistles and burdocks. Besides these, which are purely human devices, it serves as a means of rapid transit to the squirrels and chipmunks, and its posts at the re-entering and salient angles serve as pulpits to them from which to address the clearing population generally, and me in particular. In the matter of simple transit, the two little fellows have each their own method, and, as it were, social position. The squirrel, who represents the aristocracy by reason of his having his residence in a real live tree, takes the topmost rails to run along, while the more plebeian chipmunk who lives, at the very best, in the basement, but more generally in a hole at the foot of an old stump, runs along the lower ones, or, if he is of an aspiring disposition, will even get as high as the middle rail, but no higher. But this social distinction vanishes into thin air directly they catch a sight of me, who am only a member by sufferance of the clearing, and, apparently, a very objectionable one at that. At these times, Mr. Squirrel or Chipmunk, as the case may be, makes for the nearest upright post, and sitting on the very top of it will thence deliver an oration that for impassioned eloquence beats any fashionable clergyman that I ever heard, and far surpasses in fury and invective any member of the opposition, whether Liberal or Conservative. I should like to know what is said on these occasions; but no! on second thought I wouldn't: I can form a very tolerable idea, and as for the rest, " Where ignorance is bliss, 't is folly to be wise." " Don't stir up Camarina," said the heathen oracle in response to a certain enquiry. Camarina was not the name of the enquirer's wife, or his best girl, though you might very naturally think so, but of a certain fountain in Greece whose waters were phenomenally clear, and whose bottom was phenomenally muddy. The warning, or advice, is expressed in the old adage " Let well enough alone :" if you see one of those hornet's nests that look like coarse wrapping paper, don't poke your finger in the hole at the bottom to see if it is finished inside ; if anybody should offer you ten dollars for your Thomas cat just about the time that the elections are coming off, don't insist upon knowing the causes for the sudden rise in the market value of cats, and then you won't be called on to explain them to the judge in the subsequent contested election trial ; if your wife is more than usually attentive to your comfort, and more than usually affectionate, "take the good the gods provide you " in thankful silence, remembering that the spring fashions are just in, and content to keep the knowledge to yourself—if you can.

There are things that it is vitally necessary, and others that it is greatly desirable to know, but the number of these is limited, and beyond them the less a man knows the happier he is. That is the reason why I myself, and all philosophers, are happy men; we know very little more than the fact of our ignorance, and that knowledge is about as much as a man can conveniently carry: some men never attain to it all their lives, notwithstanding all the efforts of their friends and acquaintances to enable them to do so. If you do not absolutely know a thing you are entitled to imagine just what you please about it, and what you imagine is pretty certain to please you. Facts are hard things, and we break our heads and our hearts in coming into contact with them; castles in the air are rosy-colored and soft, too ethereal you think for any wise man to talk of living in them, and yet it is wonderful how great a proportion of our lives from the cradle to the grave is passed in them. Hope, Faith, Trust, Love, what are all these but castles in the air? No! don't think that I am decrying them. If castles in the air are found in the clouds, remember that the clouds are real, and no figment of the imagination any more than are the gorgeous hues of purple, crimson, and gold with which their snowy battlements are topped. However, I am wandering away from my subject, and shall act like a man and a philosopher; that is to say, I shall put into practice the very opposite to what I have been preaching. We all do that, and therefore, as my Camarina is just at this moment sitting on the post opposite me, and making a tremendous racket, I am going to disturb him by throwing a stone at him. He is off, and the vexed air is at peace again. Can you draw the lesson from that? There are times when Camarina ought to be disturbed; it depends upon how you do it, and for what reason.

Moreover, there is a lesson that Camarina herself—that is to say, in this instance, the squirrel who has been sitting on the topmost peak of the fence indulging in unwarrantable abuse of me,— that Camarina herself, I say, may learn; to wit, that fences were not made to sit on. It is only very small people that can do it with any ease to themselves, whether they take their seats with both legs on one side, or sit straddle-wise. You never see a cow sitting on a fence ; or a horse ; or even an ass; it is only small things like squirrels or birds. Similarly a boy, or a girl may assume that position, and I have even caught Nathan doing it, though not for any lengthened period. But Nathan has not yet come to years of discretion; he wants to marry Bloomah ; and Bloomah will sometimes sit on the fence, concerning whose discretion, the same thing may be said; she doesn't want to marry Nathan ; but wise people, like myself, do nothing of the sort ; we recognize that a fence is intended for a dividing line, and is therefore too narrow to afford a sufficient base to sit on comfortably. The position is also not a desirable one : it is just sufficiently elevated above the common to incite those on the ground to throw stones at its occupier, and it is not enough so to keep him out of danger from the missiles.

These remarks are applicable not merely to the small fry that seat themselves on the literal, but also to the people that pose in a similar manner on the metaphorical fence. There are plenty of them that do so, but the most frequent, and perhaps most easily observed case, is that of the politician, or newspaper editor. These are continually getting on the fence, and therefrom proclaiming their own independence and the servility of all the rest of the world. The rest of the world, very naturally, begins to throw stones at them till they get off again, and dump themselves down on one side or the other, according to which they find the most convenient. It is a very great mistake to suppose that the mere fact of sitting on a fence changes a man, or that he is a whit the more worthy of respect and confidence because his feet are, for the moment, unclogged by the blue marl of the Conservative turnip field, or the red clay of the Liberal brickyard : he is only debating whether turnips or bricks will prove the more profitable investment, and in the meantime he is the mark for clods from both fields until he comes down. Moreover, it is only the smaller, and more stupid members of either class that sit on the fence; the prominent and intelligent members have no need to do it : they are satisfied in their own minds as to the relative market values of

turnips and bricks, and, if they have anything to do with the fence
at all——they jump it.

I have taken my illustration out of the political world because
it is one that is open to everybody in this nineteenth century,
even the women being unable to keep out of it, but the principle
I am endeavoring to lay down holds good everywhere, and in every
state and condition of life, social, commercial, labouring, and moral.
The material fence represents the metaphorical one, the dividing
line between Honour and Dishonour, Right and Wrong, Life and
Death, and all other opposites. It is narrow, and a seat on it is
uncomfortable to the sitter; it is conspicuous, and exposes its
occupiers to attacks provoked by the prominence it gives; and since
it is these two, it is untenable. Where questions of principle are
involved there is no such thing as a middle way, there is only a
dividing line, which, if a man straddles, is not productive of
advantage to him. You recollect the tale of the old Scotchman
who put half-a-crown in the collection-plate instead of a penny,
and, instantly discovering his mistake, wished to rectify it. On
the collector refusing to allow this he solaced himself with "Weel!
weel! I'll get credit for it up abune, Jamie." "Na! na!" was the
reply, accompanied by an emphatic shake of the head; " Ye'll juist
get credit for the bawbee ye intended to gie."

16

The Creepers.

THERE'S a big red-vested bully of a robin has just got hold of an unwary worm by the head, and is trying to pull him over the door-step of his own house, and then "run him in" for vagrancy. The worm objects, as is very natural, and just at this present moment a "tug of war" is going on between the two, as to the issue, of which most men would back the robin. He has not got all the odds in his favor though: I expect Mrs. Worm is holding on tight to Mr. Worm's tail, so that it is two to one, in the first place ; and, in the second place, while Mrs. Worm can let go for a brief space to get a better grip on her husband, Mr. Robin can't do anything of the sort, for, if he did, the worm of contention would pop back into his hole like a flash of lightning. He is far better off, in this respect, than one of his big cousins whom I once saw acting as a vermicular championship medal between two water-newts who had seized him, one at each end. The "joint commission" plan worked very well at the commencement, as joint commissions generally do, but, also as joint commissions generally do, when the final settlement had to be reached, it didn't work at all. At first, all went well, for the worm, being held at both ends, couldn't wiggle and make his captors' jaws ache, so each proceeded to swallow his part down with the greatest equanimity, until suddenly, to the great surprise of both, a good hearty swallow apiece brought their noses into violent contact. It was a very embarrassing, not to say distressing, moment, and the more so because it never occurred to either of them to bite off what he had in his mouth and have done with it. In a physiological point of view, the situation was extremely interesting. We have most of us heard of two hearts beating as one, and have regarded the expression as a mere poetic metaphor, but here were two stomachs digesting as one, with a big lob-worm forming a bond of sympathy between them, and

converting their owners into reptilian Siamese Twins. I have
heard of somewhat similar instances occurring in which two
snakes have got hold of a squirrel, but in those the larger snake
arranged matters satisfactorily by swallowing the smaller one,
but here the newts were of about the same size, neither could
contain the other, so that solution of the difficulty was out of the
question. The only one that remained was for the larger one to pull
what had been swallowed by the other out of his stomach and
swallow it himself as he proceeded; haul it in, as it were, hand
over hand; and this was accordingly done. Mr. Robin hasn't got
this resource; he has only nipped his victim by the head, and all
he can do is to hop back a little bit every time Mr. and Mrs. Worm
"give"; if he opens his beak for a second the game is all up.
No! it's not, what you suppose, a mere question of time; at any
rate, in this case. Mrs. Worm has evidently got a strong pre-
emption claim, and I fancy that the matter will reduce itself to a
compromise. I thought so. The strain upon Mr. Worm has been
too great and he has gone pop in the middle. Mr. Robin would
fall head over heels if he did not very promptly back himself up
with his tail, and Mr. Worm has disappeared in his hole; minus
his head, it is true, but that makes no difference; he can easily
grow another, and in the meantime he won't be subject to headaches,
or dyspepsia, for he can't eat, or curtain lectures, for he can't hear
till he gets another head. There is always some good or other to
be got out of our misfortunes, even when they are as great as that
of losing our heads: and the next time you lose yours, my son,
which will be the next time you get into a rage, let the remembrance
of this help you to the speedier cooling down. You may take an
example, too, from Mr. Worm, who, you may be very certain,
when he had parted with his upper end did not go home and abuse
his wife, and make things unpleasant for his family, generally.
Come to think of it, he couldn't very well, there being nothing left
of him but his little tale of grief, but that need not detract from
the lesson I am giving you. You remember what the late Bill
Nye, (or was it Artemus Ward?) said about the Father of his
country, "George Washington couldn't tell a lie; I can—but

won't ?"   Very well ! Say to yourself " Mr. Worm couldn't make
a row with his family when things went wrong with him outside ;
I can, but wont." We are all poor worms of earth, why should
we be above learning from an earth-worm ?

So the fierce contest, which threatened to involve issues no
less important than those of life and death, has ended, as such
contests most frequently do, in a compromise : it is only in minor
differences that a complete surrender takes place on one side or
the other ; where important interests are at stake, and the strength
of the opposing parties is not too markedly unequal, the ultimate
result must be a compromise.   It is very necessary to see this
clearly, because it has an important bearing, not merely on our
own private disagreements, but also on the settlement of political
"live" questions, and of the too frequent fallings out between
Labour and Capital.   In trifling matters, a disputant, whether man,
party, or combination, will yield, provided the opposition be strong
enough, rather than incur trouble, annoyance, and expense ; but in
important matters there must either be a war of extinction or a
compromise.   This being the case, the sooner a compromise is
effected the better, and the aim at the beginning of a dispute should
be to make arrangements for its termination, and not for its
continuance.   It may be noted, also, that the sooner a compromise
is effected the more it is to the advantage of the weaker party : if
Mr. Worm had been willing to settle matters at once when Mr.
Robin seized him by the scruff of his neck the minute he put his
head out of the hole, he would only have been minus head and
shoulders ; as it was, he prolonged the argument until he was drawn
half way out and had to snap off at his waist, very nearly losing
his stomach into the bargain.   Doubtless, Mr. Worm felt very sore
on the subject when the thing was all over, and he had leisure to
reflect on it ; and doubtless, Mr. Robin did not feel as well filled as
he had calculated on being, but that is an essential of a compromise.
Neither party feels satisfied, and vents his discontent more or less
openly.   Unreasonable, perhaps, but natural.   It is not what he
has got, but what he hasn't got, that is of the most importance in
a man's eyes, although the actual value of the two may be really

reversed. It does not detract from the merits of a compromise to have both sides grumbling at it.

What with one thing, and what with another, a worm has a very hard time of it. If he makes his appearance above ground during the day, or gets up a little too early and comes out before it is dark, there is always some horrid bird looking out for him to snap him up. If he comes out at night, (so far as the clearing is concerned), there are the shrew-mice ready for him, and, I shrewdly suspect, the field-mice also. If he stays at home and reads the paper, he is never certain that Mr. Mole won't suddenly burst into his parlor and eat him up. Besides these, man calls him an "angle-worm," as if he were created, like artificial flies, expressly for fishing purposes, and after digging him up, impales him on a barbed hook and proceeds to drown him. It is not at all surprising under these distressing social conditions, that he is of a retiring disposition, and generally considered incapable of affection. That he really is so I don't believe. I see no reason for concluding that he is an exception to the general law, and has not the marital, paternal, and social instincts which are more or less evident in the other members of animal creation. Of course, he is not likely to be very enthusiastic on the subject of singing birds, which are the class that chiefly regard him as an *article de cuisine*, and I don't suppose he would much care to have them hung up in a cage in his parlor, if it were big enough; but with regard to man the case is different. Certainly man treats him more cruelly than the birds do, for they only swallow him alive as we do oysters, whilst man tortures him before killing him; but this consideration does not appear to have much weight with the lower living creatures, as is shown by the horses or dogs that evince a deep attachment to their owners in spite of cruel treatment, and yet I have never heard of a worm being made a pet of. I have heard of tame fish, tame butterflies, tame spiders, even of tame snakes, but never of tame worms. I recommend this to the serious attention of those engaged in cultivating new fads. An earth worm that would come at your call, and play tricks, would be quite a refreshing novelty.

I am glad that Mr. Robin did not succeed in his murderous

designs, for there are not many worms in the clearing, so far as I
can find out, and we can't afford to lose one. There goes another
of the clearing creepers of a different sort, who is supremely
indifferent to Mr. Robin and all his clique, and doesn't care a
button whether he is around or not. He is a stout burly little
fellow, all covered with reddish bristles, and he goes by the name
of Woolly Bear among the children. He is fussy: for all the
world like those little, round, red whiskered and red faced men that
we meet with that are always in a hurry, and can't take anything
coolly. Woolly Bear is just the same. When you see him he is
sure to be running as fast as ever he can go; never walking. If
you put a stick before him, he has seldom any time to reflect that
it wasn't there a minute ago, and has no business to be there now,
and so crawls over it as if it were a matter of course, and hurries
on. Sometimes he will take a fancy to see where the stick leads
to, and run up it so nimbly that he is on the hand that is holding
it before one has time to realize what is happening. Then you
drop the stick and shake him off. That rather astonishes him;
and when he reaches the ground, he incontinently curls himself
up, and presents a hairy emblem of eternity. I suppose he thinks
of the occurrence till he goes to sleep; and after a bit he will wake
up, stretch himself to see that he is all right, and scurry off again
as if determined to make up for lost time. No bird will touch
Master Woolly Bear; a mouthful of bristles is not an alluring
thing. He is the caterpillar of the Tiger moth, and perfectly
harmless; not so his cousin, the caterpillar of the Fox moth, which
is longer, and better proportioned. This gentleman is the porcupine
of the insect world, and his bristles come off when touched, producing irritation and swelling in the hands, as I know from sad
experience. However, he does not belong to our clearing, and,
indeed, I do not know whether he is a Canadian or not. When I
had the pleasure of making his acquaintance, it was in the North
of England.

　　There are a few cherry trees in the clearing, wild and choke,
known to botanists as Prunus Pennsylvanica, and Prunus
Virginiana, though why Pennsylvanica and Virginiana more than

Canadensis I cannot say. On these trees you will find large webs looking like exaggerated spiders' webs made up into bags, which are the dwelling places of another creeper, the tent caterpillar. I am sorry to say that I can scarcely find a good word for these gentry : they are insect gipsies, and just as objectionable neighbors. I am told that they are great pests and do a great deal of damage to the shade trees, and in orchards, which I can well believe, as they kill any branch of the cherry tree here on which they may set up their tents ; but as I have nothing to do with shade trees and orchards, and as there will always be enough apples to be had to supply my wants, I have no great quarrel with them on that account; neither do I very much grudge them a branch or two of the wild or choke cherry, but they are dreadfully dirty little wretches and make messes. Now we are not much to look at in the clearing, but we are clean; even the black on our stumps is pure charcoal, and the dust is clean dust. The tent caterpillars, therefore, are an eye-sore to us ; not because they are caterpillars, but because they won't wash. They object to be rained on, which no true habitué of the clearing ever does; and they make their preposterous tents to keep themselves from getting wet. A rainy day is a fast day for them ; and it is the only one that is. At other times they do nothing but eat, eat, eat; but then, they have to stay in doors and stew. Consequently, they are not nice : they are offensive to the touch and to the olfactories, so much so that though they are destitute of any other means of defence, no respectable bird will eat them. The blue jay is fond of the eggs that produce them ; he is fond of other eggs than these, the gorgeous thief; but when once out of the shell he cuts them entirely. The only proper treatment for them is to cremate them—nest and all.

A Clearing Out.

"OF the making of books there is no end." There is this peculiarity about language that you can scarcely put half-a-dozen words together to form a sentence to which different persons will not attach different meanings. I suppose that this really arises from the actual poverty of language, through which one word is made to do duty for a number of ideas, partly through local associations, partly through the lapse of time, though I have sometimes wondered whether man's intellect was not a more complex thing than we imagine it to be, and that what we call an idea might not, on analysis, be found to consist of several ideas, just as in chemistry bodies at one time regarded as elementary have subsequently been found to be capable of solution. It seems a paradox to say that every simple statement of fact is a complex one, but after all it is only another form of saying that Truth is many-sided. Solomon was a very wise man, and though I don't go the length of asserting that he meant more than he said, yet I am inclined to believe that he intended more than he is generally supposed to have done. Now, the sentence with which I have headed this chapter may be taken generally to state that fresh books are continually being written, and will be to the end of time. That is the generalization; the particularization in my own individual case is that when you sit down to write a book it seems as if you were never going to get a chance to stop: the making of a book is like the cable which Paddy was reproached for being so long in hauling up; " Be jabers, sorr! some one must have cut off the end av' it." Now that I am approaching the close, and clearing out of the clearing, I may as well confess that I have frequently felt as if I were never going to get through. It is not impossible that my readers may have felt the same thing. In that case I may feel confident of the success of these pages, for no author can

hope to win the favour of the public unless he can establish a bond
of sympathy between his readers and himself. If, then, we both
of us thought that I was never going to get done, the requisite
fellow-feeling is at once established.

I said in the beginning, that is in my preface which wasn't
the beginning, that I stood to win in either event ; I love consistency, and therefore I repeat the remark at the end. Those who
have read so far without being bored will have derived some
pleasure from the reading ; those who have not will be happy to
find that the work is done ; so that both classes will be contented,
and I shall have been, in my humble way, a benefactor of my
fellow-men, which is a highly satisfactory thought. When I was
at college, any man desiring to change from one college to another,
or from one university to another, had to provide himself with a
certificate of character from the authorities of his institution, which
was given in the words "Bene discessit." This was generally
taken to mean, " He has left in good standing," but I have known
cases in which it would have required a considerable exercise of
Christian charity on the part of the authorities to give such an
interpretation to the phrase, and I hold that in these the more
accurate translation of it would be " It's a good job he's gone." In
this final chapter I am appealing to the reading university to give
me my " Bene discessit," and I am not without hopes of getting it
in one sense or the other.

" What on earth induced me to write ? " Well ! that, as Hamlet
remarks, " is the question." I don't think I was actuated by any
feeling of malevolence to my species ; I am very certain it was
not ambition ; I know the average fate of authors too well to
expect a financial success. Really, I can't say what was the
motive power, except it might be a want of something better to
do : it is a want that is responsible for a great deal of unintentional
mischief in this world. And after all, I haven't really written a
book. I intended to do so, but instead I have simply committed
to print the trivial conversation that might take place between any
old friends, such as I have felt my possible readers to be. In one

17

of the manufacturing towns in England an honest artisan, who was a member of a Goose-club, one Michaelmas Eve bore home in triumph to his wife a fine specimen of that fowl, and instructed her to prepare it for the next day's dinner. "And what's I to stuff it wi' John," enquired the inexperienced housekeeper. "Owt at's green;" (anything that's green); "Owt at's green, ma lass" said John, and thought no more about it. The goose was served up in due time, and John plunging in his fork for the stuffing, drew out yard after yard of a long green string. "What on airth is this?" he demanded. "Why, John," she said, "thee tellt me to stuff it wi' owt at's green, and I had naught green i't hoose but a skein o' green yarn." She had stuffed it with green worsted! Well! she had done the best she could, and, after all, there was the goose, if the stuffing was exceptionable. De me fabula narratur. I have done the best I could, and if the inside of the book is nothing but green worsted, at any rate you have got the binding. That's all right; there's nothing the matter with that. There are more geese, I mean books in the world than this, whose chief merit is on the outside and not in the stuffing. Console yourself with this reflection, and so,

VIVE, VALEQUE.

CONTENTS.